DIRTY LAUNDRY

'I want it!' I pleaded. 'Now!'

'No,' he answered, 'you're going to be seen by some more people first. Come on.'

He had a firm hold on my hand, pulling me along the path, towards the lay-by. I went, thinking of how I must look with my tear-streaked face and my soaking dress, a truly sorry state. I'd done it on purpose, too, I knew that, and I wanted to be punished for it, spanked with my soggy panties pulled down, or stuffed in my mouth, while I was beaten.

We reached the lay-by, and a car passed almost immediately, another behind it. I was sure both had seen, but neither slowed. The third one did, an old white Fiat, and I caught the driver's eyes, staring right at me, his mouth open.

'Now bend down,' Monty ordered. 'Show the next one the wet patch on your bum.'

DIRTY LAUNDRY

Penny Birch

This book is a work of fiction.
In real life, make sure you practise safe sex.

First published in 2002 by
Nexus
Thames Wharf Studios
Rainville Road
London W6 9HA

www.nexus-books.co.uk

Typeset by TW Typesetting, Plymouth, Devon

Printed and bound by
Clays Ltd, St Ives PLC

ISBN 0 352 33680 3

Dedicated to Lucy, Sue and Nicky
for invaluable experience

One

I slid my hand down between my cheeks, into the smooth, powdery valley, parting them with two fingers and applying a third to my jelly-smeared bumhole. It was more than I could resist not to have a little feel, just stroking the slimy little ring, my fingertip caressing the tight, sensitive star shape before popping inside to the warm, wet embrace of the hole. The lubricant went in with my finger, making a rude, squelching sound, and I began to work it up my hole, my mouth coming open in pleasure as I did it.

It was so tempting to masturbate like that, with my bottom stuck out and a finger well up the slimy hole between the softness of my cheeks. A few dabs to my clitty and I'd have been there, in my dirty, anally obsessed heaven, just from the pleasure of lying nude on my bed with a finger up my bum, or over thoughts of being caught like I was, perhaps spanked, and then buggered.

I had to force myself to stop, pull my finger out and get on with what I was supposed to be doing: giving myself an enema before my date. The nozzle was on the towel beneath me, and I groped for it, finding the well-lubricated tip instead of the handle. With my fingers slimy with jelly, I poked it between my cheeks, feeling the cool, hard metal push between them, to my anus.

My mouth came open again as my ring spread around the nozzle, the thick end sliding up my juicy hole to give me a new flush of dirty pleasure. I poked it up, right up, until my ring closed on the narrow neck. I was already breathing heavily, with my pussy wet and my nipples in a state of straining erection, and as I reached back for the valve my fingers were trembling so hard I had trouble holding it.

I got it though, between finger and thumb, and held tight, teasing myself by withholding that awful, glorious moment, before I twitched it open and felt the cool water start to flow up my bum. Immediately I was in heaven, my eyes shut and my mouth hanging wide as my rectum began to fill, with the helpless bloated feeling building slowly inside me as I wondered how on earth anybody could fail to find the experience of an enema sexual.

It is sexual, it has to be. I mean, it's so intimate, so dirty, so intrusive. OK, so I didn't have to do it in the nude, or so that I could see my rear view in the mirror, with my pussy lips peeping out from between my thighs and my bare bottom with the thick red tube protruding obscenely from between my cheeks. It makes it better though, and I could think of absolutely no reason why I shouldn't indulge my dirty mind while I cleansed myself.

I opened my eyes, glancing at myself in the mirror, then moving to watch the bag as it slowly emptied its contents into my body. There was a pint of it, and I started to pant as my rectum filled, with the pressure growing and my urgency growing with it. It was getting hard to keep in, and I was clenching my hole on the nozzle and wiggling my toes, with the dreadful feeling of helplessness and panic growing in my head. I needed to run to the loo, urgently, desperately, but I held back, forcing myself to lie there and take it, until at last the full pint was in my rectum.

Even then I held still, shaking my head and gasping in air, revelling in what I had done to myself and the

2

ghastly certainty that if I didn't move soon I was going to make the most disgusting mess imaginable of my bed and my bedroom floor. By the time I gave in I was nearly screaming, and at last I could hold myself no more and pulled out the nozzle, jumping up from my bed and dashing for the loo, knock-kneed, with my bumhole clenched shut against the awful pressure inside me.

I made it, as I always do, because I know exactly how much I can take and still hold it in. Sat bolt upright on the loo, I let it all out, a feeling almost as good as taking it, a sense of relief close to ecstasy. It left me feeling weak, but only briefly, while I also felt light, and clean, and very, very naughty. The date was going to be good, I was sure of it, and now I was just in the mood for getting pleasantly drunk, indulging in some nice dirty foreplay and fucking until the morning. I could also be buggered with impunity, or at least as much impunity as is possible for a woman having a man's cock forced up her bottomhole.

I showered, powdered and made up at leisure, not even bothering to look at my watch. I was sure to be late, but it didn't matter, and anyway, if Damon had any sense, he would prefer me clean, fresh and happy but late to hot, flustered and on time. It was what he was going to get anyway.

He was just what I needed: young and good looking and modern, the very opposite of Percy, my pet dirty old man. I was cross with Percy, who had refused to come back from France at the end of summer, simply because he wanted to be in Bordeaux for the vintage. It was really unfair, because I'd had to come back and I was missing my regular spankings and all the other dirty things that only he can really provide. I'd been sulking for over a week.

Being asked out had provided the perfect opportunity to get my own back. While Percy has no claim on me for fidelity, I knew he would hate the thought of me going with someone as highly strung and possessive as Damon. Not only that, but there was something about Damon which appealed to me, a self-absorption that made him callous, cruel even. Not only did that make me hope for some dirty, abusive sex, but it would be the perfect excuse to get rid of him when Percy finally condescended to come back from France.

I'd met Damon at the *Café Eperney*, my favourite Covent Garden bar, where my friend Ami Bell had been standing him lunch in an effort to get him to sign up for the PR firm she worked for. He was a film producer, making very intense, arty stuff, which was either completely over my head or crap. It was all he talked about, and Ami seemed genuinely fascinated, although I was more taken by his dark good looks and assertive manner. The feeling was obviously mutual, because every time he looked at me his eyes would flick from my face to my chest. Sure enough, once Ami had returned to her office he'd suggested dinner. I had accepted immediately.

What I wasn't sure of was how to dress. Even the underwear was a problem. It seemed to be too much to hope for that he was actually a spanker, and even if he was it was unlikely that he'd appreciate the sort of English schoolgirl look that Percy enjoys – tight white cotton panties and a plain bra, preferably with old-fashioned stockings and suspenders. Something loose in heavy black silk would have been my own choice, but I didn't want to risk anything really nice getting torn or pinched for a souvenir. Then again a sporty look didn't seem to suit his character, while I was sure a G-string and no bra would be too overt.

For a while I sat in a pile of underwear, trying to decide what would make me seem at once alluring yet vulnerable. I wanted to play to his sense of conquest, which is always the best thing to do with arrogant men. He hadn't told me where we were going, which made it even harder, as I didn't want to go for an urban chick look and then end up at the Savoy, or a cocktail dress and find myself at some trendy bar in Soho.

In the end I decided to please myself, high briefs under tight white trousers to make the best of my bum, with a lightweight bra and a little top that left my tummy on show and gave just a hint of perky nipples beneath. A tiger's-eye lavabell through my tummy piercing and sandals completed the look, and if it turned out to be the Savoy then that was just too bad.

His brief scowl of irritation when I turned up nearly an hour late at the *Café Eperney* quickly turned to a smile, and from then on things went well. He had chosen a Polish restaurant in Bloomsbury, the *Borscht*, which was good, and popular: packed with people and with a real buzz to the atmosphere. It was so noisy I could barely hear him speak, which was just as well as he was droning on about the *film noir* he was making. The wine list was hopeless, but they had good beer and an excellent selection of vodkas to make up for it. I was soon drunk, and hornier than ever, just watching the calm certainty in his face as he spoke.

We had chosen a table at the back of the restaurant, well away from the door and, as we ate, the room became more and more crowded, until by the time he called for the bill we were pretty well jammed into the corner. We'd been trying flavoured vodkas, and when I got up I was unsteady on my feet, holding a chair for balance while he went for our coats.

Getting out was not going to be easy, with an enormously fat man blocking the way where he had pushed his chair back to fit in his colossal belly. The sight made me giggle, which he noticed, and when I tried to get past he wouldn't move his chair. Damon was already at the door, and I was in no mood for being messed about by some fat slob, so I told him to get out of the way, pretty curtly.

'Say please,' he answered, grinning at his friends.

'Look, just move will you?' I answered. 'I need to get through.'

'Say please and I will.'

'Just move, now.'

'Watch your manners, or I might just have to sit on your head.'

His friends burst into laughter at that and I felt myself start to colour, with my temper rising at the same time.

'Just move it, you great lard tub!' I snapped.

His friends laughed at that too, and he moved, but only after giving me a really dirty look. I joined Damon at the door, dismissing the incident as trivial. It wasn't, not to me, and not because of what had happened, but because of what he'd said. I like my sex dirty, and I like it submissive. I can't help it, and having someone threaten to sit on my head is just the sort of thing that gets to me.

It would have been bad enough anyway, but the man who made the threat had been just so gross. I mean, Percy is fat, and the fact that he's fat adds an extra touch to the sexual humiliation that I crave, especially when he spanks me. This guy wasn't just fat, he was vast. You could have put Percy inside him and nothing would have stuck out at the edges. It wasn't just his huge gut either, but everything: great fleshy arms, tree trunk legs, ream upon ream of billowing flesh around his middle, a great fat neck, several chins and a moonlike face under a bush of curly black hair. Worst of all was his bottom, with his buttocks great soft pads which bulged out to overflow the sides of his chair, a quite simply obscene volume of quivering human flesh, and he had threatened to stick it in my face.

The thought made me feel weak at the knees. It was just so obscene. I could imagine it, in appalling detail: being forced down on the restaurant floor, struggling in

6

his grip, the laughter of his friends, the sight of that vast bottom being positioned over my head, my utter horror as he undid his trousers and pushed them down, taking his underpants with them to expose the great soft, hairy buttocks and a set of grotesque genitals, my scream of consternation and dismay as I was smothered in it and ordered to kiss his anus or suck on his dangling balls. It was too much for me, disgusting yet horribly compelling, and I was nearly sick as Damon led me into Gower Street. He didn't seem to notice, doubtless thinking it was just the drink, which I was grateful for.

He hailed a cab and gave the driver the address of his flat. I didn't object. I knew I was going to be fucked. It was what I wanted, but my brain was spinning with dirty thoughts and images, and they weren't of my companion.

In the cab he held me, with his arm around my shoulder, and we were soon kissing and letting our hands wander. I wanted to get his cock out and suck it, all the while imagining I was being forced to do it to the fat man, or to be taken to some lonely park, spanked by him and the cabbie, then fucked comprehensively. Fortunately I had enough sense left not to try, and reached Gospel Oak without disgracing myself. Not too much anyway. Once there it was a different matter. Damon knew I was drunk and willing and made no effort to hold back. Nor did he make any effort to consider my pleasure, which was exactly how I'd imagined it and exactly what I'd been counting on to give me far more pleasure than any eager-to-please little new man could ever achieve.

My top was up almost before the door to his flat was closed, my bra with it, leaving my boobs bare to his groping hands. I responded, scrabbling at his fly in my eagerness, and getting pushed down for my trouble, right on to his cock as it sprang free. I gave him his blow job, right then and there, squatting in his hallway with my boobs out and his hand twisted hard into my hair. It was like he was forcing me, but he needn't have bothered, I was desperate for my portion of cock and badly wanted him to spunk in my mouth.

He did, right down my throat, forcing his erection in until I was gagging on it while he called me a slut and a bitch. I swallowed the lot, clutching at his firm, neat buttocks as he emptied himself into my mouth, but still imagining that it was the fat man who was making use of my mouth and not Damon. Even when he had finished I was still sucking, and he had to be quite rough to get me off his cock.

Damon had come and, like nearly all men, he expected that to signal the end of sex, at least for a while. I had other ideas and, even as I sat down on the hard wooden floor, I was struggling with the button of my trousers. It came loose, and I pushed them down, taking my panties with them. The whole lot went to my ankles and I lay back against the door, spreading my thighs open to him as my hand went to my pussy. He just watched, his mouth wide open, as I masturbated, rubbing and snatching at my pussy.

I was playing with my boobs too, one-handed, bouncing them and tweaking the nipples, getting closer and closer to orgasm. It felt so rude, so open, so dirty, with him looking down on me in shock, as if for all that he'd done to me, what I was doing was wrong. That was just perfect, and I was imagining myself doing it in the restaurant, on the floor with my top up over my boobs and my thighs apart to show everyone my pussy, their faces set in shock or delight, outrage or excitement.

It would have been after the fat man had sat on my head, not bare, as I'd first imagined it, but clothed, just to punish me. Only it would have got to me, and once he'd done it I'd have exposed myself and spread myself, masturbating in public like the dirty little slut I am, bare and spread, nipples hard, two fingers up my pussy, my legs so far apart my bumhole showed, coming in a welter of dirty ecstasy, in front of them all.

Then it was different, the three of them ganging up on me, the fat man and Damon and the cabbie. I'd be stripped in the cab, stark naked, my clothes thrown out of the window. They'd take me to a park and spank my bottom, hard, across their laps, punishing me for my insolence, for being a brat and a slut. I'd scream and kick and struggle, so plenty of people saw, but they wouldn't care, knowing it was just some stuck-up little tart getting her just deserts. Then they'd fuck me, throwing me on a pile of rotting leaves and taking turns with me, or better still, all together, with me mounted on the fat man, the cabbie in my mouth, and Damon up my bumhole . . .

The orgasm hit me and I screamed, at the top of my voice, then started to babble, calling out that he was a fat bastard and that I should be spanked, and buggered, and all of it in public.

I woke up in Damon's bed, stark naked, with a wet patch under my bum and a grade one hangover. At first I thought I'd wet myself, until I remembered that we'd fucked before going to sleep. Well, he'd fucked me anyway, because I'd only been half aware of what was going on. My memory of the rest of the evening came back slowly, with a mixture of embarrassment and satisfaction.

It had been good, in a way. In fact my orgasm had been great, and I knew full well it wouldn't have been anything like as powerful without the extra hit of dirtiness unwittingly provided by the fat man. On the other hand there was the truly awful memory of trying to explain to the rake-thin Damon why I had apparently called him a fat bastard at the moment of climax.

He was still asleep, lying beside me with his face turned away. For a moment I considered sneaking out and making my way home, only to abandon the idea. I needed coffee, and toast, and orange juice, and I needed someone to make it all while I nursed my head. So I shook him awake and suggested he get on with it.

Fortunately his arrogance didn't extend to expecting me to play maid to him and I got my breakfast in bed, including some Turkish coffee that nearly took the skin off my throat but proved amazing for clearing the cobwebs. He was also not the type who wakes up and expects his morning erection tended to, which I really wasn't up to. Like me, he wanted to take waking up slow and easy.

By the time I'd finished eating and had covered his bed with toast crumbs I'd decided I was up for a second date. He had been a bit of a pig with me, sexually, enough to arouse my interest anyway, and I wanted to find out how much more he had to offer. I had also got on with him as a person better than I had expected to, and I could tell that Percy would be green with envy.

It quickly became clear that his reticence was the result of the way I'd behaved, and that he was actually a bit wary of me, if not actually scared. A lot of men are like that, wanting a girl to do as they want and not really happy if she takes matters into her own hands. In the end I had to pretend to be embarrassed by what I'd done, which cheered him up enough to demand another blow job before I left.

He got it, and I walked back to Primrose Hill with the taste of his spunk in my mouth and an uncomfortable and embarrassing wet patch between my legs. Back at my flat I ran a bath and masturbated in it before lying back in the hot water to think about the previous night.

In some ways it was a bit of a waste, because the incident with the fat man had got me in such a state. If the incident hadn't happened, then I'd have been less urgent during the cab ride and Damon would have taken more time to deal with me. On the other hand, he

10

had asked me out again while I was still swallowing down his sperm, so it looked like I'd get it in due time.

The fat man was another matter. I had no idea who he was, and that was just as well. If I'd known, the temptation to indulge my filthy fantasy might have proved too much for me. I'd have done it, adding to the already considerable risk of it becoming common knowledge just how dirty I was.

I'd been seeing Percy for three years, and so far I'd managed to hide the fact from all those of my friends who would disapprove. I'd also managed to hide the fact that I enjoy my bottom spanked, or at least from most of them. There was an exception, Jo Warren, who I'd foolishly thought might be up for spanking me. I'd asked and she'd been horrified, but as I had more dirt on her than she did on me I felt fairly safe. I'd ensured her boyfriend was safe by seducing him, and he was so wet I knew he wouldn't dare tell, which only left her therapist, Gabrielle Salinger, who she was sure to tell but who could be relied on not to break a professional confidence.

If I'd gone with the fat man it would have been just my luck to find out I knew his sister or something, which would have been a disaster. Being revealed as a spankee would have been awful, but getting off on being humiliated by fat men was worse. It's the way society is unfortunately, that while girls are supposed to be out and proud, certain things are very definitely taboo. Enjoying being spanked is one of them, but fat is worse, far worse. Unfortunately that's the way my sexuality works. If it was really cool to go out with fat men I wouldn't have been interested, because the fantasy wouldn't have been humiliating. I'm not into fat, it disgusts me, which is exactly why the idea of being abused by a fat man appeals to me.

Nevertheless, it was a shame, because I still had that image of his huge backside poised over my face fixed

11

firmly in my mind. It was what was in my head as I lay back in the warm, soapy water, along with thoughts of my horror and humiliation as it was done to me, in a crowded restaurant, for everyone to see.

I knew I was going to masturbate again, even as my finger pressed down between the soft, fleshy lips of my pussy. I could just picture myself, perhaps held down on the floor by his friends, with my brown curls spread out around my head and my mouth and eyes wide in ghastly shock. He'd make me suck his balls first, dangling them into my mouth and telling me he'd let me off if I was a good girl.

He'd be lying though, because once I'd done it, sucking at his fat, hairy scrotum with my face screwed up and his friends laughing their heads off at my plight, his arse would go in my face. I'd be struggling as I was smothered, my hands beating on the floor and my legs kicking in a futile protest that would only draw more laughter from the onlookers. He'd tell me to kiss his anus and I'd hold back, even though I'd be suffocating. I'd do it in the end though, putting my lips to his coarse, hairy bumhole as the rest of them cheered and clapped to see me given what I deserved.

Then it would have to be into the restaurant toilets to be fucked over the lavatory bowl. He'd leave the door open so that the others could see, crowding in behind him as he forced me to kneel. He'd flop out my boobs and have a good feel, then undo my trousers, his fat hands opening my button, fumbling at my zip, easing my smart white trousers down and taking my panties with them.

With my bum bare I'd be spanked, hard, crying out my pain and emotion into the lavatory bowl until he shut me up by cramming my mouth with loo paper. With my bum smacked rosy, he'd lay his huge belly on my hot cheeks. I'd feel his cock against my pussy, prodding at me as he wanked it against my flesh. Then

12

he'd be in me, fucking me, jamming my body against the hard porcelain of the lavatory bowl as the others watched and laughed and clapped and jeered.

My will would break, and I'd reach back to masturbate, rubbing at myself in my filthy ecstasy to everybody's utter delight. They'd be calling me a slut and a bitch, the way Damon had, insulting me for being promiscuous even though I hadn't asked for the treatment I was getting. Nobody would insult him though, or try and stop him, not even the women who would be watching with as much delight as the men. They'd be complimenting him on knowing how to handle a brat, and egging him on to fuck me harder.

He'd do it too, his great lardy body slamming against my poor little bottom, his hands locked on my hips, jerking me about like a doll as he grunted and panted his way towards orgasm. He'd come up me and, at the last moment, he'd push my head down into the lavatory bowl and flush it, filling my mouth with dirty water even as he filled my pussy with sperm, and I'd come myself, soiled and filthy, stripped, abused and fucked, coming and coming and coming . . .

Which was exactly what I had done, for the second time in a row, with my hips pushed up to bring my pussy out of the bath water and the muscles of my legs locked in ecstasy.

When the last shivers of my orgasm had died down I lay still in the bath for a long time, feeling thoroughly satisfied and slightly ashamed of myself. I was also gladder still that I was unlikely ever to see the fat man again. I knew for sure that I'd have wanted sex with him, and what I want I tend to get.

Not that the fantasy was realistic, because if he'd tried anything of the sort he'd have been arrested on the spot, but that didn't matter. He was fat, enormously fat, so he was sure to be hard up for sex. He was probably a pervert too: after all, he wouldn't have threatened to sit on my head unless the idea had been there in the first place. In fact he had probably been watching me during the meal and thinking of what he'd like to do to me.

It wasn't going to happen, fortunately, and instead I was going to have a brief and intense fling with the moody and attractive Damon, getting my kicks and making everyone jealous at the same time. That was a much more appealing idea, and when I'd finally managed to drag myself out of the bath and get dressed I went down to the *Café Eperney* in the hope of having a good gloat.

The first person I recognised was Ami, at one of the outside tables, looking very serious with her big glasses and her long dark hair held back with an Alice band. I went to sit with her, putting a deliberate bounce into my walk and smiling happily as I said hello.

'You look cheerful,' she greeted me. 'Won the lottery?'

'No,' I answered, 'but not far off. Guess who I spent the night with?'

'Search me. Knowing you it could be anyone.'

'Thanks! No seriously, guess. It's someone we both know.'

'Animal, mineral or vegetable?'

'Stop messing around! He's a client of yours.'

'What? Not Damon Maurschen!'

'Is that his surname? I never asked.'

'You didn't! You bitch!'

'I did.'

'Natasha Linnet, you are the absolute end! Do you know how much I fancy him?'

'Ah, but you can't have him, can you? Very unprofessional, bonking your clients.'

I sat back, making no effort at all to hide the grin on my face. She was so jealous, and it was great just to watch her reaction.

At that moment someone came out of the café, a fat man and, for one moment, I thought it was *the* fat man and I found the blood rushing to my face. It was just an instant, and then I realised that the man was a lot older and not quite so fat, but it was enough, because the expression on Ami's face had changed.

'Tasha? Are you all right?' she asked.

'Fine,' I managed.

'Who was that?' she demanded. 'Did you know him?'

'No,' I said quickly. 'I mean, I thought I did, but I don't. Forget it.'

She shrugged and took a sip of her coffee, then leaned forward on to the table.

'Tell me then,' she demanded, 'about Damon. Everything.'

I told her, embroidering it a bit to make it sound more romantic and leaving out the incident with the fat man and my dirty fantasies. She was impressed, and not only by the sex but by the way he had treated me in the morning, which I had also tweaked a little bit.

'Lucky cow,' she said when I'd finished, 'and what do I get? Chris, who's asleep five minutes after we've finished.'

'He's not so bad, surely. Good looking anyway.'

'That makes it worse. I mean, I really can't handle it sometimes. He makes me so horny, and if he's watching football he won't even come to bed until it's finished. He's really destroying my self-esteem.'

'Stand between him and the telly and give him a striptease.'

'I couldn't, I do have some self-respect! Besides, I tried ... something similar anyway. He just told me to get out of the way. I've spoken to Gabrielle about it and she says ...'

'Are you with Gabrielle?'

'I have been for months. She's the only thing that keeps me sane.'

'I thought you were into aromatherapy and shiatsu?'

'I am, or I was. Even combined they only kept my head straight for a few hours, or until something else came along to wind me up. Gabrielle's great, but you've been, haven't you?'

'Once. Whole-being therapy didn't really suit me.'

'Oh, but it's wonderful! She's so intelligent! She's explained to me that Chris's obsession with football is an attempt to accommodate his own inadequacy by projecting the success of his team on to himself. Just understanding has made it a lot easier to handle.'

'Oh, right.'

I wasn't really listening, mainly because I'd heard it all before. Chris was a prat, a good-looking prat, but a prat. I wouldn't have stayed with him for five minutes. Ami went on, expanding on Chris's inadequacies and praising Gabrielle until I jokingly suggested she ought to dump Chris and go out with Gabrielle.

'I'm serious here,' she answered me. 'Anyway, she's suggested I do something to restore my self-esteem, to make myself feel wanted, as a woman.'

'I could have told you that for free.'

'Well I'm going to do it. I'm getting some of the girls together and we're going to go down to Brighton for the day, where I intend to let myself get picked up and bonked silly. You'll come, won't you?'

'Is Jo Warren coming?'

'No, I invited her but she and Hugh had booked something up. You quarrelled with her, didn't you, in France?'

'Yes, it was just one of those things,' I said hastily, although my heart had seemed to jump straight into my throat.

'Right,' she went on, 'that's a shame. She won't be there, anyway, but there's Amy McRae, and her girl-friend, and Isabel Mintower. It should be fun. Please come?'

It sounded all right, and in any case she looked so earnest that I found myself nodding automatically.

Two

It was two weeks until the Brighton trip, which was enough time for me to get bored with Damon Maurschen. The trouble was, that while he had the right attitude, he had no imagination. I mean, being held by the hair so that I can't get away while I'm made to suck cock and swallow is fine, but not every time. He wasn't a spanker either. In fact, he wasn't particularly interested in my body at all, except as a receptacle for his cock. When I came on to my period he reacted with disgust, as if I was unclean, which I hate. He wasn't even into striptease or making me show myself off in front of him. When we did fuck it was in missionary position, except for once, when he said I should go on top, which he seemed to think was some sort of sacrifice on his part.

I kept seeing fat men too. I'd never really taken much notice before, but suddenly they seemed to be everywhere, and each time I saw one I thought of the man who had insulted me. It wouldn't get out of my head, and I was still fantasising about having rude things done to me by him, even while having sex with Damon, even when he was inside me. That was what finally made me decide that the relationship was a waste of time. I would still have stuck with it anyway, just so Percy would be jealous, only Damon got into a temper when I told him I was going to Brighton with the girls, which he simply

17

had no right to do. I told him to get lost, and I was still smarting over his sheer arrogance the next day.

The others were going down by train, but I took the TVR, driving fast with the radio at full volume, which did a lot to improve my feelings. I parked well away from the front and took a bus down to meet them at the base of the pier. I was the first there, and spent a while just filling my lungs with air. There was plenty of it, because while it was sunny, the wind was coming in straight off the sea, emptying the beach and sending spray over the marina wall.

When they arrived it was all together. I spotted them from a long way off; Ami Bell with the sunlight glinting off her big glasses, Amy McRae with her short cropped blonde hair, Isabel, small and blonde, another girl, small and dark, who I took to be Amy's girlfriend, and one other. The fifth girl was the tallest of them, very slim, with straight, cropped brown hair and glasses. It took me a moment to recognise her and then I realised that they had brought down the therapist from hell, Gabrielle Salinger.

Unfortunately Ami spotted me before I could make up my mind to do anything, and that was that – my day was ruined. Gabrielle knew much too much about my dirty laundry for comfort's sake. It was impossible not to imagine her studying me, analysing me, thinking of what a pervert I was.

It got worse. They all seemed to worship Gabrielle, even Amy McRae, who edits *Metropolitan* and is about as tough as they come. Ami Bell was the worst, hanging on to Gabrielle's every word, and Isabel was nearly as bad, while Amy's girlfriend, Gina, was too shy to say much at all, but just looked on with a sort of dumb adoration.

Gina was small and very pretty, with a fragility about her that I could well imagine Amy enjoying and which appealed to me as well. Not that I was going to do

18

anything about it, as I could only see it ending in trouble, while Amy gives me far too many commissions for me to risk pissing her off.

So I spent what should have been a really fun afternoon trying to act naturally while trying to avoid Gabrielle and not make my attraction to Gina too obvious. Being bisexual when nobody else knows is usually great, because I can admire girls in a way no male could ever do. This time I had to hold back and, with Gina in a little floaty skirt that kept blowing up in the wind, it was not easy.

Ironically, Gabrielle seemed to want to talk to me more than any of the others, and that was really worrying. It was obvious that her interest was professional, and she kept trying to get me alone, doubtless to ask some hideously intimate and embarrassing question. I felt like a specimen under a microscope, and by the time we came off the pier I was really nervous.

We ate at an Italian, and I took care to sit between Ami and Isabel. I badly needed a drink and was knocking down glass after glass of Copertino as we ate, until at last I began to relax and join in the fun. It was a mistake, because by the time we'd finished I was having serious difficulty keeping my eyes off Gina. The sun was low, with the light striking through her dress to show off the outlines of her breasts, which were braless, and also her hips. The wind was getting stronger still, and twice her dress blew up high enough to flash her panties, sending her into fits of giggles.

I wanted her so badly I could have cried and, to make matters worse, she was being really friendly to me, as if she knew. It was just possible that she did, and I began to wonder if she wasn't teasing me to see if I'd play. That set me thinking about what it would be like with Amy and her together, which made it even worse.

We sorted out our hotel rooms and then went down to the bar. I wanted to stop drinking, but they had noticed I was a bit down and assumed it was something to do with Damon. So they kept buying me rounds and I got more and more drunk, until I was having serious trouble keeping my hands off Gina. She was giggly too, and focusing more and more on me, until I could see that Amy was starting to get jealous. Gabrielle was getting more insistent too, doubtless thinking she'd get something interesting out of me if I was really drunk, and I knew that there was every chance she'd succeed.

By the time we left the bar we had our arms around each other in a line as we made for the club we had chosen. I'd tacked on at one end, to Gabrielle, because the other choice was Gina and I wasn't at all sure I'd be able to keep my hands off her bum. Even then it was difficult, because I could feel the gentle curve of Gabrielle's hip and the soft flesh of her waist. I hadn't been with another girl since coming back from France, and after two weeks of Damon it just felt so good to have a female body next to mine.

I could see what was going to happen. We'd get to the club and dance and drink and I'd either make a move on Gina, let myself get picked up by the fattest bloke in the house, or pour out my heart to Gabrielle. All the options were going to be disastrous. I had to get away.

Even that wasn't easy. I pretended to need the loo, but Isabel said she did too and they waited for us. We had reached the club before I could find another excuse and were quickly inside. It was crowded and hot, the air thick with smoke and the smells of perfume and sweat. It was loud too, with a furious bass rhythm that drowned out all possibility of conversation, for which at least I was grateful. I said I'd get the drinks, but Gabrielle insisted on coming with me to help.

There was nothing I could do, and when we got back to the others I found they had jammed themselves into an alcove. There was only one place to sit, the end of a bench, right next to Gina. I had to take it, and as I sat down I felt my body press to hers, with the outline of one little breast against my arm. Amy's arm came up around Gina's shoulder in a clear gesture of possession and I managed a weak smile as I passed her drink, catching a warning look in return. It was as if she was reading my mind, and I had to get out, right then.

I made an excuse, mumbling something about feeling sick, and left the table. Ami made to follow but I pushed in between two tall men and hurried off through the crowd to the exit and out into the night.

I'd only been in the club a few minutes, but the fresh air hit me like a hammer. My head was swimming with drink and confusion and erotic thoughts, all mixed up with self-pity and anger. It just wasn't fair!

I started to walk along the front, with the wind whipping at my hair and the taste of salt in my mouth. I was vaguely aware that there was a really major storm blowing up, but it didn't seem to matter. There were plenty of other people about, laughing as they dodged the spray that was beginning to blow over the wall, or huddled into coats, hurrying for shelter. I wanted to be alone, to get my thoughts in order, even to masturbate, and I walked on, as fast as I could go.

It was just by the sign marking the start of Hove that I saw him, seated at a bus stop: the fat man from the restaurant. I knew it was him, even though I'd been seeing him in every fat man I'd passed for the last two weeks. It had to be, every great, bulging ream seemed familiar, and I was sure the orange anorak he was wearing had been on the back of the chair in the restaurant.

I should have walked on, and he'd never have noticed, but I had to look, and for a moment our eyes met. My head filled with all the filthy images I had conjured up since our encounter and I found my mouth twitching up into a nervous, scared smile. That was it, but it was enough and, as I hurried past the bus stop,

21

from the corner of my eye I saw him get up. Immediately my heart was in my mouth.

He was following me, I knew it, but I didn't dare turn round. I was scared, but as much of my own response as of him. He was fat, huge, I could outrun him easily, even drunk. Anyway, he probably only wanted to tell me what an ill-mannered little bitch I was, to try to make me feel bad for the way I'd spoken to him, to try to make me feel small, to humiliate me . . . Oh, God!

I'd stopped, and turned back. He was coming towards me, slowly, his great flaccid body backlit by a street lamp, his face in shadow. I didn't know whether to be angry with him or to apologise, to tell him to fuck off or to try to be friendly, but there was a part of me hoping that he would make some obscene threat.

When his face did come into the light I saw that he was as nervous as I was, his little blubbery mouth twitching at one side, his piggy eyes uncertain. For one moment I wondered if it really was him, but he had to be, or why else follow me? After all, no one as gross as he was could possibly think I'd be interested.

'Going for a walk?' he said.

I nodded.

'Nice weather for ducks, eh?'

It was such a stupid thing to say that I found myself smiling, and I realised that he wasn't going to have a go at me. What he was going to do was try to chat me up, and that was worse.

'Can we go for a coffee?' he asked, a line guaranteed to make most girls run a mile. Not me, not then.

'No, I don't want one,' I answered. 'I'm just walking.'

'How about it then?' he went on.

'How about what?'

'A fuck.'

'Jesus! You bastard!'

'Well it's what you're after, isn't it?'

'No it is not!'

'Get real. Dressed up like a dog's dinner, all on your own. I can see you're not a pro, so what else would you be doing?'

'Going for a walk! Getting some fresh air!'

'Yeah, sure.'

It was the most clumsy, inept, hopeless come-on I had ever heard, and I've heard a few. He had to be mad, thinking that someone like him could pick me up. I mean, if Brad Pitt had just walked up and asked me for a fuck I'd have told him where to get off, but this guy! Well it was either that or he knew how he'd got to me in the restaurant, which was impossible.

I turned, willing myself to walk away, but he fell into step beside me. His great, podgy arm came around my waist and I didn't pull away, even though a voice inside me was screaming to slap him in the face, to kick him in the balls, to run. Then his hand had closed on my bottom and he was pulling me into his arms.

He may have been fat, but he was far stronger than I was. I got pulled in close, both his hands now on my bottom, kneading my cheeks through my jeans as he pressed his blubbery mouth against mine. His tongue touched my lips and before I knew what I was doing they were coming apart and we were kissing, with his great slobbery mouth wide over mine and his tongue halfway down my throat.

It was disgusting, really gross and, to make it worse, he tasted of fish and chips, but I couldn't pull away, only put my arms up to his chest and let him have his snog and his feel. In the end it was him who broke the kiss, but not before he'd had a really thorough grope of my bum. I was so glad I was in tight jeans and not a skirt, because I knew it would have been up, with his horrid sweaty hands down my panties. There were other people about too, which made it worse, far, far worse.

'People are watching!' I hissed.

'Yeah, right, let's go somewhere private.'

'No, I mean . . .'

He had taken me by the hand, pulling me after him. I went with the pressure, with my sense of erotic humiliation burning in my head. It was too much, I couldn't stop myself. I was going to let him have me, to make me suck his cock and lick his balls, even to fuck me, even to carry out his horrid threat and sit on my face.

'I know a place,' he was saying. 'A great place. Come on.'

I went, and all the while I was wondering what the hell I was doing, with my mind swinging from open rebellion to a desperate urge to really bury myself in all the disgusting fantasies I had thought up over the last two weeks. I thought he was going to take me to some sordid bedsit, but he continued down the front, almost dragging me and stopping over and over to snog me and grope my bum and boobs. Once we were beyond the main front he even pulled my top up, jerking my bra with it to spill out my tits for a feel. I let him, and I thought he might even fuck me, right there, in the shadow of a bus shelter with the sea spray blowing over us.

He didn't, but contented himself with a feel and a suck of my nipples, then told me to leave my boobs out. Half of me wanted to, but I covered them, sure someone would see and report us. In response he slapped my bottom and with that I was really lost. The next time he stopped I let him pop my jeans button and he felt down the back of them, putting his disgusting sweaty hands into the back of my panties and pulling them up into my crease.

By then I was as urgent as he was, kissing back as his fat fingers took hold of my panties, jerking them up to tug the material against my pussy. My arms were around him too, feeling the huge billows of flesh around his middle and the obscene bulging shapes where the

24

cleft of his buttocks rose out of his trousers. It was so dirty, and I was dying to be used, really used, the way I had imagined him do it, cruelly, revelling in my shame and disgust as he enjoyed every aspect of my body and forced me to indulge his every, filthy urge.

He only stopped when we reached a row of garages, well beyond the area I knew, with the black bulk of Shoreham power station visible against the dull orange sky. It was where I was going to be fucked, it had to be, and sure enough he led me down the slope by the hand, aiming for the gaping mouth of one of the few garages that still had its door attached. It was opposite a street lamp, the interior illuminated with a dull orange glow, showing a stained concrete floor, a mangled supermarket trolley, a squalid mattress, surrounded by a litter of beers cans and the torn remnants of some squalid pornographic magazine. It must have smelled, and I imagined it, yet it didn't seem to register, only the sight, only the overt, dirty maleness of the place. He beckoned me inside, glancing guiltily back towards the town and, even as I followed him, for all my drunken lust I was thinking that I had to be absolutely crazy for what I was doing.

I did it anyway, and no sooner was I inside than he had pulled the door down and we were plunged into absolute darkness. That made it so much easier, and as he took me in his fat arms and pulled me down on to that foul mattress my fantasies were running strong. I wanted to be made to suck him, to take his balls into my mouth, to have my bottom spanked to a glowing ball, to be made to kiss his monstrous buttocks, all of it, but most of all I wanted him to sit on my head.

He wasted no time, his hands all over as I melted into his embrace, kneeling together on the mattress. He was groping for the button of my jeans, wrenching my top up to once more flop out my boobs. I hadn't realised how cold I was, until I felt his hot, clammy hands on my bare tits. He was groping, squeezing them hard, so that it hurt, tweaking my nipples, then sucking on them as he went down. I could only sigh as his hands found the waistband of my jeans, pulling them hard down and taking my panties with them. He left them like that, around my thighs, so that I was bare from boobs to legs, everything he wanted showing, breasts, bottom and pussy. A finger found my sex, burrowing firmly between the cleft of my lips, finding my hole, to be pushed roughly inside. His mouth went lower still as he fingered me, kissing my belly, then licking it, his saliva running down my skin as he sucked at my tummy piercing. His lips found my pussy, mouthing at my pubic mound and mumbling obscenely about how he liked a girl to be shaved. Then his tongue had found my clitty and I was moaning aloud, with my boobs in my own hands, stroking my rock-hard nipples as he licked and fingered at my sex. His other hand was on my bottom, his fingers in the crease, then right in, touching my anus, tickling it before pushing into the tiny, wet hole.

I was going to come, just like that, and I was so ashamed of myself, for letting a gross, leering fat man strip me and lick my pussy, for letting him grope my boobs and touch my bumhole. Worse still was what was going through my head, the thoughts of what he might do to me, make me suck his cock, fuck me, make me kiss his bottomhole . . .

With that I came, imagining the hideous humiliation of being forced to kiss his anal ring as his tongue flicked and lapped at my clit. I cried out loud, a wordless scream of ecstasy and shame, and then he had stopped and was holding me, once more kneading my buttocks as he pulled me against his bloated body.

Somehow he'd managed to get his anorak off, and I could feel the coarse wool of a jumper against my bare flesh as he started to kiss me again. I responded, thinking of what I'd let him do. It wasn't what I had expected. It had been dirty, yes, disgusting even, because he was so gross, but he had been body worshipping me, something Damon had never done at all. I knew it was because having a girl to play with would be so rare for him, but that didn't stop me feeling grateful. That was just as well, considering what was sure to be coming.

'Now my turn,' he said, his voice thick with passion in the darkness, as he pulled back from me. 'First, let's have your kit off, right off. I'll do it.'

I let him strip me, peeling my top and bra off over my head, then rolling back so that he could get at my jeans. He pulled them off, my shoes, socks and panties going with them, to leave me stark naked. For a while he just groped, before taking me by one wrist and pulling my hand down to his crotch.

His cock was out, his balls too, a good handful of hairy, greasy flesh, obscenely male. He was kneeling, thighs spread, my arm touching the solid fat of his gut as I started to feel him up, cupping his balls and using my thumb to roll his foreskin back and forth.

'Oh, you know how to do it, don't you,' he breathed. 'Just keep doing that and I'll soon be hard.'

'Shouldn't you undress too?' I asked, giving in to the filthy urge to find out what that much flesh really felt like in my arms.

'Who needs to?' he answered. 'It's the girl who ought to be stripped.'

'I understand,' I said quietly and began to tug harder at his cock.

He'd touched a sensitive point, even if it had been entirely by accident. There's something wonderfully submissive about being stark naked when a partner is fully dressed. It really puts me in my place, especially for a spanking, when I've got everything showing, not a scrap of modesty left to me, and whoever's punishing me hasn't a stitch out of place. It was the same now. He needed his cock and balls out, to deal with me, but that

27

was all, at least until his trousers came down so that I could be made to kiss his anus.

'Now suck it,' he ordered and leaned back so that I could get my mouth to his cock.

I went down right away, without hesitation, sticking my bum up in the air as I nuzzled my face into his genitals. He was big, and sticky, and not very clean, but I took his cock in my mouth anyway, sucking quickly to clear away the awful taste. It was so humiliating, not only from the taste and being nude on my knees in front of him, but because his great fat belly was pressed to my forehead. Even if I couldn't see him, I knew what he looked like, and it was just a pity that there wasn't enough light to let him see me.

He was taking his time getting hard, even though I was sucking and tickling his balls at the same time, and I wondered if he hadn't already come in his pants while he was feeling me up. He certainly tasted like he had, slimy and salty, with a greasy, sweaty feel to his skin. Eager to get him properly erect, I began to mouth at the head of his cock, rolling his foreskin back with my lips and sucking at the turgid bulb of flesh within.

'Oh, yeah, nice,' he groaned. 'Yeah, you're good. You're like something out of a porno movie. I saw a girl do this, in one, gobbling some black guy.'

That explained a lot. It was easy to imagine him wanking over dirty videos. In fact it explained his whole attitude to sex, including expecting to get into my panties within minutes of meeting. Some men are like that, with everything they know about sex straight from videos and magazines. Well this time he'd struck lucky.

'It was great,' he went on. 'She was a waitress, and he did her in the restaurant, with her stripped off and his fucking great log of a cock in her mouth. He did his load in her face too, right over it, in her eyes and everything. How'd you like that, a load of spunk, right in the face?'

28

I nodded around my mouthful, wanting to accept any humiliation he felt appropriate for me. He'd got me feeling so submissive, and I was putty in his hands, naked and willing, ready for any obscenity he chose to inflict on me. He was hard now, too hard to let me get it all in my mouth, and I was struggling a bit as he reached down under his belly and took hold of it.

'Maybe you'll get lucky,' he said, 'but not yet. I want to fuck you, on your knees, arse up.'

'Don't you ... don't you want to do what you threatened?' I asked, pulling off his cock.

'What?' he demanded.

'You know, to punish me, to ... to sit on my head. To make me kiss your bottom.'

'What? You want to kiss my arse?'

I nodded, stupidly, because he couldn't have seen me, but I just couldn't bring myself to say the actual words, to ask to kiss his anus. Even with my head reeling with drink it was too dirty, too shameful. He did it for me.

'You mean, like, on my arsehole?' he demanded.

'Yes,' I sobbed.

There was a pause, as a great bubble of shame and self-disgust rose up in my throat. I'd pushed it too far, suggested something too dirty for him, a great fat pig like him, and what I wanted was too dirty. Only it wasn't.

'Well, yeah, all right,' he said suddenly. 'Whatever turns you on. I've never had a girl kiss my arsehole before. But I want to fuck you first. Come on, get in doggy position.'

'Yes,' I answered and began to scramble round on the filthy mattress.

I put my head down and lifted my bum, choking with humiliation as his fat thumbs found my cheeks and spread them. He was going a fuck me, a great, fat slob, with his cock up me from the rear. Worse, once he'd had his fun with my pussy he was going to make me kiss his anus, and I'd asked for it.

There were tears in my eyes as he prodded his cock at my hole, guiding it with his hand. I was whimpering too, a really broken, miserable sound, but he took no notice, sliding his cock up my pussy and taking me by the hips. My hole was so wet he'd gone straight up, really easily, adding a fresh stab of shame as he started to fuck me. His belly was right up against my bum, and I could feel the sweaty flesh sticking to mine and moving, peeling on and off. He had his thumbs under it too, holding my bumcheeks apart.

'I love doggy,' he puffed, his thumbs digging into my bottom to spread the cheeks wider still, stretching my anus. 'I wish I could see this. I bet you look fucking great. You've got a lovely arse, lovely knockers too. You're a fucking doll. I could spunk up you so easily.'

'Don't,' I panted, 'but fuck me faster, for a bit.'

Immediately he slammed into my bottom, really hard, knocking the breath out of me. He kept going too, again and again, puffing and panting as he rode me, too fast and too hard to let me catch my breath, crushing me down into mattress with his weight, until I couldn't breathe at all, only to stop as suddenly as he had begun.

'I'll spunk if I do that,' he gasped, slowing, then stopping. 'I'm going to spunk anyway.'

'No!' I begged. 'Not up me! You're going to make me kiss your hole!'

'Fuck, but you're a dirty bitch!' he swore, but he pulled back and began to turn me by my hips.

I went with the pressure, surrendering myself and hoping he'd just make me do it and not beg for it or anything still more humiliating. Sure enough, he rolled me on to my back and crawled up beside me. I could hear him fumbling with his trousers, my heart hammering in my chest as he prepared to force me into the obscene act I'd wanted so desperately.

He climbed on to me, forwards, and I was imagining his great cock rearing up over my face, slimy with my

30

own juice. I could smell it, both him and myself, and then he was settling his vast backside across my neck and the hair of his scrotum was tickling my face. I opened my mouth, wide, expecting his balls in it.

I got them, right in my open mouth, sucking them in to make him gasp. I felt his hand touch my nose as he folded it around his cock, wanking, right in my face as I sucked at his balls. I could taste his sweat, and my own juice where it had run down as he fucked me. My legs were coming up and apart, spreading my pussy to the air. I was going to masturbate as he did it, and I couldn't stop myself.

Out came his balls, pulled away as he lifted himself, then laid back wet and sticky with saliva, across the bridge of my nose as he lowered his bottom into my face. It was going to happen, now, and I had found my clit as he sat slowly down, his great wobbling backside touching my mouth, spreading across my face, soft and heavy, the cheeks coming apart, my lips puckering out, and I was kissing his anus.

I just came, the instant my lips touched that bloated, filthy hole, screaming out my ecstasy, only to be shut up as his bottom settled fully on to my face. I was still coming, but I could hardly breathe, panting the scent of his balls through my nose with my mouth crushed to his anus and my face screwed up in utter disgust and utter ecstasy. The orgasm went on and on, with my back arched and my head just burning with utter, complete humiliation. In the end my tongue came out, up his dirty fat hole and then it was just too much. My orgasm was breaking and I couldn't breathe at all, my hands thumping on the mattress to try to make him stop.

He took no notice at all, just jerking furiously at his erection, his fist hitting my nose with every stroke. I tried to struggle, panicking, my feet drumming on the mattress, my hands beating on his back and sides. He kept on, hammering at his erection, his balls slapping in my face, grunting as he rubbed his anus over my mouth as I writhed and struggled under his weight, only to groan and splash hot come over my face as he came.

'Fucking nice!' he grunted.

I was still hitting him and he climbed off pretty quickly, leaving me gagging and spitting on my back.

'You are one great little arse-licker!' he panted, and sat down heavily against the wall.

I couldn't answer. My face was covered in spunk although, as I tried to wipe it out of one eye, my fringe fell back into place and I discovered that most of it had gone in my hair. All I could do was grope a tissue out of my bag and wipe up as best I could, but there was nothing I could do about the taste in my mouth, while for some reason the effect of the alcohol seemed to be ten times worse than before.

I kneeled up, feeling sick, my head swimming. He was doing something behind me, but I didn't care. All I could think about was the state I was in and the awful shame running through my head, made worse by the fact that I knew full well I'd end up masturbating over the experience. I thought I'd got over sexual shame and guilt, but I'd been wrong.

Suddenly needing to cover myself, I groped for my panties, finding them right beside me, on the mattress. I struggled into them, pulling them quickly up, and it was only then I realised that he'd wiped his cock on the seat.

Three

It was not the best of awakenings. The first thing I was really aware of was the cold, then the taste in my mouth, which was absolutely revolting. I was half under his coat, in just my top and panties, which had dried and stuck to my skin. The fat man was still asleep, snoring, with his trousers still undone and halfway down over his pasty white bottom, which reminded me of what I'd done.

I felt really ashamed of myself, but good too, in a way, because I'd realised my fantasy, which sometimes takes a lot of strength. Not only that, but I still didn't know his name, or vice versa, let alone his number or address. It was clearly time to leave, as quietly as possible. That way I could put the experience behind me, something I could masturbate over from time to time, when I was in a dirty mood, but not something that was going to have any repercussions.

In any case I had managed to avoid either making a play for Gina or spilling my heart out to Gabrielle. I was fairly sure that if it hadn't been for the fat man I'd have ended up going back to the hotel. After all, it had been a pretty wild night, and the little bit of concrete visible under the garage door was still wet, even though it now seemed to be blazing sunshine outside. If I had gone to the hotel, there would have still been a fair chance of fouling things up.

I began to dress, as quickly and quietly as I could. My bag was by the mattress, and for one horrible moment I had a vision of him rifling through it while I was asleep, but it hadn't been touched. My clothes were damp, and dirty too, but I ignored the discomfort as I struggled into them, covering my boobs first and pulling off my soiled panties before putting on my jeans.

He was still asleep by the time I'd finished, and it occurred to me to leave him my panties as a souvenir, which I was sure he'd appreciate. I was even laying them on the mattress when I had an awful vision of him trying to get them on and changed my mind, balling them into my fist instead, for disposal in the first convenient litter bin.

The door was bent and rusty, creaking so loudly as I pushed at it that I was sure he'd wake up. He didn't, but as I ducked out beneath it I discovered that we were not alone. There was a man sitting on the dirt bank opposite the garages, looking right at me. He was a mess, with filthy clothes and matted hair, one hand clutching an open beer can, with several more littered around him. I tried not to make eye contact, edging to the side and wondering if I ought to just run for it.

'Bitch, fucking in my bed!' he snarled suddenly and spat on the ground.

It was only then that I realised that that was exactly what I had done. I hadn't really given it thought, assuming the garage was just somewhere the local boys brought their girlfriends for a fuck. Now that he said it I had no reason to doubt him. I hadn't just let the fat man have me, I'd done it on a tramp's bed. It was too much for me. I just ran, dropping my panties as I went.

'Fucking bitch!' he roared, and threw the beer can at me.

As I dodged it, my toe caught in a crack in the concrete and the next moment I was down on my knees as beer splashed over my top and into my hair. His laughter rang out behind me and I cursed as I scrambled up, rubbing at my right knee. It hurt, and I turned, intending to give him a piece of my mind and then run like crazy.

'Bastard! Fucking your whore on my bed!' he was yelling at the fat man, who had come out of the garage.

The fat man started towards me, and I was going to run, but there was beer dripping out of my hair and all down my top, and I badly needed someone to help me. He was the only choice.

'You all right?'

'Yeah, fine,' I answered. 'He just threw beer all over me. Look, you're local aren't you? Because I really need to clean up.'

He laughed, and I nearly slapped him, but the vagrant had picked up a lump of concrete, so we beat a hasty retreat, up on to the road, from where we could see right along the coast. I hadn't realised just how far we'd walked the night before. Even the West Pier seemed to be almost on the horizon.

'Where do you live?' I asked, praying it was going to be nearby.

'In London,' he answered. 'I'm borrowing a mate's flat for the weekend. We can go there. I'll sort you out.'

The flat was in Peacehaven, miles away, and we took a bus. I started out feeling really embarrassed, but he wasn't brash, as I'd expected him to be. In fact, he was seriously insecure about himself, and while he kept giving me funny looks, he seemed to be pretty grateful for the fact that I was with him. That was fine by me, because it put me in control of the situation. There's nothing quite so easily led as a man frantic for sex.

He talked on the way, almost non-stop, as if he thought I was going to disappear if he stopped. I let him, and when I found out that he was a computer programmer and lived in Croydon I even told him my real name. After all, it wasn't as if we moved in the same

35

social circles. His own name was Monty, Monty Hartle, and he was younger than I'd imagined, in fact a year younger than me, at 26, which improved my authority even more.

As he talked I realised that he didn't see himself as fat. He was aware of it, obviously, he could hardly not have been, but it was rather like the way that I'm aware that I've got brown hair but I don't see myself as a brunette. To me, words like 'brunette' and 'blonde' just objectify women, and he clearly viewed being fat in the same way, although to me it was the overridingly important thing about him.

By the time we got to the flat I was feeling a lot better about myself, mentally anyway. Physically I was both exhausted and uncomfortable. The more friendly I'd been to him the more in awe of me he had become, and I could see no reason not to take advantage of the fact. So I told him to run me a bath, and pinched his mate's dressing gown before stuffing my clothes into the washing machine.

He had hovered outside the bedroom door as I undressed, obviously wanting to look, but not daring to. His sheer desperation put a smile on my face, and I deliberately left the robe loose at the front so that he got a teasing slice of bare boob when I came out. At my suggestion he started to get a coffee together, which I needed badly, and I sat down at the kitchen table while the bath ran. He'd gone silent, but spoke as he poured boiling water into the mugs.

'You know last night . . . it was all right, yeah?'

'I was so drunk I don't really remember,' I lied. 'But, yes, it was all right. I don't mind, if that's what you mean.'

'Great,' he answered, and there was so much feeling in that word.

I was beginning to enjoy myself. He was a bit like Percy in a way, really attentive, but, where Percy keeps

36

me under quite strict discipline and won't stand too much nonsense, Monty really seemed to worship me.

The bath was full and I took my mug into the bathroom, sipping at it before shrugging the robe off. With some coffee inside me I felt better still, and I left the door slightly open, as much to tease him as to allow us to continue talking. Getting into the water was lovely, sheer bliss as I relaxed into it and all my stiffness and discomfort began to fade away. As Percy says, to really appreciate a pleasure you have to experience the reverse, and it was certainly true about that bath.

I put my head back, letting my hair soak to get rid of the spunk and beer, with my ears underwater so that I couldn't hear. Taking the soap, I began to wash, my tummy first, which is always so soothing, then the caked mess between my bumcheeks and pussy lips. When I finally lifted my head I realised that Monty had said something, a question.

'Sorry, what was that?' I asked.

'I said, may I watch?' he answered.

'Watch me in the bath?'

'Yes.'

I hesitated. He sounded really insecure, urgent too, as if just seeing my naked body was a really big deal. Obviously it was.

'Do you have to?' I demanded.

'We fucked last night,' he said, his voice mixing resentment and longing.

'Oh, all right,' I said. 'If you have to.'

I was enjoying his discomfort, his lust too, and as his owlish face appeared around the door I gave him a dirty look. His guilt was plainly written on his face, but he came in, sitting down on the loo with his fat hands folded in his lap. I began to soap my legs.

'You're a real pervert,' I told him. 'A peeping Tom.'

He coloured and shifted uneasily, but his eyes were fixed on my body, flicking between my legs and where my boobs showed above the surface of the water. There was so much lust in his face, which had started to go red.

'You're just a dirty little boy,' I went on. 'Aren't you? A filthy, dirty little boy. Honestly, wanting to watch a girl in her bath.'

'What's wrong with it?' he said, now defensive.

I just laughed, because that wasn't what I wanted, not to make him feel bad. Anyway, not so bad it stopped him getting off over me.

'You can wank if you like,' I offered. 'That's what you'd really like to do, isn't it?'

He nodded, the colour of his face growing suddenly richer as he reached down for his fly.

'Uh, uh, not yet,' I chided him. 'First you're to wash my hair, but no touching anywhere else.'

He swallowed, the lump clearly rising in his throat. It was great. I had total control over him. Why he put up with it after the sluttish way I'd behaved the night before I don't know. If I'd treated Percy the same way he'd have spanked me with the bath brush.

I sat up a little and put my head back as he reached for a bottle of shampoo. His hands were trembling, and he was really clumsy, squirting out so much that it ran over the side of his palm. He got down on his knees and I shut my eyes as his hand went to my head, smearing the shampoo liberally over it.

'Rub it in well,' I ordered, 'with your fingertips.'

He complied, clumsy, but effective, with his big, podgy fingers actually just about ideal for the job. It was soothing too, and he didn't seem in any rush to stop, while I knew full well that his eyes would be fixed on my body. I was enjoying myself more and more, and I wanted to drive him crazy with lust and make him feel really guilty at the same time.

'Now rinse,' I said and arched my back to dip my hair into the water and incidentally stick my boobs up high. 'In the water first, then from the tap.'

I could hear his breathing as he washed the shampoo out of my hair, and I was wishing there had been some conditioner so that I could make him go through the whole thing again. My nipples were hard, and it was as if I could feel his eyes on my chest. I let him do my hair, until his hands began to sneak lower, massaging my neck. It was nice, but it wasn't what I wanted, and I sat up.

'Uh, uh, don't get dirty with me,' I chided. 'Now out with your little cock and I think you'd better wank it off.'

I needed a towel to dry the water off my forehead, and by the time I opened my eyes he was back on the toilet seat, with his fat thighs wide apart and his cock and balls hanging out of his trousers. It looked really obscene, just the way I had imagined it the night before, and my dirty feelings started to rise again, urging me to crawl over to him and lick and suck at his gross genitals, but I held myself back.

'Soap your knockers, please,' he rasped as he began to stroke at his cock.

'Dirty bastard!' I answered, but took my boobs in my hands, with the soap bar as well, smoothing it over them in circles as his cock grew in his hand.

'That's great,' he moaned. 'Oh you've got gorgeous knockers, Natasha, really gorgeous ones.'

'You like them do you?' I taunted. 'You like to wank over girls' boobs, I suppose. I bet you go down to the beach to watch.'

He nodded, now tugging hard at a fully erect cock. It looked perfect, so utterly obscene, with the great thick shaft straining up over his ball sac and his free hand holding his gross belly out of the way. I wanted to laugh at him, but I wanted to suck on his cock at the same time. He was getting frantic, and I went on soaping my boobs, which were covered in lather, with the nipples poking up through the froth, rock hard and very sensitive. I thought he was going to come, but he slowed suddenly, panting, obviously unable to make it so fast.

I laughed, I couldn't stop myself, just from his desperate, urgent lust, and all because I'd let him jerk his dirty cock over the sight of my body. He swallowed, struggling to regain his breath, then began to wank again, more slowly now, stroking his balls as he did it, then gradually faster as he feasted his eyes on me.

'What do you like to do?' he urged. 'I bet it's something grubby, something really grubby. Come on, you can tell me.'

'You just want me to talk dirty, don't you?'

'Whatever turns you on.'

'It doesn't turn me on, Monty, it turns you on, you pervert.'

I was lying, but I was getting so high on tormenting him that I didn't want to stop. He was red in the face, with sweat running down his cheeks as he hammered at his cock, all the while with his eyes glued to my body. I could sense his guilt and shame, just like my own for what I'd had him do to me, and it was great, revenge and sadistic delight at the same time.

'You love this, don't you,' I went on. 'I bet you do it all the time, over porn, you dirty bastard, in your bedroom, wanking over some poor girl's tits and bottom. Imagine it, Monty, some poor girl who's so hard up for money she has to pose in a dirty magazine, hating every minute of it, and what are you doing? You're wanking over her, aren't you, you filthy little pervert, wanking your cock over her bare body, just like you're wanking it over mine. Jesus you're dirty. Look at you, with your cock out and your eyes fixed on my tits. Do you want more? How about some pussy, with my legs apart? How about some bum, with my cheeks nice and wide so you can see the hole? That's what you'd like best, isn't it? I bet it is, jerking off your filthy little cock over the sight of my bumhole, isn't it?'

It was what I wanted, badly, and I rolled in the bath as I spoke, sticking my bum up out of the water and pulling my back in to make my cheeks part and show my hole, the rear of my pussy too. I was looking back, and I could see his face, bright red and wet with sweat, while his hand was jerking frantically at his cock. He was staring at my bum, his eyes fixed on my most intimate details, and at last it was too much for him and a spurt of white fluid jumped from the tip of his cock, then another, to splash across his belly and run down over his fingers.

'Pervert,' I told him one last time as he slumped back against the toilet. 'Now get out.'

I wanted him out because I needed to come myself, and having taken charge it didn't seem right to let him watch. He went, not even stopping to clean up, but waddling out of the room with his cock still hanging out of his fly. My hand went straight to my pussy as I rolled on to my back, my eyes closing in bliss. I was grinning as I masturbated, imagining his shame and confusion as he brought himself to orgasm over the sight of my body. I'd made up the bit about glamour models hating it, and it was probably rubbish, but I'd guessed it would make him feel worse, so much worse. He'd come though, and I was sure he'd felt as much of the guilt and shame he'd made me suffer for two long weeks.

That was what got me to orgasm, as much as the feel of my soapy body and the thought of what an exhibition I'd made of myself: sheer sexual revenge. When I opened my eyes it was to find him peeping in at the door, so I threw a sponge at him and called him a pervert again as he beat a hasty retreat.

What was left of my coffee was cold, but I drank it anyway, and finished washing before climbing out of the bath and putting on the robe. Monty was in the kitchen, stuffing his fat face with jam sandwiches. I made toast for myself, not really sure what I should say, until he broke the silence.

'You liked that, didn't you?' he asked.

41

'Of course I did,' I answered. It seemed pretty pointless to deny it.

'You're a dirty girl, aren't you?'

There was something about the way he said it, 'dirty girl', as if it was something clear cut, classified, and my mind went back to my thoughts of brunettes and blondes. There was something really smutty about the concept, humiliating too, as if it gave him the right to use me, because I was dirty, soiled goods.

'I can be,' I answered cautiously.

'You are,' he said with certainty. 'You asked to kiss my arse last night, you did, and you call me a pervert.'

'You are,' I replied. 'Peeping Tom. I was drunk last night.'

I'd said it, but without much conviction in my voice. He knew.

'Drink brings out the truth,' he said. 'Come on, dirty stuff turns you on, doesn't it? What do you like best, that, kissing a man's arse?'

'No.'

'What then? Come on, tell me, please. I want to know what really turns you on.'

'Oh, all right, it is that, sort of, sexual submission anyway. You really got to me when you threatened to sit on my head, if you must know. That's why I went with you, why I wanted to kiss you like that.'

'Hang on, it was you who asked me to do it!'

'No, before that. The first time.'

'First time?'

'You know. In the *Borscht*.'

'The what?'

'The Polish restaurant in Lamb's Conduit Street, you know.'

He shrugged.

'Stop messing about! You were there. I called you a ... something nasty and you threatened to sit on my head to teach me my manners.'

'No.'

'You must have been there, you must have!'

I was pleading, I could hear the tone in my own voice, but I knew he was telling the truth. He wasn't the original fat man at all.

All the way back to London I thought about what I'd done. I kept telling myself that I could handle it, that it was no worse than many of the other things I'd done. After all, I'd kissed Percy's anus often enough. He liked me to do it to him to say thank you for beatings, and he was fat enough, and more than twice my age into the bargain. It didn't matter, there was just something irrevocably obscene about Monty Hartle. There was also something funny about him, almost clownlike, with his great wobbling body and fat face. That made the thought of sex with him yet more humiliating, and it also made him seem safe, completely unthreatening.

I was doing over a hundred most of the way up the M23, until I saw the flashing blue light of a police car on one of the bridges, which sobered me up considerably. After that I was careful, and when I got to the M25 I turned west for Dorking and Box Hill, which seemed the ideal place to be alone to just think.

I'd spent most of the day with him, waiting for my clothes to dry, in nothing but one of his T-shirts, although that covered me completely. I was still knickerless under my trousers, because I hadn't been able to face the offer of one of his pairs of underpants, which I'd have had to tie off at both sides in any case.

He'd given me his address, plus his landline, mobile and email, really eager that I should see him again. I'd taken them, but declined to give mine in return, although I had a sneaking suspicion he'd gone through my bag at some point. He'd even asked me out, in his inept way, using words I hadn't heard since I was a teenager. Naturally I'd refused, but I had said I might

43

get in touch with him, which was as far as I was prepared to go. Really I needed to get my head round the whole thing first.

Box Hill itself was quite crowded, with dog walkers and families out for a Sunday stroll. I needed to be alone, and struck off on a footpath, off the National Trust land to a bit of woodland that looked lonely enough for my purposes. I knew I was going to masturbate, I had no illusions about that, or shame. The problem was what I was going to masturbate over.

I would have liked to strip nude, and it was just about warm enough for it, but I didn't really feel secure. Anyway, if I stripped I was likely to come just over the exhibitionist thrill of being naked in the open air, and I had a reason for masturbating other than simple self-indulgence. What I wanted to do was let my mind drift and see what I came over, then I would know if I ought to take the thing with Monty any further, or drop it.

Not that the practical reasons for what I was doing stopped me having fun with it and, as I looked for a safe place, a deliciously naughty feeling was growing inside me. I'd done it quite a lot in France, where it's so much easier to find lonely places, but nearly always with Percy watching, to stand guard as well as to enjoy the view. Now I was alone, and vulnerable, and excited.

There is always that thrill of wondering what would happen if I got caught when I masturbate outdoors, but I make very, very sure it never happens. After about half an hour of trying to choose a place, and all the while growing more edgy and more aroused, I settled on a bank of fern right at the edge of the wood. It was perfect really, because I could sit with my back to a big beech tree and see down the slope through the fronds, although there was no chance of anyone seeing me.

I still felt seriously nervous as I undid my fly and eased my trousers down over my hips. Being knickerless gave me a nice hit of pleasure, with my pussy immediately bare, only to discover that the beech leaves I was sitting on tickled my bum. So I made myself a little seat of fern leaves, forcing myself to do it with my trousers still down to add to the thrill. It was a lot more comfortable sitting on them, and I relaxed back against the tree, with my legs wide and my jeans down around my ankles.

It felt very good indeed, and I began to stroke myself, concentrating on my belly and thighs and deliberately avoiding my pussy. After a while I pulled my boobs out, which felt ruder still, especially when I remembered that was how I'd been while he licked me out in the garage.

I had been drunk, very drunk, but I'd done it, and at heart I knew it was what I'd wanted to do anyway. Lying to myself was futile, especially as I'd been perfectly sober when I'd been fantasising about it before, and when I'd masturbated in front of him in the bath. Watching him had been good too, as well as making me feel a lot better about myself. He was obscene, so fat, with his great greasy cock and huge balls, all hanging out beneath his massive belly.

It was getting too much for me to hold back, and I began to stroke my boobs, cupping them, one in each hand, and running my thumbs over the nipples. I was near naked outdoors and it felt really nice, and I was going to come, over one of the rudest things I'd done in my life. I'd been right not to strip too. It felt better half-dressed, dirtier, less decent, with everything that mattered showing, with my boobs in my hands so that it was quite obvious that I was no sunbather, but a slut, playing with herself for the pleasure of it.

For a while I just toyed with my boobs, letting the arousal build up slowly inside me. I knew that if I really needed more sex with Monty I'd come over it, but there was no point in forcing the issue. Instead I tried to think of something else, Damon and the way he liked to force me to swallow his spunk, but it was no good, that was past and I'd had my fill.

I tried Gina next, thinking of how much fun it would have been to turn her over my lap in the club, to flip up her little floaty dress and pull down her panties, to spank her bare bottom in front of all those hundreds of women and men. It was good, especially imagining how she would have kicked and struggled, squealing out her protests as I exposed her and punished her for being such a little flirt. Unfortunately it was impossible not to imagine Amy's reaction. She's taller than me and fitter than me, and it would have been me who ended up getting punished.

Not that that was so bad either. A bare bottom spanking in front of several hundred leering watchers is just my thing, at least in fantasy. Amy would have done it hard too, really making me kick and thrash, showing off my pussy and bumhole as I was beaten, then making me grovel on the floor to kiss her feet in abject apology, with my bare red bum stuck up in the air for everyone to see.

She would have made me apologise to Gina too, kissing her little white pumps. Gina would have giggled and pulled up her dress, pointing to her pussy and ordering me to lick it. I'd have done it, in front of everybody, with my tongue well in as Amy watched in delight, Isabel and Ami in shock, Gabrielle with a detached, scientific interest. That would have been the worst of it, Gabrielle Salinger, cool and aloof, watching me lick pussy. I'd have masturbated too, unable to hold back, just as I was now.

I'd closed my eyes and my hand had gone to my pussy, stroking and kneading, still clear of my clitty, but close enough. I was wet, and as I pushed two fingers to the mouth of my vagina they slid up easily, into the warm, moist mouth, feeling the wet, bumpy tube within, then out, and to my mouth, to suck up my own juices just the way I'd licked them off Monty's balls.

46

That was too much, and my fingers went to my clitty as I thought of the taste of his balls, sticky with my own juice from where he'd fucked me, doggy style, on all fours like a bitch on heat. It had got worse though, so much worse, with his fat, blubbery bottom in my face, right in my face, smothering me, making me kick and writhe underneath him, forcing me to kiss it, to kiss his anus, his arsehole . . .

I really screamed as I came, choking it back only when I remembered where I was. That broke the orgasm before it was really over, and I hastily covered myself and scrambled up, retreating through the wood instead of down the slope. Fortunately, nobody seemed to be about, and I returned to the car without incident.

It was nearly dark by the time I got back to my flat in Primrose Hill, to find the doorway piled up with red roses, bunch upon bunch of the things.

Four

The roses were from Damon, inevitably, which was a real pain. For a moment I'd thought Percy might have come back early, until I'd read the card.

It was the usual stuff, a mixture of grovelling apology and the use of his strength of feeling for me to justify trying to tell me what to do, along with a touch of condescension. I'd heard it all before, and I wasn't impressed. It was just a nuisance. I'd hoped he would be so full of himself that he wouldn't bother to chase me. I'd been wrong.

My first thought was to take the moral high ground, saying that I'd met somebody else in Brighton and that it would be wrong of me to see both of them or to dump the new man. It would leave Damon with some of his pride and, when men get dumped, it tends to be their pride which is really hurt, more than any other emotion. On the other hand, I could hardly present Monty as the new man and, anyway, I didn't see why I should leave Damon with any of his pride, roses or no roses.

He didn't seem the type to give up so easily anyway, but I wasn't going back with him. I'd had my fill. Nor did I want to make a big scene of it. All I wanted was for him to go away quietly, but I had a nasty suspicion he wouldn't.

I didn't know what to do with the roses either. There were twelve dozen of them, and they weren't even good ones, just the sort people who look like they're illegal immigrants try to sell you at traffic lights. If I put them in water and he saw them he was bound to assume he had melted me. I didn't want to do anything melodramatic, like stuff them in the outside bin or shred them all over the pavement. In fact I didn't want to do anything that displayed emotion at all, good or bad. What I wanted to show was indifference.

In the end I took them to a local church, where the vicar accepted them, trying to look grateful, but quite obviously wondering how he was going to find receptacles for so many of the things. I dodged the issue with Damon too, deciding to ignore him and hope he'd go away.

On the Monday I got down to work, of which there was no shortage. Percy and I had been to all sorts of places in France, and tasted wines you don't normally see in Britain at all. I wanted to get the best out of it before Percy got back, mainly so that I could pretend I'd 'discovered' things that in fact he'd shown me. Inevitably it would mean a dose of the cane, probably more than one, but I knew where that led.

I stopped at five, because I wanted to be very firmly out for the evening. I also felt the need of some serious pampering, and decided on a trip to Haven, which meant no men and the perfect chance to think. It was exactly what I needed, because I was still considering the pros and cons of seeing Monty Hartle again. I knew I wanted what he had to give – I'd come over it – but I didn't want him getting involved with my life in general.

So I walked across the park, to Marylebone, and was soon lying back in a steam room with nothing on but a couple of towels. Damon, Monty, enforced cock sucking and fat men's bumholes seemed a world away, and I'd lulled myself into a nice, sleepy haze when Ami Bell came in, looking far from happy.

'Bastard!' she said as she came to sit beside me.

My first thought was to be pissed off that she didn't seem in the least worried about my disappearance in Brighton, but my curiosity quickly overcame that.

'Who's a bastard?' I asked.

'Men, all of them,' she snapped. 'But most of all Chris!'

'Why?'

'He went up to Manchester at the weekend, to watch some football match. I mean, what is the point of me have a night to myself if he goes off as well?'

'Well . . .'

'Anyway, that's not all. He went with a tart, I know he did.'

'Oh.'

'His shirt stank of perfume, something really cheap and nasty. It's horrible! I can't bear to touch him!'

'Did he admit to it?'

'I haven't asked! I can't bear to. I know he'd just deny it anyway. I feel really soiled.'

'Dump him.'

'How can I? We're buying the flat together, and I do love him. I think I do, anyway.'

'Have an affair.'

'That's what Gabrielle suggested. I want to, but I can't. I found that out in Brighton. Several men tried to get talking to me, but I just couldn't respond. I didn't fancy any of them. What happened to you, anyway?'

'I just felt sick. I was actually. I really couldn't face coming back to the club with all that smoke and noise.'

'Oh, right.'

She sighed, leaning back against the wall and closing her eyes. Her hair was wet, and she hadn't bothered with a towel for it, leaving the strands plastered to her head and shoulders. She still had her glasses on too, and they were rapidly steaming up, making her look yet more bedraggled and pathetic.

'What else happened?' I asked.

'Nothing, really. After the club we went back to the hotel. Amy and Gina went to their room and Isabel, Gabrielle and I sat up talking. I had a rotten head the next day, and when I got back I found Chris asleep and his shirt stinking of that awful perfume. Oh God!'

A really good idea had occurred to me. Ami might not have fancied any of the men in Brighton, but she did fancy Damon. If I could somehow get the two of them together it would solve my problem and hopefully make her happier. Having said that, she never really seemed content with her life, whatever she did, but I would be rid of Damon. There was the difficulty of him being a client of her firm, but it had to be worth a try. There was also the thought of how her pretty, innocent face would look while she gagged on his cock. Not that I'd get to see it, but I'd know.

'You should go with Damon,' I suggested.

'Damon? Damon Maurschen?'

'Who else?'

'I can't! He's a client. Anyway, I thought you and he ...'

'Not any more. It didn't work out. He wouldn't commit, so I told him to get lost.'

'I wish I could be as assertive as you, or Amy. She's so empowered. She snogged Gina in the club, quite openly!'

I shrugged, wondering if she'd be so impressed by my behaviour. Outright lesbianism is cool, bisexuality isn't so easy to get away with, never mind being a complete slut. There was envy in her voice too, and I wondered if it was because she wanted to be as strong as Amy McRae, or whether she wished it was her who'd been snogging Gina, or Amy for that matter. Suddenly dumping Damon on her didn't seem such a good idea.

'I saw Gabrielle earlier,' she went on. 'She suggested taking colonic hydrotherapy. Apparently by purging myself physically I can effectively purge myself mentally. She's so intelligent!'

'So everyone keeps saying.'

'It's true, she's wonderful! Whole-being therapy is like nothing I've ever tried before, or maybe like everything I've tried before rolled together. I'm not sure about the colonic hydrotherapy though. Wouldn't it hurt?'

I couldn't resist it, there's just too much mischief in me.

'It doesn't hurt at all,' I assured her. 'It's a wonderful feeling.'

'You've done it?'

'Yes, I do it regularly.'

'What's it like.'

'Wonderful, like I say. Really cathartic, with the tension building up as it goes in, then all flowing away as it comes out.'

'Isn't it a bit dirty, messy?'

'Not if you do it properly. I could show you. I'll even help you if you like.'

'Would you?'

'Sure, why not. Let's take a shower and you can come back with me.'

She did. I had no idea of what Gabrielle's colonic hydrotherapy involved, but the chance of giving Ami Bell an enema was just too good to miss. She has a lovely bum, round and just cheeky enough to be spankable. So spankable in fact that as she climbed up the stairs in front of me with her lovely cheeks moving inside her tight jeans I was wondering if I couldn't bullshit her into believing that a spanking or a caning had some sort of cathartic value. Punishment does, actually, for me, but I couldn't see her buying the idea and decided to content myself with the enjoyment I was going to get out of her enema.

Like I say, it's beyond me how anybody could fail to find the experience sexual. I mean, you're naked, or at least the most intimate parts of your body are on show, and there's a tube up your bumhole! I was shaking before I'd closed the door to my flat, but Ami seemed completely oblivious.

I poured us a glass of wine each and told her to go into the bathroom and undress. She did it, and I watched, with both my arousal and my sense of mischief rising and rising as she peeled off her clothes. Her panties were big, and white, which was just perfect, while she had a Wonderbra on in a vain effort to make something of her tits, making her more vulnerable than ever when they came bare. She took off everything, except her glasses, and nude, with just the big, round spectacles and her still damp hair, she looked so sweet. I wanted to spank her, or make her lick me, with her face buried in my pussy and her big brown eyes looking up at me through the lenses. Naturally I couldn't but what I was going to do was nearly as good.

'Aren't you going to undress too?' she asked as she folded her panties on top of the little pile of clothes she'd made.

She bent nicely as she did it, giving me a fine view of her bum, then took a towel and wrapped it around herself.

'Me?' I asked.

'Yes, I thought you were going to show me first. Anyway, I know it's silly, but I feel a bit shy with no clothes on in front of you while you're still fully dressed.'

'That is silly! Take a towel if you like.'

'Will you show me?'

'Yes, of course.'

I began to undress, and while she didn't watch openly, she kept glancing at me out of the corner of her eye. She had taken a towel, and sat down on the edge of the bath. I stripped very casually, not showing off at all, but my suspicions were growing and I was wondering just how far I could push her.

'I wish I had breasts like yours,' she sighed, as I reached up for the medical cabinet. 'You're so lucky.'

I smiled back. After all, my boobs are just about perfect, not too big, not too small, and firm. Certainly the boys have always been complimentary, girls too. Hers were like bee stings. Unfortunately it wasn't the moment to invite her to have a feel.

'This is the kit,' I explained. 'The water goes in this thing like a hot-water bottle. A pint's about right, and it ought to be warm. This nozzle goes up your bum . . .'

'Ow! It's really thick. Doesn't it hurt?'

'Not really. You put some jelly up first, of course, and some on the nozzle. Anyway, it's not nearly as thick as a man's cock.'

'A cock!'

'Sure, haven't you ever . . .'

'No I have not! I could never do that! You haven't, have you?'

I just laughed. I hadn't realised how innocent she was. She was blushing, making her look sweeter than ever, while the thought that the bumhole I was about to penetrate was virgin was almost too much for me.

'Look, this is what you do,' I said, changing the subject before she could lose her nerve completely.

I am such a show-off. I took the tube of jelly and spread my bumcheeks, right in front of her, making sure she could see every detail between them. With it stuck right out, I used two fingers to keep my cheeks open and squeezed out a worm of jelly between them, right on to my hole. It felt deliciously cold and, as I stood up, it squashed between them, which was glorious.

Going to the sink, I measured out a pint into the reservoir and hung it on the shower rail, all the while with the jelly squishing between my cheeks as I moved. She watched everything, her mouth slightly open, looking like a surprised owl with her big glasses. I turned my back to her again, put one foot up on the bath and stuck my bum out, letting her see every detail of my pussy and the greasy spot of my bumhole. Taking the nozzle, I put it between my cheeks, just above the hole.

'It shouldn't hurt at all,' I told her. 'Not if you're properly lubricated. You just have to relax. Look, watch my anus.'

I let my sphincter go loose, feeling my anus push out and open a little. It felt so good, and so rude, showing off my greasy little bumhole for her, with her eyes fixed on it. I slid the nozzle lower, rubbing in the slimy, mushy flesh, then up, inside, my ring opening to take it, deep, and closing on the neck.

'There we are,' I said. 'No pain at all.'

'What does it feel like?' she asked.

'Not much,' I said. 'I can feel it in my hole, but it's not really big enough to stretch me inside.'

'Oh.'

She sounded so timid, and I wanted her to keep talking, as intimately as possible, while I showed myself off. I turned the valve, making sure she saw, and gave a little gasp, only half voluntary, as the water started to flow up my bum.

'There aren't really any nerve endings in the rectum,' I said, 'but you can feel it stretch, like when you need to go to the loo badly. It gets like that with the water, a sort of bloated feeling. It's getting like that now.'

'Isn't that unpleasant?'

'No, I like it. It's a bit . . .'

'What?'

I'd paused deliberately, knowing she was bound to ask what I'd been going to say.

'Never mind.'

'No, what Tasha?'

'Like being buggered. My bottom feels full, heavy. It's like it goes to my head, and it's the same with a cock up the bum. It's not that different from having a cock up the pussy, not so nice, but . . .'

I trailed off again, this time because I felt I might have gone too far. What I wanted to say was that being

55

buggered felt dirtier, even if the physical sensation wasn't so good. With my bottom spread bare in front of her and the nozzle held up my bum, it was getting hard to hold back, and she was just staring at me, looking more owlish than ever.

'How . . . how could you let a man do that to you?' she asked suddenly. 'It's so degrading!'

'Not if you want it,' I answered, and trailed off with a sigh.

There was plenty of water up me, most of the bag. It was making me want to pant and I was having to squeeze my bumhole to keep it in. Ami was watching in absolute fascination, and I wondered if I dared expel in front of her. I wanted to expel over her, on her tiny tits and in her face, but of course it was out of the question.

'I'm quite full now,' I said. 'I'm having to hold it in. Oh . . . it does feel nice . . . oh . . .'

I pulled the nozzle out of my bum and sat quickly down on the loo. For one moment I held it, and then I let it come, spraying out of my bottomhole into the pan beneath as I let my breath out with a long sigh. I was acting up a bit, but it did feel good, and all the better for being done in front of her. She watched as I did it, and when it was all out I turned to her with a grin.

'That is wonderful now,' I said. 'I feel cleansed. Gabrielle's right, there is a mental effect as well as a physical one.'

Ami nodded, looking stunned. I was bubbling inside, really turned on and so, so full of mischief, but I tried to act nonchalantly as I wiped my bottom and stood up. What I couldn't resist doing was spreading my cheeks and asking her if I was properly clean, to which she nodded again.

'I think I'll step under the shower for a minute anyway,' I said. 'It's nice to clean up properly afterwards. Then it's your turn.'

Once more she nodded. She was pink faced and fidgeting, clutching her towel to her chest, her other hand shaking as she picked up her wine glass. I stepped into the shower, not bothering to close the curtain, and made a big show of washing my bum, with plenty of soap. I was sure she'd realise that I was showing off, but I really couldn't stop myself, and I even put a finger up my bumhole, in plain view.

When I'd finished I dried myself and put a little powder on, under my boobs and between my bum-cheeks. As when I'd stripped, she pretended not to watch, but I knew her eyes were on me. She was in quite a state, and she'd drunk most of the bottle while I'd been giving myself my enema and cleaning up, making me more hopeful still. It made sense to give her the enema and then masturbate over the experience in peace, but sense was coming to have less and less to do with it.

'Right then,' I said happily, once more picking up the enema bag and the jug. 'You'd better bend over the bath, so your bum's stuck out towards the loo. We don't want any accidents.'

'Accidents?'

'It can be a bit of a shock, the first time. You wouldn't want to do it on the floor, would you?'

'Couldn't I just sit on the loo?'

'No. I need to see what I'm doing. I might hurt you otherwise.'

'Oh.'

She was really hesitant, wonderfully hesitant, but she did it, placing her hands on the side of the bath, bent down, looking back over her shoulder with a worried expression on her face as I poured the contents of the jug into the reservoir.

'You'll have to stick your bum out a bit more than that,' I chided. 'I can't see your anus.'

She let out a sob of pure humiliation, but she did it, sticking her bottom out so that her lovely round cheeks came apart, revealing the neat pink dimple of her bumhole, with her pussy lips peeping out below, pouted and hairy, also damp at the centre. I wanted to touch, so badly, and my fingers were shaking hard as I took the tube of jelly and squeezed some out over her bumhole. My hand went down and I was touching her, lubricating her anus, around the hole, then up, sliding my finger deep into the hot, wet tube of her rectum as she gave another of her soulful little noises.

I wanted to keep my finger in, and to slide another up her pussy, but I knew she wasn't ready, not yet. I had to try though. All thoughts of giving her the enema and then masturbating over the experience afterwards had gone. She wanted it, and she wanted it as badly as I did, physically.

'There we are,' I said, pulling my finger out with a sticky pop.

He anus closed immediately, tight, to make a little pink star, greasy with jelly. I could tell she was virgin, because she was a lot tighter than I am. She'd still be able to take the nozzle, but I was going to have to be careful. Hurting her was the last thing I wanted to do.

'Now just relax,' I instructed her, picking up the nozzle. 'Let your anus go loose. Don't be nervous, just imagine you're on the loo.'

She gave another of her sweet little sobs, but her bumhole started to push out, opening. I touched the nozzle to the greasy dimple of flesh and watched her ring spread open, taking it. She let out a little, low moan as it went up, hanging her head down so that her long hair dangled as the nozzle slid up her anus to the neck. Her ring closed, tightening to hold the nozzle in, and I let go, rocking back on my heels to admire her penetrated bottom.

I was wishing I had a strap-on dildo to hand, so that I could make a proper job of fucking her bottom. She just looked so sweet, bent over, with her little round bum in the air, her head hung down, her titties dangling, and the tube sticking obscenely out of her anus.

'I'm going to turn it on,' I said. 'You won't feel much at first, because the water's pretty close to blood temperature. After a while you'll feel your tummy start to swell and you'll want to go to the loo. Just take it, and tell me when you need to expel.'

She nodded, saying nothing and I tweaked the valve open. The tube rounded out and she gave the softest of gasps as the water started to flow up her bum. I watched, trying not to smile too openly.

Slowly her breathing changed, becoming deeper and slower, and her bumhole began to bulge out. I wanted to masturbate, coming as I watched her, or burying my face in her beautiful rear and licking her to orgasm as her rectum bulged out with water. It was impossible not to at least touch myself, and I sneaked a hand down between my thighs, finding my pussy swollen and wet. So was hers, the lips puffy with blood and her hole marked with a bead of white fluid.

Again her breathing changed, suddenly growing faster. I reached out, stroking her bottom as it became a rhythmic, urgent panting. She was nearly full, I could tell, with the area around her bumhole pushed out and her ring clamped tight on the nozzle. I glanced up, and sure enough, the reservoir looked close to empty.

'Hold it,' I said. 'Keep it up your bottom for a while, let the water do its work.'

'I can't!' she panted. 'I can't, Tasha. Oh!'

'There, just try and relax,' I soothed, again stroking her bum.

She was shaking, and wriggling her toes, struggling to hold her enema in. I wanted to lick so badly, and I put my other hand to her bottom, feeling her cheeks.

'What are you doing?' she demanded, still panting.

'Helping you,' I told her. 'Just go with it, Ami, let your feelings take you. I'm going to take the nozzle out now, but hold the water in. OK?'

She nodded, her hair bouncing to the movement. Slowly I eased the nozzle from her bumhole, watching as she tensed it, held tight against the pressure. I was so turned on that I was wondering if I couldn't find some excuse for her to have an accident, to do it over me, all down my front, over my boobs and belly, even in my face. Suddenly her bottom tensed, her cheeks clenching as she cried out.

'I can't hold it!' she squealed. 'Oh, Tasha, I can't! It's going to happen! It's going to happen!'

At the last possible moment she swung her bottom over the loo, sitting down heavily as her anus gave and the contents of her rectum exploded out into the bowl. Her head was back, her mouth open, her face set in an expression of utter bliss as she emptied herself. I watched her do it, trembling, knowing that if she wouldn't let me have her I was going to force her legs apart and lick her pussy until she gave in.

'Oh my!' she sighed as her body at last went limp. 'That was ... that was ... I feel so strange.'

'Come on, I'll clean you up.'

She let me, unresisting as I wiped her bottom for her and led her into the shower. I was trembling with need, and I just wanted to grab her and have her, pushing her down on her knees in the shower to lick my pussy until I came in her face. Her nipples were hard and her lower lip was trembling. I knew she was ready, I was sure she was ready.

I held back, willing myself to wait for the right moment. She let me soap her, saying nothing, with her nipples straining to erection and her lower lip trembling nervously. My hands went to her bum, soaping her cheeks, then down in her crease. I found her bumhole again, wiggling my fingertip in the tight entrance as I began to stroke her wet hair, very gently, with my other hand. She was trembling so hard I could feel it through my body.

60

I had to do it, I just couldn't hold back anymore. I kissed her hair, her forehead, her nose. She sighed and her arms came up, to my shoulders, around my neck. Our mouths met, opening together and we were kissing, cuddling together as I pulled her in to my body. She was as urgent as I was, kissing me with real passion, and that broke my last efforts to take it slowly.

Still wriggling one finger in her bumhole, I let my other hand go lower. My fingers found the swell of her pubic mound, delving between her lips, to the soft, wet flesh of her pussy. She gave a little gasp, trying to pull back, but I held on, masturbating her.

'Don't,' I soothed. 'Don't fight.'

Again our mouths met, kissing gently now as my fingers worked on her sex. Quickly she started to push herself against my hand, cuddling on to me, tighter, until I pulled back, to kiss her chin, her neck.

'Oh, Tasha, no,' she moaned. 'Not that.'

I ignored her, kissing lower, on to her breasts, taking each nipple between my teeth, lower, down over her tummy, to her belly button, lower still, and she gave a low groan as my lips found her pussy. For one instant she held back, and then she was pushing herself into my face and her hand had gone to the back of my head, the other to her breasts. I began to lick, exploring her pussy with my tongue, tasting her juice and teasing each little fold of flesh. She was moaning, stroking her breasts, with her head back and the water cascading down over her face.

'Don't stop, never stop!' she gasped.

I kissed her clitty, sucking the little bud in between my lips to make her cry out before going back to exploring her.

'Oh, you're good, so good!' she moaned. 'Chris has never done anything like this ... so nice ... so good.'

With that she came, her thighs tensing against my face, spasms running through her flesh, her hand

61

locking in my hair. I kept licking, kneading her bottom as well, my finger still in the tight bud of her bumhole, which was pulsing as her climax ran through her.

She had come, and I was going to take my turn if I had to sit on her head. In fact, that seemed the perfect thing to do. I took her hand, leading her out of the shower. She looked so pretty, with her bedraggled hair and her steamed-up glasses, which she hadn't taken off at all, perfect to be smothered in pussy and made to lick.

'What are you doing?' she asked as I eased her down on to the floor. 'Do you ... do you want me to ... to you?'

I nodded, straddling her body as she went down. She seemed confused, nervous, but not at all unwilling, looking up at me as I mounted her, my pussy right over her face. I gave her a moment to realise what I was going to do, then sat down, smothering her mouth with my pussy. Her pert little nose pressed to my clit, which I began to rub on her, wriggling it in her face.

She began to lick, clumsily, but well enough, her eyes staring up at me through the big, round glasses. It was such a sweet sight, and I could feel everything, my bumcheeks spread over her face, my anus pressed to her chin, her tongue in my vagina, her little nose on my clitty. I wiggled down, masturbating on her face, thinking of how lovely she had looked, nude, bent, with a tube up her bum and her pussy sticking out behind, her head hung in shame and confusion as her belly swelled with water. It had been so good, so rude, so mischievous, a seduction by enema, a successful one, because now I was mounted on her face and she was licking my pussy out ...

I came, screaming and writhing my bottom into Ami's face, squirming and wriggling as she struggled to lick at me. For one moment her tongue lapped at my bumhole, and I caught the thought of how it would have felt to expel my own enema in her face, and watch

62

the mess run down her cheeks and drip from her hair, her glasses spattered with it, her mouth wide in shock and disgust. Then she was licking my clitty and everything was forgotten but pure pleasure as I held the moment, on and on, until at last I could take no more.

I saw Ami off in a minicab at nearly three in the morning. She was still giggling as she left, and gave me a wave from the window as the car moved off. We'd had sex again, stroking and licking at each other in my bed until we had both come. After our second orgasms we'd lain together in each other's arms, content to cuddle until she finally decided she had to go home. I went straight to bed, and more or less straight to sleep, feeling thoroughly pleased with myself.

I've known girls to get in a state after having sex with me before, even ones who were a lot cooler about it than Ami had been. So I wasn't all that surprised when my phone went in the early afternoon and it was her, with something close to panic in her voice.

'Tasha? I need to speak to you!' she blurted out.

'Sure, what about?' I answered, trying to be as cool as possible.

'What about? About what we did together!'

'No problem. Calm down.'

'Calm down? How can I calm down? I can't handle this at all. I don't know if I'm a lesbian or what!'

'Ami, Ami, please, get a grip. We only had a little play, it's nothing to get in a state over.'

'A little play! We had sex, Tasha!'

'So? Haven't you ever been with another girl before?'

'No I haven't!'

'Oh. Well, still . . . look, you enjoyed it, didn't you? I did.'

'Of course I did, you know I did. That's the trouble. I enjoyed it more than I do with Chris! I think I'm a lesbian, Tasha!'

'Well that's all right, isn't it?'

'No it is not all right! What I am supposed to say to my mum?'

'Don't tell her.'

'How can I not tell her? It's a really important lifestyle choice! And I'm not sure she'll understand. And she's always wanted me to have kids.'

'What's stopping you?'

'Being a lesbian?'

'You're not a lesbian, Ami. We were a bit drunk and we got a bit carried away with each other, that's all. It's nothing to worry about. It happens.'

'You've done it before?'

'Yes. It's nice, just think of us as closer friends.'

'Closer friends?'

'Yes, why not? Look, I gave you your enema, didn't I? That's pretty intimate, and it made you feel good. I made you come as well, and that made you feel good too. What's the difference?'

'It's sex!'

'And taking the enema didn't turn you on?'

'No! It . . . I . . .'

The phone went dead. I waited a moment, expecting her to ring back. It was hard not to smile, because she was always talking about women's rights to express their sexuality and so on, and now she was in a fine state, just because she'd been to bed with me. It wasn't even as if we'd done anything kinky. Well, the enema, but that wasn't really sex, or at least she hadn't seen it that way until too late. I was fairly sure she wouldn't even tell anybody. Not that it mattered, because we hadn't done anything our friends would view as perverse. Well, again, the enema, but I was absolutely sure she wouldn't tell them that it had turned her on.

It was only when I put the phone down that I realised there was another thing I could be absolutely sure of. She would tell Gabrielle Salinger, everything.

Five

I had formed a picture of Gabrielle's office in my mind, with a file on the desk about two inches thick, labelled 'Natasha Linnet – Sexual Deviant' or some such title. Now she could add to it, with some new details on my perversity, adding sexual enjoyment of enemas to wanting to be spanked.

It really was too much, and I was still holding my head in my hands and cursing Ami for not being able to handle her sexual feelings when the phone rang again. Naturally I thought it was her, and I picked up without looking at the number on the display, intent on inviting her out for a drink in an effort to explain that it was perfectly reasonable to have sex with your girlfriends.

It wasn't her, it was Damon, and that threw me completely. I just didn't know what to say. The whole business with him had slipped my mind, and I simply didn't have an answer ready. After all, I could hardly say I didn't want to see him because I'd started a lesbian relationship with Ami Bell, although it was tempting. It just wouldn't have been fair on her.

'Did you get my roses?' he asked.

'Yes,' I admitted. After all, I could hardly deny it.

'I bet they're all over your flat,' he laughed.

'Er . . . yes,' I answered, immediately realising that it was not a sensible answer. Nor would 'no' have been.

'Look, I am sorry,' he went on. 'I realise that I was getting, well, maybe a bit possessive. It's only because you're so wonderful, so free in yourself . . .'

What he meant was that I was a dirty slut who didn't mind him getting off on forcing me to swallow his spunk, but I didn't say it. He kept talking, while I struggled to think of a good excuse to turn down the date he was quite obviously leading up to asking me for.

'. . . there's this new place,' he was saying, '*Chez Fabrice*. I think even you will be impressed by the wine list . . .'

'It's crap,' I said, struggling to buy time and making a complete mess of it. 'No, I didn't mean that . . . it's . . . it's not really my thing.'

'It's great, you'll love it. I know the patron, I've booked the best table . . .'

'You arrogant bastard!'

'Natasha!'

'What do you mean by booking a table before we'd even made up? How dare you? What do you think I am, some little airhead you can buy off with a few cheap roses and a meal? Who the fuck do you think you are?'

I slammed the phone down, almost in tears. I hadn't wanted to make a fuss, but I'd had no choice. It had been that or accept a date with him, because I knew him. If I'd made some lame excuse he'd have just kept picking at me until I gave in, and I knew full well that if I'd tried to let him down gently he'd have come round. Then I'd have had the problem of explaining the absence of his precious roses.

In fact there seemed to be every chance that he would come round anyway. I needed to be out. For a moment my hand hovered over the receiver, as I wondered if I should call Ami and try to make her see sense. It would mean a really intense conversation though, and that was the last thing I wanted.

I got the TVR out of the garage and just drove, out on to the Westway at first, then south, down through

Hammersmith and over Putney Bridge. I was telling myself all the time that I was driving at random, but I knew perfectly well where I was going, and I ended up parking in the street where Monty Hartle lived.

Normally if I get really fed up I go to Percy, and get a really good spanking, even a dose of the cane or belt. Physical punishment really brings the world into perspective, thrown down nude or with my clothing in disarray while a dirty old man thrashes me until I'm in tears. Everything else always seems so much less important afterwards, especially while he's got his cock inside me.

There were one or two other people who could have been relied on to give me much the same treatment, but Monty was the man of the moment, and he hadn't had a chance to punish me yet. I was sure he'd want to as well, or at the very least that he'd do it. Certainly I couldn't imagine him going on about respecting me too much to do it, or it being against his moral principles, the way some men have been known to do. To the best of my knowledge Monty didn't have any moral principles.

The difficulty was that it was far too early for him to have got back from work. So I sat in the car for a while, then walked to the end of the road and back, to try to soak up the atmosphere of the surroundings he lived in.

I don't really go out into the suburbs a lot, or at least, not to stop. There had to be thousands of streets just like his in England, maybe tens of thousands, but to me it was really quite unfamiliar territory. For a start it was oddly quiet. Other than the background hum of traffic that you can never really get away from in London, there was only the faint sound of a radio, nothing else. It was also deserted, and I was the only person in the street, despite there being fifty or so houses on either side. They were all the same too, more or less, other than the occasional coat of paint or pebbledash front. It was uniform, humdrum, the sort of image of suburbia pop singers like to paint. I was sure that was superficial, having read somewhere that more strange sexual practices go on in the suburbs than anywhere else. I was sure it was true. Anyway, if it wasn't, then it would be soon enough once Monty got back from work.

At half past six he appeared, rolling around the corner at the far end of the street. I watched him for a while, just admiring his bulbous, sacklike body and enjoying the intense erotic shame he gave me. He had a completely blank expression on his face, and I could see that he was miles away, probably in a certain garage in Brighton.

When I got out of the car he did a wonderful double take, before his fat face broke into a beaming, lecherous grin.

'Hi, Monty,' I greeted him.

'Natasha, hi,' he answered. 'I didn't expect to see you here.'

'I bet you didn't expect to see me at all.'

'Well, maybe. So what's up?'

'I wanted to see you. I need to have my bottom spanked.'

'Wow.'

He'd been fishing his keys out of his pocket as we spoke, and he dropped them. I laughed. That was the great thing about him. I could say what I meant, straight out. I didn't care what he thought, and I didn't have to worry about the consequences.

Retrieving the keys, he fumbled them into the lock.

'You're into all that bizarre stuff, aren't you?' he said, pushing the door wide open.

'I suppose so, if you want to call it that.'

I followed him through the door, squeezing past him so that he could shut it. My boobs brushed his chest as we passed and he caught one in a hand, squeezing it. I let him fondle, after all, once he'd beaten me I knew I'd be up for anything he wanted to do to me.

'So what's with the spanking?' he asked. 'Coffee?'

That was great, so casual yet so dirty, feeling me up and asking about spanking, then offering a coffee.

'Sure,' I answered. 'Black, no sugar, unless it's instant, in which case white. It's complicated about the spanking. Let's just say I need discipline from time to time.'

'A school thing?'

'No. There was no corporal punishment at all at my school. Sorry to disappoint you.'

He shrugged as I followed him into the kitchen. It was small, and poky, with a strong smell of curry. He wasn't the tidiest of people, with the remains of last night's takeaway still on the table, but it was no worse than I'd expected. I could see why he was fat too, because he appeared to have eaten the contents of six aluminium packs and two heat-saving bags. Of course there was another possible explanation.

'You did say you lived alone?' I asked.

'Sure,' he answered.

For a moment I had a truly dreadful vision of his mother walking in and catching me across his knee with my panties at half mast. It made a great fantasy, and the humiliation would have been unbearable, especially if she'd dealt with me herself for being a tart, only of course it wouldn't have worked like that.

'Look, if I give you your spanking, will you be my sex slave?' he asked suddenly.

'Maybe,' I answered. 'It depends what you want to do to me.'

'Make you crawl around on the floor, that sort of stuff, like in this German video I saw, where the girl's on a lead, like a dog . . .'

'Well OK, so long as I get a stop word.'

'What, like if I go too far?'

'Exactly. I usually use "amber" for slow down and "red" for stop.'

'Yeah, whatever.'

'And no bondage, I don't know you well enough.'

'Sure, but I can fuck you?'

'You know you can.'

'Let's do it then! Fucking hell, you're hot!'

'Great. Do you want to beat me first? I'll be a lot more obedient once I've been punished.'

'More obedient? You are something else. I've already got a stiffy.'

'That's what all the boys say,' I answered, and gave his crotch a squeeze.

He was hard, rock hard, his cock a solid bar in his trousers, sticking up to one side. Just looking at him, and knowing the thing in my hand was going in me, was almost too much.

'Come on then, punish me,' I urged. 'Put me over your knee and spank my bare bottom, or cane me. Have you got a cane, like a school cane?'

'A school cane? No.'

'A spoon then, you must have a kitchen spoon?'

'Sure.'

'Then use it on me. Come on, Monty, I'm getting urgent. You'll make me kiss your bum afterwards, won't you?'

'I'll make you lick it!'

'You'd better do me hard then. Have you ever punished a girl before?'

'No.'

I'd been squeezing his cock as we spoke, but I stopped, scared he'd come in his pants and spoil everything. Too many men go off on guilt trips after they've come, which was the last thing I wanted.

'Just make sure you keep all the smacks on my bum,' I told him, 'and make a big deal of exposing me.'

'Count on it,' he answered, passing me the coffee.

He left the room, which puzzled me for a moment, until he came back, holding the most enormous spoon

70

I'd ever seen, about three feet long, with 'The World's Biggest Stirrer' painted on the handle. The expression on my face had changed at the sight of the horrid thing, and he noticed, giving me one of his dirty leers.

'Get in position, then,' he said, hefting the spoon.

It was going to hurt, a lot, but it was good, because it added an air of ridicule to the whole thing. I always like to think there's something comic about a girl getting a spanking, because it deepens my humiliation. Monty with his huge spoon was as comic as it gets, but it was me who was going to get bent over with my bare bum showing, me who was going to get spanked.

'I'm bound to make a fuss,' I told him as I pulled the chair out from the table. 'Just ignore me, unless I use my stop word. Give me a dozen, hard ones.'

'I've got a better idea. You have to throw dice to see how many you get. Look, see.'

He rolled something out on to the table, where it came to a stop against a curry container. It was a die, not an ordinary one, but a huge yellow multifaceted thing. The number nine showed uppermost and there were sides to spare.

'Twenty sides,' he said proudly, 'a role-playing dice. I throw, and if you don't like the result you can buy a reroll, with, let's see ... yeah, you get your knockers out. If you want a second reroll you have to take it with something up your cunt, an egg. I've got eggs. All right?'

I nodded dumbly. He might never have beaten a girl before, but he was a natural sadist, forcing me to choose my own fate and adding a touch of extra humiliation with it. I went to the table, moving the remains of his dinner carefully to avoid getting stale curry on myself, and climbed on to the chair, kneeling. I leaned forward, placing my elbows on the table and lifting my bum. He was grinning as I looked back, and squeezing the bulge in his crotch.

My shivering was getting really strong, and I hung my head as he stepped towards me, trying to calm myself down. It didn't work and, as his fat arms closed around me, groping for my trouser button, I felt the muscles of my tummy twitch. He was right up against me, his belly pressed to my bum, his cock too, rock hard against one cheek. My breathing was getting heavy, and it was impossible not to give a gasp as my jeans button popped open and a little whimper as my fly was peeled down.

'I haven't even started yet,' he said.

'You're going to though, aren't you,' I replied. 'You're going to beat me. Oh God!'

He had put his hands in the waistband of my jeans, stepping back as he pulled at them, tugging them off my hips, then down, over the seat of my panties. I was in white ones, the kind Percy likes, and which I've become addicted to, plain white cotton and just a size too small. He smacked his lips as they came on show, a disgusting, blubbery sound.

The jeans were settled down to my knees, and I pulled my back in a little more, rounding out my bum to stretch the panties taut across my cheeks. He grunted and blew out his breath, and I looked back once more. He had his hand on his crotch, massaging his erection through his trousers. I could see it, his balls too, outlined against the fabric beneath the overhang of his gut. His eyes were fixed on my panty-clad bum, really staring and, as I watched, his tongue flicked out and he smacked his lips again.

'Pull them down, strip me bare,' I begged.

'You love all this, don't you?'

'No. I hate it. Now pull them down, show me off.'

'Say it. Ask nicely.'

'Pull down my panties. Please, Monty.'

'You can do better than that.'

'Oh God, you bastard! Please, Monty, sir, pull down my panties. Spank me. Pull down my panties and spank me like the dirty little brat I am. Come on, do it, pull them down, make me show my pussy, make me show

72

my bumhole, then beat me, hard! Then you can fuck me, put that lovely big cock up my pussy. You can bugger me if you want, right up my bumhole . . .'

'Shit!' he swore.

'Idiot!' I cursed as a wet stain appeared on the front of his trousers, just by the tip of the bulge that marked his cock.

'What's the matter?' he demanded.

'You've come in your pants. That's what's the matter!'

'So?'

'Well, OK, never mind. Come on then, pull them down.'

He didn't even bother to clean up, just reaching out to take hold of my waistband. I shut my eyes, my head swimming with blissful shame as he peeled my panties slowly down, exposing the top of my crease, my cheeks, my bumhole and at last my pussy, to leave it all showing, bare behind, utterly exposed, without a scrap of modesty left to me, the way a girl about to be punished should be.

'Nice,' he said. 'I like a shaved cunt. Do you shave in your arse crack too?'

I couldn't even answer him, the question was so humiliating, but I shook my head, letting out a sob as I did it. It was really getting to me, and I knew it wouldn't be long before I was in tears, at least once the beating started.

'I bet you do,' he went on. 'Right, let's see how many you get.'

He rolled the die out on to the table, right in front of me. It landed on a four and I felt a sharp surge of relief, then disappointment. He gave me a wry smile.

'Roll again,' I demanded.

'Reroll? Get your tits out then.'

I kneeled up, pulling my top high over my boobs before reaching back to unclip my bra. He watched, no less eagerly than he had before he'd come. I snipped my bra catch and felt the sudden extra weight of my breasts as the support went. Pulling it up, I twisted around, letting him see both of them. He grinned and nodded.

I took my bra right off and kneeled back down, now with my boobs swinging from my chest, just brushing the table. He adjusted his cock in his trousers, pushing it down. The stain was still spreading on his crotch, adding an extra element of dirtiness to what was being done to me. I liked the idea of a man who could come in his pants over the sight of me bent over in my knickers. It was a little scary, though, and the more so for the way he was gloating over me.

He reached forward to retrieve the die, treating himself to a feel of my bum as he did it. Again he rolled it, and it settled on nineteen. That was too much, with the huge spoon, and I couldn't see him being gentle. I wanted to be spanked, not beaten black and blue.

'Reroll,' I said immediately.

'That means an egg up your cunt,' he reminded me.

I nodded, setting my knees a touch further apart to give him easy access to my pussy. He went to the fridge, bending down to take an egg from a box. Behind me again, he pressed it to my pussy and I felt the mouth of my hole start to stretch around it. It was a big one, and I really felt it, filling my hole, then popping inside. I'd half expected it to break, but it had held, round and firm in my body. I could feel it squeezing out, so I tensed myself, holding it in place, with just a little bit showing in my hole. He had began to play with my pussy, cupping my mound in his hand and rubbing at me, until I began to pant, when he stopped abruptly.

'Now you get it,' he said. 'Roll.'

I took the die, shook it in my hand and rolled it, watching it tumble out of my palm and across the table, again settling among the curry cartons. It showed an eighteen, so I'd got off one stroke at the cost of having him shove an egg up my pussy.

'Spank me then,' I sighed.

He picked up the spoon as I stuck my bottom up as high as it would go, still squeezing to hold the egg up myself. Monty hefted the spoon and patted it against my bottom. I felt the cup settle on my flesh, holding a good share of one cheek, and I wondered just what I was going to look like after I'd been beaten with the horrible thing.

I shut my eyes, unable to look as he hefted the spoon, then screamed, my body jerking forwards across the table, my face going right into the mess of his dinner as he slammed it down across my bottom, far, far too hard.

'Ow! Ow! Ow!' I heard myself squeak. 'Ow, Monty, not so hard! Please! Amber, amber!'

My face had gone in a carton and there was a blob of curry sauce on my nose, which I wiped away before getting back into position, trembling hard, my whole body shaking in reaction.

'Sorry,' he said. 'How about this?'

He brought the spoon down again, firmly, making me jump and cry out once more. It hurt, and my instinct was to tell him to stop it, to tell him to go to hell, but underneath I wanted my spanking, and I wanted it done properly.

'OK,' I managed, panting. 'A bit harder, maybe.'

The egg was still trying to get out, and I tensed my pussy, drawing it back up, only to get the third smack when I wasn't expecting it, harder than before. Again I yelped and bucked, but he gave me another, immediately, and another, to leave me gasping over the table, with my feet kicking and my mouth wide in pain and misery.

It really hurt, so much, as he went on, whack after whack across my poor, burning bottom. There is nothing fake about the pain of a spanked girl, just because she likes it. It hurts every bit as much as it would for anyone else, and there's always a barrier, which I have to force myself over. I was kicking madly, hammering my fists on the table, sobbing and whimpering, trying to count, ten, eleven, twelve, when the egg burst in my hole, spattering fluid across my pussy and down my thighs. Immediately it began to drip into my panties, filling the air with the stench of rot.

That was too much for me. I burst into tears, really howling as the filthy, slimy mess oozed down between my sex lips. It was full of bits of shell and I could feel them in my hole, rough and scratchy as my pussy closed on the broken pieces. Monty had stopped, presumably because I was in tears, but I stayed in place, struggling to cope with my feelings, until at last I succeeded, sticking my bottom back up properly so that he could watch the filth dribble out of my hole. I was still snivelling, and there were hot tears on my cheeks and arms. My bottom felt huge, and very open, my anus wet with sweat, my cheeks hot and dry.

'Go on,' I sobbed. 'Finish me off.'

He hesitated for one moment, and then the spoon smacked down across my bum, and again as once more I cried out in my pain.

'Fourteen,' he said, and smacked me again. 'Fifteen.'

I was crying, openly, with my head lifted, the tears running freely down my cheeks. He gave me the sixteenth and my mouth came open, a trace of drool running from one side. I cupped my boobs, squeezing them, then put my face down, pushing the curry cartons aside with my head, looking back at him. I could smell the curry, and the rotten egg, and my own sex. He gave me the seventeenth and I reached back to masturbate, finding my pussy wet with juice and slimy, rotting egg.

'Last one,' he called.

'No,' I breathed. 'One more hard, but keep going, gently, little pats, and do as I tell you.'

Again the spoon came down, hard, making me gasp, then again gently, patting my aching bottom, and again, setting up a slow, rhythmic motion as I started to rub at my filthy pussy. I could feel the egg, slimy and thick over my flesh, and full of bits of shell. A fibrous bit was hanging out of my pussy, and I snatched at it, pulling out the yolk, which I slapped to my clit, bursting it across my flesh. Monty kept on, saying nothing, his piglike eyes fixed on the filthy, bruised mess he had made of my bottom, then on my tear-streaked face, eye to eye.

'Keep doing it,' I moaned. 'A little harder, and call me dirty names, anything you like. Oh God, I wish you hadn't come. I wish you could put your cock up me like this, up my dirty hole, in all the mess, and fuck me, and spunk up me . . . Harder! Now beat me, you fat bastard!'

I was nearly coming, right on the edge, with the egg slimed all over my pussy, rubbing harder at my clit. The spanks got harder, and harder still, until I was gasping again, fresh tears bursting from my eyes, my orgasm building in my head, higher and higher with the pain and awful, burning humiliation of it all.

'Less of the fat, you stuck up bitch!' he snapped and gave me a really hard swat. 'Look at you, with your red arse in the air and your knockers showing. I was right, you do belong in a porno video, the dirtiest sort, the sort where the girls piss over each other, the sort where they piss in each other's mouths and drink it, or in their knickers and show it off to the camera . . .'

I screamed, really loud, coming in blind, helpless ecstasy, beaten and degraded, bringing myself off to the filthiest, filthiest suggestion, and as I came I knew full well that he'd watched one where that was exactly what happened. That was what my mind fixed on as my orgasm went through me, some young girl, with her skirt held high and her bum stuck out in pure white panties, only with the rear pouch sodden with her own pee, showing it off. That would be something to be spanked for, really spanked.

The spanking stopped as I slumped, breathless on the table. I'd made a real show of myself, masturbating with my pussy stuck out right at him, my bumhole pulsing and my legs and bottom twitching to my contractions. I half expected him to mount me, or drag me down on the floor and fuck me on my back. He wasn't ready though, and just stood back, grinning to himself as I slowly recovered my senses.

'Thank you,' I managed, when I could finally speak. 'That was good, one of the best.'

'Don't forget you're going to be my sex slave,' he reminded me.

'Sure, but let me clean up and relax for a bit first. Then I'll do anything you like.'

'Fine,' he answered.

I cleaned the decaying egg off my fingers and then went for a shower. His bathroom was as sordid as his kitchen, but there was a mirror, in which I inspected my bottom. I was in a pretty sorry state, with big, spoon-shaped bruises covering both cheeks and a general, all over red colour. I knew it would be a good two weeks before I could show my bum without it being obvious I'd been spanked, but it had been well worth it, the best orgasm I'd had since getting back from France.

My panties were full of egg, so I put them in the sink to soak, making a mental note to remember to put a spare pair in my bag the next time I came to see Monty. There was even some in my jeans, so I took them off and scrubbed the crotch, leaving me in just my top. That left my pussy and the cheeky bit of my bum showing under the hem, which I was sure Monty would appreciate.

He was on the phone when I came back downstairs, with a pizza menu in one hand. He gestured to me as I came in, tapping the menu and I leaned close, pointing at one which came with capers and smoked ham. He nodded, finishing the order off as I sat down.

'We'll start when the pizza gets here, shall we?' he asked, putting the phone down.

'Whatever you say, Master,' I answered.

My tone had been cheeky, almost sarcastic, but he didn't rise to the bait, instead getting up and waddling into the kitchen. He came back with a pack of beers, one of which he peeled off and gave to me. It was strong ale, which isn't really my thing, but I was thirsty, and I was sure that the experience to come would be easier with a shot of alcohol inside me.

'Don't bother with the Master bit,' he said. 'Just do exactly as I say, without question. In fact, I don't want you to talk at all.'

'I'll try,' I promised.

We talked as we waited, about Brighton, cars, drink, even the complicated fantasy games he was into, which I'd barely heard existed. It all seemed really weird, with me sat there on my freshly smacked bottom, nude below the waist and waiting for a session as his sex slave. It also highlighted the differences between us, as I don't think we agreed on anything. Finally the bell went.

'Get it,' he ordered.

I was going to protest, but I remembered what he'd said and shut my mouth. The idea was obviously that I answer the door with my pussy on show, humiliating me by making me flash in front of the pizza delivery boy, and no doubt doing a lot for his image locally. I didn't mind – after all, we were in Croydon – but I completely forgot that we'd be expected to pay for the pizzas.

That meant not just giving a brief flash of my pussy, but walking back down the passage with my bright red, heavily bruised bumcheeks peeping out from under my top. I did it though, not even bothering to close the door, which I could have done, and gave the astonished delivery boy a big smile as I took the boxes from him.

I also queried the order, because there were four huge boxes and two bags, which seemed excessive, even for

Monty. It was right though and, as I walked back, I wondered if it was really humanly possible for a man to eat three family-sized pizzas and most of a fourth, because all I wanted was a slice and some of the garlic bread. I wanted to ask, but I remembered what he had said about not speaking and came to kneel meekly at his feet, holding out the boxes. I had no idea what to expect, but was hoping he might want to feed me by hand, which Percy likes to do occasionally. He took one of the boxes and opened it, revealing a pizza well over a foot across and a good inch thick.

'Deep crust, fifteen inch, family-size Mexican Caramba,' he said. 'That's spicy beef, spicy pork, fresh garlic, double green chillies, jalapeno peppers, onions.'

I made a face, it was impossible not to. He held it out, letting me sniff it and I was praying he was going to eat the lot in front of me, to torture me, only it would have been no torture at all, just gross having to watch. I couldn't possibly eat the thing myself anyway, it would have fed me for days.

'You're going to hate this,' he assured me. 'I bet you're really obsessed about your weight, aren't you? Well now you're going to have to eat this up, off the floor, like a dog, like a bitch.'

He didn't actually tip it on to the floor, but he put the box down. I'd been hoping for something more overtly sexual, which I could get off on as well as him, but he'd given me my spanking, and done it well, for a novice, so it seemed only fair to try to play.

With my face well down, I nuzzled the pizza with my lips. It was hot, but not unbearably so, and I took a bite from the edge. It was a bit sickly, but not too bad, and I began to eat. So did he, starting on a much plainer pizza from one of the other boxes. He was soon ahead of me, and paused, leaving for the kitchen.

He came back with a bowl, into which he poured the remains of my beer, then another from the pack.

Clicking his fingers, he pointed to it and I shifted my position, lapping it up and actually quite grateful for the fluid. He sat back down again, undid his fly and raised his bottom off the chair, pushing down his trousers and underpants together to expose his cock and balls. It really was gross, because his cock was still slimy with come from the accident he'd had during my punishment.

With his genitals showing, he went back to eating, taking a single mouthful, then once more clicking his fingers as he pointed to his cock.

'Lick it clean,' he ordered, 'and you forgot to kiss my arsehole.'

That was true. It had slipped my mind completely in the ecstasy of my spanking climax. Now I was going to have to do it, and even in my dirtiest fantasies I had never imagined mixing arse-licking with my dinner. I nearly used my stop word, but again it seemed unfair to deny him. I had promised. I'd even asked for it. I crawled over, quickly swallowing my mouthful of pizza and beer. His legs were far too fat for me to get my face between them, so I kneeled back on my heels, meekly waiting for instructions.

'Kiss this,' he said, and rolled his legs up, holding them behind his knees.

The position left his bottom stuck out over the edge of the chair, and spread. It had been dark in the garage, now it wasn't. I could see every lewd, obscene detail, the huge, pasty white buttocks, the great, hairy sack of his scrotum, his big, flaccid cock, shiny with sperm, and worse, his anus. It was a broad, lumpy ring of dun-coloured flesh, surrounded by hair and cut with little lines, running down to the hole at the centre. I swallowed and looked at his face, hoping for some sign of mercy.

'Kiss it,' he ordered. 'You've done it before. What's the matter?'

The matter was that I could see what I was supposed to be kissing, and that I was sober. There was a huge lump in my throat, and a voice in my head screaming at me not to be so dirty, so disgusting.

'Kiss it, you stuck-up little bitch!' he spat. 'Kiss my arsehole!'

In my fantasies I'd always been made to do it, forced, sat on or dragged by the hair. Now I couldn't do it, not like this.

'Make me,' I answered him, really softly, hardly hearing my own voice.

Immediately he hooked his foot over the chair arm. His hand came out, gripping me by the hair. He pulled, far too strong to resist, and my face was smothered, in hot, sweaty male flesh, his balls squashing out over my nose and eyes, my lips pressed firmly to his anus. An agonising bubble of humiliation burst inside me as I puckered up my lips and kissed his ring, and then I was licking, my eyes tight shut, slobbering at it, like a dog, and up to his balls, gulping his fat cock into my mouth and sucking off the spunk, then back to his bumhole, licking, kissing, probing with my tongue until at last he pulled me back by my hair.

I was breathing really deeply, almost panting, and I felt suddenly weak. He laughed, reached out to dab a stray smear of sperm off my nose and cuffed me gently in the face.

'That's for not obeying immediately,' he said. 'Now get on with your dinner, bitch.'

I went back to the pizza and the bowl of beer. It was different now. I was eating not because it was fair to play his game, but because my master had ordered me to. He watched as I guzzled it down, eating with one hand while he played with his cock with the other, breaking off occasionally to take a swallow of beer.

My pizza was about half gone when he finished his. By then his cock was fully erect, and glistening with grease from his food. He was really excited, and I could actually smell his cock, despite my face being covered in bits of pizza, which wasn't easy to eat on my hands and knees.

I thought he would fuck me, and maybe push my face in the remains of my food as he did it. He held back, opening another box to start on his second pizza. I continued to eat, mouthful after mouthful, although I was beginning to feel bloated. I finished it though, every last scrap, which left my tummy hard and round, feeling fit to burst. There was a sickly feeling in my throat too, and I was hoping he'd let me digest for a while before doing anything rude to me.

'Right,' he said, 'number two. Same again, only this time a special I made up, just for you: tuna, tandoori chicken, pepperoni, spicy pork, pineapple, green chillies and extra cheese. Come and get it, bitch.'

He put the box down open, and I could only stare in horror. My stomach already felt bloated, a round, hard ball inside me, and I knew I would be unable to finish. It was a horrid combination too, and as I put my face down the smell hit me, making me feel queasy. I had to try though, and took a bite, tearing it off with my teeth. He chuckled and went back to his own, stroking his cock as he ate.

I was going to be sick, I knew it, as I forced myself to swallow mouthful after mouthful, always putting off using my stop word, until at last I knew that if I took one more mouthful I would really be sick. I paused, looking at him in the hope of sympathy. He was still eating, licking the topping off a slice in the most disgusting manner. His cock was already filthy, because he had changed hands several times. I was pretty sure I was going to have to suck him clean, but I was still taken aback when he folded the remains of the pizza slice around it and began to masturbate with it. He was smearing cheese and tomato up and down the shaft, over his balls too and, as I watched, the sick feeling in my throat grew stronger.

'Suck it,' he ordered.

I crawled forwards as he spread his thighs, so grateful that he'd let me stop eating, despite what it meant. The smell of cock and pizza grew stronger as I rested my arms on his legs, so strong I had to swallow to stop myself retching. It hadn't seemed a big deal before, when I'd been made to kiss his bumhole, but now it was overpowering, and sickly. I swallowed again as he took my hair, but let myself be pulled on to his cock, taking the thick, greasy shaft into my mouth and sucking on it.

His grip tightened, twisting in my hair, and I wondered if he was going to do the same as Damon, making me suck and swallow what came out. He certainly had his cock deep enough in my throat, so deep I was starting to gag and was unable to swallow my mouthful of cheesy saliva, until he finally let me up a little. I quickly swallowed my mouthful as he started to fuck my mouth, with long, slow strokes, each of which ended with the head of his cock jamming into the back of my throat. I could taste everything, not just the cheese, but cheap tomato paste, anchovies, garlic and most of all, cock.

If he didn't stop I was going to be sick all over his cock and balls, which was going to bring our session to an abrupt end. I tried to mumble my slow down word around my mouthful and slapped his leg gently, looking up at him. He grinned and eased my head off his erection.

'Can't take it?' he said. 'Eat this then.'

He held out the piece of pizza he had been wanking with. I opened my mouth, my need to be a good girl warring with the urge to be sick. His cock looked fit to burst, and I knew he wouldn't be able to hold back much longer, so I just needed to keep myself together a few minutes more. The pizza slice was pushed into my mouth and I bit off the tip, chewing and trying to ignore the taste. He passed his beer can and I took a gulp, which only made it worse, with the horrible tinny taste of the beer on top of everything else.

I felt my gorge rise, but I swallowed, trying to be brave. His hand was on his cock, jerking at it, held out with the end pointed at my face. He was breathing heavily too and I knew it was going to happen at any moment.

'Take it,' he puffed, pushing the pizza slice at me. 'Hold it under my cock. I'm going to give you a spunk topping and watch you eat it, I am, you little bitch, you stuck-up little bitch . . .'

Suddenly it was all too much for me. I felt the contents of my stomach coming up, rising in my throat, and I was running for the loo, clutching my mouth. He gave an exclamation, annoyed, then burst into hysterical laughter. I made it, just, but as I pushed open the door it all came up, into my mouth and hand. I held it in, sinking to my knees with my head over the bowl, to puke into the lavatory, again and again, spasm after spasm, completely unable to stop myself. At last I managed to choke it back and I was left coughing and spluttering into the bowl, my head well down, with my hair hanging into the mess beneath me.

I never even realised he was behind me until I felt his hands on my hips, and the next moment I'd been lifted and impaled on his cock. It went straight up me, really easily, with his fat belly squashing against my bum as he pushed it in to the hilt. I tried to protest, but another spasm hit me and I was choking and gagging into the loo, utterly out of control, my body jerking to his thrusts, my boobs slapping against the cool plastic of the lavatory bowl.

I was sick again, twice, as he fucked me, but he didn't seem to care, humping away at my bottom, harder and faster. He let go of my hips, grabbing my head to shove

85

it further down the loo. I squealed in protest, more of my hair going into the sick. Then suddenly he had taken my boobs in his hands, squeezing them hard, jerking my body like a doll, grunting and mumbling, calling me a stuck-up bitch, over and over as he emptied his spunk up my pussy.

His cock came out with the last push, sliding up between my bottom cheeks to leave a slimy trail of sperm and pussy juice from my bumhole to the top of my crease. I was still gasping, totally unable to speak, let alone get up. He had sat back, and I could hear his breathing, really heavy from the exertion of the way he'd fucked me. For what seemed like ages I stayed like that, utterly spent, occasionally coughing or spitting bits of pizza into the bowl, until at last I found my voice.

'You bastard!' I spat. 'You find that sexy, fucking me while I'm being sick?'

'No,' he answered. 'I find it sexy watching a girl like you lose control.'

Six

I felt so much better for my session with Monty. There really is nothing like a good spanking. I had no illusions about our relationship. He was easy to control and he appealed to my love of erotic humiliation, that was all. In return, his sadistic attitude towards me seemed to come from an odd mixture of body worship and resentment. I was slim, and pretty, and I suppose privileged too, from his point of view. If he wanted to take out what was probably a lifetime's worth of rejection by women on me, that was fine, although what he'd done to me had taken me right to the edge.

The spanking had worked anyway. My head was completely clear, and I felt up to handling Damon Maurschen, Ami Bell, even Gabrielle Salinger, and without losing my cool. In fact I was in such a mellow mood that I even felt a bit sorry for Damon. On the other hand, I couldn't see what else I could have done. I didn't want him, and that was that. I either had to be nasty about it or give in to him, which was no choice at all. Ami was different. After all, I had seduced her, after a fashion. I liked her too, and I wanted to make up. I wasn't sure how, but I was determined to make the effort. Gabrielle was harder, as in her case I didn't really have any control.

There were six messages on my answering machine when I got in, at nearly midnight. The first was the

87

editor of a wine magazine, asking if I could do an article on Cahors, which cheered me up even more. He was an old friend of Percy's and I knew I wouldn't have got the commission otherwise.

The second was from Damon. It was in much the same tone as his note had been when he sent me the roses, apologetic yet also condescending. He admitted that he had been wrong to book the restaurant table without asking me first, but adding that he hadn't realised how 'sensitive' I was. By sensitive he obviously meant immature, and that was really infuriating. Certainly it had been immature of me to throw a tantrum, but that wasn't the point. The point was that I didn't want to be with him, and he was refusing to take no for an answer.

It was beginning to look as though he was one of those men who would get more and more desperate for me the more resistant I became. That was just what I did not want and, to make matters worse, I was sure he had no real affection for me, just a desperate need to salvage his pride. I was obviously going to have to do something drastic, or very clever, and I was trying to think what as I listened to the rest of his message. There was lots of it, and eventually I'd stopped listening and was drumming my fingers on the telephone table, waiting for him to finish.

Finally he did. The next three messages were from friends saying they'd call back, then came another female voice, but with a different accent, which I recognised immediately. It was Gabrielle.

'Natasha? Hello. This is Gabrielle Salinger. Sorry you're not in. I would like to talk to you. I . . .'

There was a click and the little red warning light came on, telling me the memory was full. I could have kicked Damon at that moment. Because he'd wittered on for so long I'd missed the end of the message from Gabrielle, which was far more important. I didn't know if she was going to call back, or if she wanted me to call her, or what, and I wasn't even sure if I still had her number.

I could think of only one reason why she would want to talk to me, which was to grill me about what had happened with Ami, and with Jo Warren too. Unprofessional it might me, but she hadn't seemed too worried about that in Brighton, openly discussing a case with Amy McRae of all people, and only holding back the client's name.

That was a worrying thought. What if she wrote something for Amy, on sexual dysfunction, using me to illustrate her remarks? She might not give my name, but people would guess. Maybe that was why she'd rung me up.

It was ten minutes past midnight, hardly the best time to call somebody, especially on a week night. I didn't care.

I tapped in 1471, praying nobody had called me since. The number that came back was unfamiliar, and I pressed the 3. It began to ring and I blew out my breath, trying to calm myself as I wondered if it was best to be aggressive, or conciliatory, even whether I should try and make a joke of the whole thing.

She answered, her voice sleepy, but still with that touch of formality I always found unnerving.

'Salinger, hello?'

'Hi, Gabrielle,' I answered, my confidence dissolving rapidly. 'It's Natasha, Natasha Linnet. You called me earlier, and . . . it's just that my answering machine didn't pick up the message properly. Some idiot had left a really long message on it. The memory ran out. Did I wake you up? Sorry.'

I trailed off, feeling really stupid. Now she was going to think I was a lunatic as well as a pervert. I could see the file growing fatter.

'No. Not at all. I was just reading in bed,' she answered me. 'I . . .'

'I'm sorry,' I cut in. 'I just thought it might be urgent. I'll call back tomorrow, shall I?'

'No. Do not. Hang on.'

The was a rustling noise and a snap, which I imagined was her getting her glasses out of a case.

'That is better,' her voice came again, firmer now. 'Yes. I called you. I was hoping to see you.'

'Professionally?'

'No. Not at all.'

'Oh.'

'In Brighton, you said you were a wine writer. You have been to Alsace?'

'Yes. I was there earlier this year.'

'I am from Colmar. Did you know?'

'No.'

'It would be good to talk. I think. If you like. Perhaps at lunch?'

'Well, I . . .'

'Tomorrow, at the *Café Eperney*. Perhaps one o'clock, if you are free?'

'Yes. I mean, no. I'd have to check . . . Yes, I am.'

'I will see you there, then. Thank you.'

She put the phone down and I was left holding the receiver.

I'm normally good at reading people's emotions in their voices. With Gabrielle it was next to impossible, especially over the phone, with her precise, formal English and her odd accent, between French and German. So far as I could tell she had sounded genuine, but I didn't believe a word of it.

Her excuse was too thin, not impossible, but thin. Then again, she was a psychologist. Possibly she had chosen the excuse precisely because it was thin, to unsettle me. It was convenient though, convenient enough to be true. It might even be true, but that didn't alter the fact that I knew exactly why she really wanted to speak to me.

She had been hard to refuse too. Impossible in fact, as I had found myself accepting her invitation without even checking my organiser. It had been her voice, full of calm certainty, as if there was no possibility of me refusing, as if she was used to people doing as she told them, without argument. A little shiver went through me as I put the phone down, a very familiar shiver.

My first thought, in the morning, was simply not to go. That lasted the length of a coffee and a piece of toast, after which I decided that it was too cowardly an option. I would go, and talk to her, and take control of the situation. If she genuinely wanted to talk about Alsace, then fine, I would do so. If she wanted to dissect the intimate details of my sexuality then I would refuse politely, making it quite clear that I was happy with myself and considered my sex life private. I would show her that I was as strong as she was.

I took a cab down to Covent Garden, in a fairly bloody-minded mood, but by no means downbeat. It was a challenge, after all, and a real one, with real consequences. With what she knew, she was quite capable of making my life unbearable. My only defence was her sense of professional confidentiality, which I knew wasn't all that strong. I couldn't afford to put her back up, but I was determined not to give in either.

When I got to the *Café Eperney* she was already there, reading *Metropolitan* as if she was criticising a rival's paper. She hadn't seen me, and I watched her for a moment, studying her face. There was no doubt she seemed naturally strong, with her firm jawline and perfectly regular features made stern by the short hair and small, steel rimmed glasses, the image of an old-fashioned librarian. It was in the way she dressed as well, very neat and formal, and the way she held herself, as if she was under constant scrutiny, yet perfectly confident.

She looked up as I came in, smiling and shutting the magazine with a single, quick motion. The table she had chosen was in a sort of cul-de-sac to one side of the bar, the quietest part of the café. Also, she was seated against the wall, forcing me to take a chair which left me with my back to the door. Obviously she had arrived early to establish herself in a commanding position, but that sort of simple ploy wasn't going to work on me.

'I was reading Amy's article on women in religion,' she remarked, gesturing to the magazine. 'Have you seen it?'

'Yes, it's very interesting,' I answered.

'Perhaps,' she said, 'yet it is a shame Amy must take so populist a line. The evidence for what she says is no more than anecdotal, while there is a sensationalism to it that trivialises very real concerns, to an extent.'

'She has to make *Metropolitan* sell,' I countered. 'Too much science bores people.'

It was an obvious attempt to gain the upper hand, demonstrating her intellectual superiority. I was having none of it, not on her terms anyway.

'What shall we have?' I asked, picking up the wine list.

'There is a Sylvaner,' she answered, 'for fifteen pounds. At my home it would be a typical café wine, in a carafe, at perhaps thirty francs.'

'You'd still be disappointed,' I told her, glancing down the list to find the wine she was talking about. 'It's just a co-op wine, nothing special. We should have Alsace though. There's a Tokay here, from Jean-Paul Dard. Let's have that. You know him, I suppose?'

'No,' she admitted.

'No? He's based in Kayserberg, a few miles outside Colmar.'

'Kayserberg I know.'

'His wine is very much in the new style, delicate, with the emphasis on balance rather than power. Perfect for lunchtime.'

I ordered, feeling thoroughly pleased with myself for demonstrating my superior knowledge. Also my buying power, as the bottle cost thirty pounds, twice as much as the one she had suggested. If she thought she was going to play dominance games, she had picked the wrong woman.

'I was there in the spring,' I went on. 'Have you been back recently?'

'I was there last Christmas,' she said, 'but I do not go often. My family are very traditional. They do not like what I do.'

'No? I'd have thought they'd be proud of you?'

'It is not so. My mother is very religious. My father is in local politics. Both think I should have married by now, and be producing children to carry on the family. I am an only child.'

'Me too, but Daddy's not like that. He'd do anything for me . . .'

I trailed off, realising that she had already made me admit one of the most important things about me, along which lay the key to my sexuality. I'm spoiled, and it's from there that I get my need for punishment. Not only that, but a lot of my confidence and security comes from being able to rely on Daddy, which I did not want her to know, especially as her own seemed to be innate.

'They find my rejection of Catholicism difficult to accept,' she went on. 'Impossible, in fact. I have been an atheist since my adolescence, yet they still think I am going through a phase.'

She laughed, a very light, carefree sound. I smiled and shrugged, now cautious of her easy, intimate manner, not wanting to get pulled in again.

A waitress appeared with our bottle, in an ice bucket, and glasses. I sat back, deliberately letting Gabrielle pour for me, which she did without any sign of self-consciousness. I sipped the wine, which was excellent, although it would have had Percy complaining about modern techniques, and she continued.

'It was not easy to shake off the imprinting of my childhood, even though I understood it. Meaningless

93

guilt, in particular, was difficult to overcome. You know, the guilt of breaching conventions and taboos, when there is no victim. In particular for sexual acts.'

I sat silent, aware of exactly where she was trying to lead me. She would convince me that I should feel no shame for what I did, and I'd tell her everything. Her manner was so confidential, almost conspiratorial, and it would have been easy to go along with her. It wasn't going to happen.

'In our culture there is a shame of femininity, deeply ingrained,' she went on. 'Woman is sin, as represented by Eve and, as such, if she is to even attempt to be pure, she must feel ashamed, merely for being female.'

'I know, it's disgusting,' I agreed.

'Disgusting, true, but a reality. One must face reality. To deny it because it is wrong is not a solution. In my work I seek to bring women above their ingrained shame, to an understanding of themselves as a rational animal, responsible to themselves, to society, but not a conceptual being, a principle function of which is their repression. By the way, Ami is all right. I have explained to her.'

'You have?'

The question had slipped out before I knew I'd said it. She had been talking as if she was addressing a convention, then suddenly changed, to something very personal and very immediate.

'Yes,' she continued, 'she came to see me yesterday. I explained her reaction to what you did, both physically and mentally. She understands now and, I think, has benefited from the experience. I didn't know you took colonic hydrotherapy?'

'I don't ... I mean, I do, obviously ... not ...'

'Not as therapy?'

'No ... Yes ...'

'For pleasure?'

'No! Yes, of course I do, you know I do. Ami told you everything, I suppose?'

It had come out in a rush and my temper had risen with it, until I had to choke myself back from telling her to mind her own business. I expected to see triumph in her eyes, maybe amusement, but she had put her wine glass to her lips, hiding her emotions, a trick I've used myself a thousand times. I was still trying to decide what to say when she put it down.

'Do you also feel shame? You seem insecure about it.'

'No, I'm not,' I answered. 'I'm fine about it. I don't feel the need for help, or therapy, or anything. The feeling stimulates me sexually, and it did the same for Ami. It's not a big deal. I'm in control, completely.'

'Perfect,' she said.

She was going to continue, but at that moment somebody called out my name and I turned to see Damon coming towards us. Gabrielle immediately stopped talking, and I caught the look of irritation on her face for an instant before she buried it behind her glass.

'Let me join you?' he said, pulling a chair up to our table.

'Do,' Gabrielle answered, although I'd been hoping she'd tell him he wasn't welcome.

I couldn't, because I'd already made too much of trying to bring our relationship to a close and I didn't want him to think that he was that important to me. For the next half hour we made small talk, with Damon trying to ingratiate himself with me. Eventually Gabrielle went, and I made an excuse not long after, gaining some small satisfaction from leaving him to pay the bill.

I needed to think, and I was feeling just faintly tipsy, so I walked home. I felt I'd managed quite well with Gabrielle, being friendly but firm. What I wasn't sure of was where the conversation had been going when Damon had interrupted us. Once she'd got me to admit I got a sexual kick out of taking enemas I'd expected her to become detached, analytical. She hadn't, and she had said just one word before stopping – 'perfect'.

As always with her it had been impossible to gain much from her tone of voice, but it certainly hadn't been analytical. It hadn't been gloating either, which in any case would have been far too obvious a reaction for her. If anything it had seemed very genuine, as if she was happy that I took such perverse enjoyment. That seemed possible, after the way she had been going on about getting rid of shame and guilt, but it didn't really make sense. Anyway, she had been so open and friendly when I knew perfectly well it was all carefully staged to draw me into an admission that I wasn't going to trust anything she said anyway.

She had managed to lead me though, for all my efforts at resistance, a piece of knowledge that gave me the same familiar shiver I'd felt after putting the phone down the night before. It was impossible not to think about it. She was a manipulative bitch, but the same skills could have been put to much better use to dominate me sexually, if only she'd been a slut. Not just that, but she had the look too, with her short cropped hair and her steel-grey eyes. The way she held herself was good too, very straight, so that she seemed really tall despite being perhaps an inch above me, no more. It was certainly easy to imagine her giving me orders.

I resisted a bit at first, not really wanting to make a fantasy figure of her, in the circumstances. Unfortunately it was just too good to hold back, and by the time I reached Regent's Park I was wondering what sort of role she'd fit best. My first thought was a wardress in an old-fashioned prison, picking on me by forcing me to perform the most menial tasks. Inevitably I'd fail to complete them to her satisfaction, which would give her the perfect excuse to punish me. It would be done publicly, in the exercise yard. I'd be dragged out, screaming and kicking, but to no avail. There would be six or seven other wardresses, enough to control me easily, and I'd be stripped, stark naked, my clothes torn off despite my pathetic struggles.

My beating would be really popular, because I'd be a tell-tale, a grass, or whatever the term would be. There would be other prisoners watching, hundreds of them, thoroughly enjoying themselves at my expense as I was strapped, nude, over a trestle, still kicking and screaming, pleading for mercy. I would already be blubbering my eyes out as I was forced down, bum high, legs wide, with my pussy gaping to the crowd, bumhole on show, bare boobs hanging down.

I'd be thrashed, really hard, by Gabrielle, with her standing over me with a really vicious switch, slashing it down across my bottom, over and over, until I was screaming with pain, until I wet myself all over her, in front of all of them, until there was blood running down my poor ruined bottom, until I passed out. They'd bring me round with a bucket of cold water, right in my face, and the first thing I'd see was Gabrielle, her skirts lifted, her pussy bare, so that I could lick her to climax in a gesture of beaten, defeated submission.

It was good, but it lacked the element of realism that I like. Anyway, I could hardly sit down on a bench and frig myself off, however much I wanted to. For a moment I considered her in the role of traffic warden, only to abandon it. The role might be authoritarian, but to a confirmed car addict like myself it was much better to imagine a warden in a submissive role, getting a bare bottom spanking from some angry motorist. I had actually been made to dress up as a traffic warden before, and punished, but it was such a lower-middle-class role, not really me at all.

Gabrielle needed to be something grander than either role, something to suit her intelligence. It came to me suddenly, a fantasy so obvious and so cruel that I knew I would have to masturbate over it the moment I got back to my flat. It involved her as she was, a therapist, but running a sort of perverts' equivalent to Alcoholics Anonymous, where dirty-minded sluts like myself could go to rid themselves of their nasty little habits.

The humiliation would be agonising. I'd have to stand up in front of a group of other women, maybe men too, and admit I liked my bottom spanked. Most of them would be nearly cured, and guilty of lesser perversions anyway, so they'd look down on me, full of satisfaction and piety because I was about to get it. I would get it too, because the cure would be for Gabrielle to bring home to me just what physical punishment is really about.

I'd have made my confession in the nude, to show proper contrition, and I'd have stayed nude as I was lectured by Gabrielle, told how I was a disgrace to women, and how awful I was for enjoying having my bottom smacked. They'd tie me to a chair, strapped up really tight so that I couldn't move an inch, with my bare bum stuck out and everything showing. They wouldn't be cruel at all, but smug, full of self-righteousness as they lashed my hands tight up behind my back and forced me to spread my knees.

It would be Gabrielle who did the beating, really hard, with a thick, knobbly cane. I'd scream and struggle in my bonds, whimpering and begging, but nothing would make her stop, because she would know it was for my own good, to cure me. She'd make a real mess of my bottom and, when she'd finished and I was snivelling brokenly and mumbling apologies with spittle running from my mouth, she'd tell one of the men to fuck me, not for his fun, but because it was necessary to complete my lesson. He'd do it, and they'd all watch with smug satisfaction, faces set in solemn approval as my beaten bottom was fucked from the rear and spunked over.

When I reached my door I was so urgent I couldn't get the key into the lock. In the end I managed, tumbling inside, up the stairs, into my flat and on to the bed, pulling up my skirt one-handed as I scrabbled in my bedside table for the vibrator. I got it, and twisted it on, sticking it down the front of my panties without preliminaries. The sensation was glorious, and I was on the way to orgasm immediately. For one thing I could feel the bruises Monty had given me with the spoon, and imagine them inflicted by Gabrielle, in that awful, cold room, grey painted, soulless, with me strapped down on a chair, howling and thrashing my way through my punishment with every eye on me and Gabrielle above me, beautiful and stern . . .

As I came I got the most wonderful image of her face, with all calm, confident strength, stern and dominant, the face of a woman to whom I ought to be grovelling naked as she thrashed my bare bottom.

When I'd finished I just lay on the bed, with my skirt still up and the vibrator sticking out of the top of my panties. It had been a good orgasm and, if I felt a little cross with myself for coming over Gabrielle, then I had to admit that it had been worth it.

Masturbating over Gabrielle was all very well, but it didn't alter the fact that our conversation had been inconclusive. I needed to see her again, and hammer things out. I might even tell her a little, if she was prepared to treat me as a rational human being and not some sort of loony. With luck that would satisfy her and, after all, if she felt that getting excited over taking enemas was OK, then maybe she felt the same over spanking. After all, as a psychologist, presumably with some sort of degree, she had to know about endorphins. Whether she could handle what went on in my head was a different matter, but I didn't have to go there.

That was clearly the most sensible thing to do. Explain to her how I enjoyed the physical sensations, and leave out my feelings. With luck she'd swallow it and that would be that.

I intended to call her that evening, but she beat me to it, saying that she was going for a detox at Haven and inviting me to join her. It seemed as good a place as any, besides which, after my fantasy, the chance to be naked in front of her was too good to pass up. So I accepted, arriving shortly after eight to find that she had booked one of the private rooms.

I went up, to find her stark naked, piling up huge pots of what looked like some sort of preparation on a bench, beside several rolls of cling film. I'd seen her nude before, but not close up, and it was impossible not to admire the smoothness of her skin, which was very pale and pretty well flawless, like polished ivory.

For a while we made small talk, mainly with her explaining the basis of whole-being therapy and how it was intended to blend physical and mental techniques to give an all-round sense of well-being. It made sense, in a way, although like so many of these things it basically boiled down to putting yourself first. I've always done that anyway.

In due course she got on to the subject of enemas which, as I knew, she didn't see as a purely physical technique.

'Physical and mental processes are inextricably linked,' she was saying as I finished stowing my clothes in the locker. 'To cleanse the body is to cleanse the mind.'

'*Mens sana in corpore sano*,' I said. 'Isn't that a bit old-fashioned for you? Victorian, almost.'

'The truth holds,' she replied. 'What has changed is society's definition of sane. Take Dr Kellogg, for instance, who was obsessed with the repression of natural sexual feelings, yet gave himself regular enemas. Did he use them as a substitute for sex? If he did, was he aware of it? Certainly he never admitted it. The same is true of other common Victorian practices: flagellation, electrotherapy . . .'

'Flagellation?'

'Undoubtedly. It can be an experience both cathartic and stimulating. You know, I think?'

'Yes,' I answered, really quite boldly. After all, there was no point in denying it. Not with the spoon bruises still on my bottom.

'You possess unusual self-awareness,' she went. 'You should treasure that, as a quality. Indeed, self-awareness is a central consideration of whole-being therapy.'

'Thank you,' I answered, cautiously.

She had wrapped a towel around herself, but I stayed nude, enjoying the feeling of being naked while she was covered. From what she had said I could finally be sure that Jo Warren had told her about my love of being spanked, and she seemed to approve, which had made my desire to be dominated by her stronger still. I knew I was going to have to admit to it soon enough, yet I was determined to be firm, and not to have a case study made of me. She could lie with the best of them, I was sure of it, and I wondered if she might even say she liked it herself, even offer me a spanking, to gain my trust. If she did, it was going to be hard to resist.

'Sex and shame have no place together,' she went on. 'Feelings of shame should be for acts that harm others, not for acts that bring pleasure.'

I didn't agree, but I wasn't saying anything. Certainly I didn't want to try to explain that, for me, a good deal of pleasure actually came from shame.

'To admit the pleasure you find in acts we are taught to think shameful is a great liberation,' she was saying. 'Not that we should assume that all those who use such techniques for their physical benefits necessarily find them sexual, or even pleasant. Take the case of enemas. In many cases an enema may be used simply to provide more direct access to the internal system than straightforward ingestion. Coffee enemas, for instance . . .'

'Coffee enemas?'

'Yes, they are particularly effective in cleansing the liver. Some also take them as a precaution against bowel cancer, although the evidence is not clear. Red wine, again, for the absorption of resveratrol, although one must be careful in the case of alcoholic solutions. Alcohol is absorbed very rapidly through the lining of the lower gut and can be potentially dangerous. I imagine you'd rather just drink it.'

I smiled, trying not to blush at the memory of the not infrequent wine enemas applied by Percy, more than one of which I'd been made to taste.

'My own choice is for a combined preparation,' she went on. 'It is an essential element of my detoxification regime . . .'

'You're going to do it, now?'

'Certainly I am. Will you not do so too? It is easier with assistance.'

'Well I might. What do you do?'

'Apply the preparation to the skin,' she answered, gesturing to the pots on the bench, 'with a little taken internally.'

'And the cling film?'

'To hold the preparation in place. As I say, it is easier with assistance.'

She was pretty keen for me to help her, and again I wondered if she wasn't trying to lull me into a false sense of security. Not that it mattered, so long as I was careful. It seemed harmless enough, so long as I kept my feelings to myself. Besides, I'd be helpless, so I wouldn't be able to get carried away and try to jump on her. Afterwards, back in my flat, I could work the whole experience up into a nice submissive fantasy.

'What's in the preparation?' I asked.

'It is complex,' she answered. 'A formula I devised myself, and which I call Balanced Mud. It includes natural exfoliants and several essential oils.'

She opened a pot, revealing a thick brown paste, very like mud. I dipped a finger into it and sniffed. The scent was intensely herbal, like a very rustic vermouth, also rich and fruity, with a touch of earth.'

102

'Pineapple?' I queried.

'Pineapple juice is an important constituent,' she admitted. 'Also tea-tree oil.'

'So you'd smear me with it and wrap me in cling film?' I asked hopefully.

'Except for your face,' she replied. 'In all therapy involving enclosure it is crucial to keep the airways free. Always.'

She sounded absolutely serious, absolutely formal, not at all giggly, as I would have been if doing something with such obviously sexual implications. Yet she knew what enemas did to me.

'So it's a mental therapy as well?' I asked.

'Certainly,' she said, 'there may be a sense of return to the womb while enclosed, and of birth when released, in addition to the mental aspects of the cleansing effect.'

'All right,' I agreed. 'Shall I go first?'

'That would be most sensible. Put your hair up. Stand over the drain and place your arms to your sides. Relax yourself.'

After piling my hair high and wrapping a towel around it, I stepped to where she was indicating, a grill at the centre of the floor, as she picked up the open tub. It was easy for her to suggest that I relax, but she was about to rub the mud preparation into my body, which meant putting her hands on my neck, my boobs, my bottom, even my pussy. Some women genuinely seem to be able to enjoy touching without any erotic implication. Not me, unless I don't want it at all. It's either sexy or has the potential to become sexy.

She dipped her hand into the pot, bringing up a good handful of the thick paste, which she slapped on to my shoulder, smearing it across my back. It was cool, and felt pleasantly slimy, until, as she added a second handful, it began to tingle, ever so slightly. A third handful went on and she began to rub it in, across my shoulders and around my neck, her long finger pressing

103

gently to my skin. She certainly knew how to massage, and I could feel the tension draining out of my body as she worked on me, more tension than I'd realised I had.

I was quickly feeling pleasantly drowsy, horny too, in an easy-going sort of way, wanting sexual things done to me but without any real urgency. The feel of her fingers on my flesh was just so nice, particularly at the nape of my neck, which she kept coming back to. Her hands were soon on my breasts, cupping them and smearing the mud upwards, which made my nipples pop up under her fingers. I was hoping she'd enjoy a good feel, but she gave them no special attention and moved lower, doing my belly and sides, then my lower back, and at last my bottom. That really was glorious, slow and sensual, with her hands spread wide, making slow, circular motions that made my cheeks lift and part.

If she didn't concentrate on my erogenous zones, then she didn't hold back either. With my bottom cheeks well smeared with the mud, her hands went down between them, quite casually, as if touching another woman between her buttocks was of no great significance at all. Her finger even touched my anus, pushing a little mud into the opening before moving lower to coat the insides of my thighs. Her treatment of my bottom left me aroused, if still strangely at ease – in fact, more so than ever – and I was wondering exactly what was in the mud, or if the feeling simply came from her skill at massage. Not that I really cared, as I was more than ready for her to touch me, in any way she wanted.

I'd thought she would leave my pussy until last, maybe even touch me off, which wouldn't have been difficult. I knew she considered orgasm therapeutic in itself, and was hoping that it was included in her treatment. After all, it wouldn't be as if I asked for it. Unfortunately she simply smoothed her hand once over my pubic mound, smearing on a good handful of mud, and briefly dipped lower, to coat my sex lips, although she did briefly enter my vagina and stroke mud on to my perineum. My arms came next, my legs last, leaving me coated from neck to toe in the stuff, with the herbal smell thick in my nostrils. My whole body felt enervated, my skin tingling gently, slightly hot, but not unpleasantly so, and while I wasn't sleepy, I was very, very relaxed and equally horny.

'Is that good, yes?' she asked.

'Yes, beautiful,' I admitted. 'You're great at massage.'

She gave a little tut of acknowledgement, nothing more, and stepped across to the sink to wash her hands. As I waited, the mud was running very slowly down my body, and I realised why she had put more high up. The tingling sensation was growing stronger too on the more sensitive areas of my flesh: my armpit and breasts, particularly my nipples, but also between my bottom cheeks too and most of all my pussy and bumhole.

Washed, she took the cling film, an industrial-sized roll a good two feet long and thick as well. I put my hands to my sides as she approached, thinking of the domination fantasies she had inspired and wanting to be as helpless as possible. Not that she was going to be cruel to me, but she was going to give me an enema of sorts, which was close enough.

Pulling the end loose, she pressed it gently to my back, smoothing it on one-handed as she unrolled it, trapping my arm. Pulling it out across the front of my chest, she trapped the other, squeezing my breasts in as she did it. That alone was enough to trigger my feelings of restriction, with my boobs bound up tight, and it became stronger as she wound more around me, quite hard, encasing my upper body until I couldn't move my arms at all. My hips followed, then my legs, leaving me standing but unable to take so much as a step, with the cling film wound tight, right down to my ankles. The restriction had become genuine, and quite severe, with the soft flesh of my bottom and belly squashed out beneath the cling film and the mud oozing into whatever cavities were left, including my cleavage and between my thighs.

'And now, to the table,' Gabrielle said as she tore the roll free.

I'd always imagined her as strong, but she lifted me really easily, certainly more easily than I'd have been able to lift her, on to the massage table, full length and face down. Helpless in my cocoon, and bottom up, it was getting hard not to show my reaction, and my domination fantasies were running wild. She could do anything to me, anything she wanted to, explore my body, spank me, indulge herself on my mouth, rub herself off over the slick film that encased my breasts. What she actually intended to do was nearly as good.

'Now,' she said, 'a little applied internally, in both the vaginal and rectal chambers, and you are done.'

I twisted my head around, watching as she went to a box of plastic gloves and pulled on a pair. As she moved the box it revealed a small tray, with a big syringe on it, maybe holding half a litre, with a long nozzle ending in a bulblike tip. Just looking at the thing had me biting my lip, but she was as cool as ever, sticking the end into the pot of mud and drawing the plunger up to fill the syringe with glutinous brown muck, glutinous brown muck that was about to be squirted up my pussy and bottom.

With the syringe full she took up a pair of scissors, coming behind me. I felt her fingers on my bottom, where the mud had pooled between my cheeks and thighs. I felt the tension go as she cut the cling film, and there was a little squashy noise as some of the mud pushed out of the hole. Her fingers went in, between my cheeks, opening them, and she was touching my bumhole. I was gritting my teeth, struggling not to show my emotion as she greased my hole, her rubber-covered fingers working the mud into my ring, opening me, probing and slipping inside, up into my rectum. It was already stinging my anus, really burning, making me tense my cheeks and wiggle my toes in reaction.

She made a thorough job of it, smearing the inside of my gut with the mud, before reaching for the syringe, still with two fingers holding my bumhole open. Just thinking of her actually peering up my bum was too much, and I let out a sigh, closing my eyes against the senses of exposure and helplessness, of shame and indignity. Then the nozzle was at my hole, pushing up as her fingers withdrew. She stuck it well up, deep into my rectum, until my anus was stretched taut and I could feel the weight of the horrible thing up my bottom, before depressing the plunger, and with that my self-control went completely.

I moaned loudly as I felt my rectum start to fill with mud. It felt heavy, solid, very different from a water enema, although I knew it was no more than a thick paste. In no time I had begun to feel bloated, with a desperate, urgent need to go to the loo building up inside me. It was going right up too, and I could feel my belly beginning to swell and the pressure rising as it pushed against my bladder.

She put it all up, the whole half litre, before pulling the syringe from my bumhole. I could hardly hold it in and I was panting, really showing my feelings. She took no notice, calmly cleaning the nozzle and refilling the syringe before once more coming behind me. Again I felt the nozzle poke in between my thighs, but lower, aiming for my pussy. It went up, deep, and then she had begun to depress the plunger and my pussy was bulging with mud, stinging too, a hot, almost burning sensation that added to the pain in my anus and the bloated feeling in my rectum.

'There we are,' she said as the nozzle pulled from my pussy. 'The tingling will soon die down. Let me put some fresh cling film on and then you may expel when you are ready.'

'Expel? In the cling film?'

'Certainly. You will find it cathartic, I think.'

I wasn't sure if I'd find it cathartic or not, but I knew I'd find it rude, deliciously, wantonly rude. I said nothing though, waiting with my bumhole clamped tight against the mounting pressure as she wrapped fresh cling film around me, from my waist down to my knees, sealing the hole. I had to lift my bottom to let her get the roll under me, and I nearly let go. It came out of my pussy anyway, squeezing into the cavity between my thighs and up between my sex lips.

Gabrielle was watching, smiling down at me in my helplessness, quite clearly enjoying the state she had put me in. She looked so dominant, tall and cool and aloof, amusing herself by making me expel my muddy enema into the cling film cocoon. I wanted her to enjoy it, and what was going on in my head too, but I still didn't dare tell her. I was wishing I could though, badly, and that she would then make good use of my helpless body to get her kicks, perhaps sitting on my face with my tongue well up her bottomhole.

I was still holding the enema, tight, enjoying the rising pain and helplessness, also the humiliation of knowing it would come out in the end, and that she would see. My bumhole was still stinging too, and my breath was coming ever deeper, my cheeks clenching, my thigh muscles twitching, and suddenly it was too much. It was coming out, thick and slow, oozing between my bum-cheeks and into the cling film. I'd shut my eyes, my face screwed up to the gloriously disgusting feeling as it began to bulge out in the cling film over my bum, squashing up between my cheeks, down too, over my pussy, then up it.

I moaned aloud as my vagina filled, unable to hold my reaction back. It was all so lewd, so wonderfully filthy, with the mud still oozing out of my bumhole, my pussy full of it and the pressure building around my bum. I wanted to pee, and I just let it come, bubbling out into the cling film to mix with the mud and pool around my pussy mound, warm and wet.

'You are peeing?' Gabrielle asked. 'Good. Let your body empty, everything. It is good, yes?'

'Yes,' I sighed.

'You are aroused?'

I nodded miserably, unable to deny it, hoping she'd say she was too, and then just use me. She said nothing, just nodding to herself as if to confirm her suspicions and returning to the inspection of my bottom. I knew it must have looked obscene, and that there was a big bulge where my cheeks met my thighs, because I could feel the weight of it. I wanted Gabrielle to slap it, to spank me for what I'd done, to treat me as if it was wrong, naughty.

The mud was still coming, but I was having to push, and I wasn't sure it was all mud, which made it yet more humiliating. I was soaked in pee too, all over my tummy and thighs, even up between my boobs, which felt tight and slimy under the film, and badly needed to be touched. Then Gabrielle's hand had settled on to the bulge behind my bottom.

'Is it all out?' she asked.

Again I nodded.

'Good,' she said. 'Then I roll you over.'

Her hands went under my hip and shoulder and I was flipped over on to my front, really easily. I shut my eyes, knowing she could see the pee flowing down over the contours of my flesh beneath the cling film, then grimaced as the squashy mess around my bottom settled beneath me.

I had no idea what she was going to do, but there were still visions of her sitting on my face running through my head. I'd have gladly licked her pussy for her, even her bumhole. In fact it would have been a privilege to stick my tongue right up that rude little hole while she masturbated in my face.

What she did was less intimate, less delightfully rude, in fact cold and clinical. Yet that seemed right – the calm, methodical manipulation of my body as she coolly pressed a ridge of cling film down into the slimy cleft of my pussy and quite simply frigged me off. It took seconds, her finger finding my clit, rubbing as my mouth came open in surprise and ecstasy, harder, all the while looking down at my body in the most extraordinarily calm, detached way, and then I was there. I cried out as I came, naturally, but when she removed her hand it was hard to believe she had masturbated me like that. There were no kisses either, and she had turned her back before I'd sat up, walking to the sink to pull off her plastic gloves and drop them into a bin.

Seven

Gabrielle never got the favour returned, because I was still washing when her mobile went. Somebody wanted to see her, urgently, and she accepted, although I could tell she was genuinely annoyed about it. Given how little she showed her emotions, that suggested she'd badly wanted to continue with me, either for the sake of her treatment or to quiz me. I suspected the latter.

I didn't hear from her in the week either, or call her, because I'd been given a rush commission which again would have gone to Percy if he'd been around. I did hear from Damon though, who was being incredibly persistent. He kept trying to arrange dates, or more exactly fix them, because I evidently wasn't supposed to have much say in the matter. In the end he told me straight out that he would be picking me up on Saturday morning to visit some obscure film festival in Cambridge. He also told me to bring my best, so it was quite obvious that he just wanted me on his arm to show off, as if I was a doll. It was not going to happen.

I'd given Monty by mobile number, which seemed safe enough, and he called on the Friday, suggesting I came and spent the weekend with him. I was tempted, but I wasn't really ready. For one thing my bottom was still a mess and it would be another week before I was really fit for anything more than spanking by hand. Another problem was that I didn't know if I could bear to live in his flat for two days. Cleaning up after our last session had been a real pain, while the thought of a diet of beer and takeaways was less than appealing. On the other hand, it was the only chance I had of some good, rude sex, while there was a lot to be said for being somewhere Damon could not find me. So I accepted, on the condition that he took me away, out of London and south or west. He agreed readily, suggesting that I drive down that night.

When I got there he was eager enough, but seemed somewhat preoccupied, as if something was preying on his mind. It came out as soon as he had sat me down with the inevitable cup of bad coffee. I'd guessed the problem and was ready for it.

'So . . . you are my girlfriend, right?' he asked, not at all to my surprise.

'Well, no . . . Look, can't we just keep this as a sex thing?' I replied. 'Think of it as an open relationship.'

'An open relationship?'

'Something like that. The thing is, I'm with someone else. We've been together for three years.'

'Oh right, Mr Perfect, I suppose, and I'm just the freak show for when you want it kinky.'

'No, don't stereotype me. Percy's over sixty and nearly as fat as you are.'

'A sugar daddy?'

'No, I pay my own way. He's very caring, we have a lot in common, and he gives me the discipline I need.'

'Right.'

'Don't get heavy with me, Monty.'

'OK, sorry.'

'I take it you haven't got a girlfriend.'

'No. I've had my share, I suppose, off and on. It never lasts. Women are a pain.'

'Thanks.'

'Not you, obviously. It's just that with women there has to be this great big song and dance before sex, like some sort of ritual. Like they're making some huge sacrifice by opening their legs.'

'Not necessarily.'

'Almost always. It's like you can't just do sex for the fun of it, there always has to be a load of crap to go with it.'

'You're out of date, Monty. Anyway, that's because the cost of sex is much higher for women, in biological terms, or at least it was until contraception came along. The social situation reflects that, and it's been changing steadily for decades. I fuck with whoever I like.'

'Yeah, but you still made a big deal out of it, at first, pretending you didn't get off on having me toss over watching you in the bath and that.'

I shrugged, not wanting to admit that he only appealed to my desire for sexual humiliation.

'Blokes are more logical,' he went on. 'We make a decision and we stick to it.'

'Go gay, or bi,' I suggested.

'Other blokes don't turn me on, or I would,' he responded. 'There was this guy, once, who caught me looking at a dirty mag in a wood. He'd put it there, like a sort of trap, then watched to see who picked it up. What he wanted was for us to read it together and take turns to wank each other off. He wasn't gay – he wanted to look at the pictures of bare girls – but he wanted someone else's hand on his cock while he did it.'

'And you wanked him off?'

'No I fucking well did not!'

'Why not?'

'I'm not into blokes.'

'What if he'd offered you a suck? Close your eyes and you'd never know the difference.'

'Yes I would. It wouldn't feel right in my head, and you know that, Natasha, you're as much into head fucks as I am.'

'I'm sorry, I was just teasing. Tell me what happened.'

113

'Nothing, I was just using him to illustrate my point. He was up for sex, easy and no strings, but he'd turned to men, even though he wasn't gay.'

'He was bi, by any standards, but I don't know why you have to classify people anyway. Just look on him as a dirty bastard.'

'Whatever. I wish women were like that anyway.'

'Pay for it.'

'That's no good. I like to get off on what's going on in their heads. How can I do that if they're just bored, going through the motions while they think about what they're going to buy with my money?'

'What if they hate every second of it?'

'That's better, at least they're responding.'

'You pig!'

'Not really, I'd feel too bad about it to get off. What I really want is a woman who's like a pet dog, always loyal, always eager to please.'

'Basically you want a woman as a sex object, and to see herself as a sex object. No one thinks like that. You've got to remember that everyone is individual, the centre of their own universe. Nobody is ever really going to see themselves as existing to satisfy you. Human beings are basically selfish.'

'What I'd really like is a perfect robot girl, so that I could program her, yet she would be able to think for herself.'

'Get real, Monty.'

'You'd be surprised, maybe in my lifetime.'

'Sure.'

'It'll happen. You're wrong anyway, about people being basically selfish. You get cases of people completely devoting their lives to the worship of another person.'

'Like obsessive fans who end up shooting the object of their desire? Great. Anyway, never mind your selfish fantasies, what about this bloke in the woods?'

'What's to tell? Like I said, he left a porno mag on an old stump and went to hide so he could see it. I came along, picked it up and out he came. He suggested we toss each other off and I turned him down. That was that.'

'Weren't you scared?'

'What of?'

'Being homosexually raped for one thing!'

'He was half my size, and skinny as hell.'

'It scares me, just thinking there are men like that around. I'd have run a mile.'

'He'd have probably run a mile if he'd seen you. I know I would, if I was having a sneaky wank in the woods and a woman came by.'

'Do you spend a lot of time doing that?'

'No.'

'But you do do it?'

'Sometimes.'

'Dirty bastard!'

'Me dirty! Look who's talking.'

'Fair enough,' I admitted, 'and I like it outdoors too. In fact, the day after we met I went up to a place on the Downs and frigged myself silly over what we'd done. I do it quite a lot actually, but I'm really careful. Girls can't afford to risk getting caught.'

He didn't answer for a while, and then he seemed to come to a decision.

'You into that sort of thing then?' he asked. 'Exhibitionism and that.'

'I like to be naked outdoors. Yes, I like to be seen, sometimes, if it's safe, by the right people.'

'We should do some of that, tomorrow. Maybe we could play the porno mag trick, and when some dirty old man picks it up you could wank him off. Would you do it?'

'Yes.'

'For real?'

'I told you I would. If I'm in the right mood. It's a really dirty idea. Right up my street.'

'Right up your cunt.'

'Maybe.'

We started work on our dirty little scheme in the morning. The first thing was to choose a regular haunt for dirty old men, otherwise we were likely to be waiting all day for nothing. He was obviously getting a big kick just out of planning it, so I let him take the lead. Besides, he seemed to have a pretty good idea of the best spots.

Sex that night had been straight, for us, with me on top of him, backwards. He was too fat to watch his cock go in and out of me properly, but he had a good feel of my bum, and his thighs and gut were nice to bounce on. To finish I climbed on top to be licked while I sucked his cock, and made him come in my face just as my own orgasm was building up, which was great. The result was that we were both in just the right mood for our escapade.

I wanted to get it right, in every detail. Dress for a start, which wasn't an easy choice. Monty wanted me to go for a really tarty look, but it felt wrong for me, while he felt that most of the stuff I'd brought with me either looked too posh or too aggressive. He was painting the sort of men we were likely to come across as timid creatures, and wanted a non-threatening look but a sexy one. Trousers were out too, in case I needed to make a hasty cover-up.

In the end I walked down to a local charity shop and picked up a plain white dress, simple, and easy to lift. They had cheap cotton panties too, coloured ones in threes, and I bought a couple of packs, just to be certain I wouldn't run out. He had told me to buy a porno-graphic magazine on the way back, which was pretty humiliating in itself. I chose the smuttiest one I could find, all smiling girls in tarty underwear, with big boobs

116

and fat bottoms, and the leer on the shopkeeper's face as I paid him was something else. Back at Monty's I got into the dress and a pair of the panties, pink ones, without bothering with a bra. In the mirror I found that I looked a little cheap, a little slutty, but not nearly as bad as the girl on the cover of the magazine. My nipples showed, and the line of my panties, but I could have passed in a club if it wasn't too exclusive.

I read the magazine in the car, marvelling over how vulgar it was, while Monty bought provisions. The poses were incredibly lewd, girls pulling their pussy lips apart, or holding their bottoms wide to stretch their bumholes out. Nothing was hidden, with pin-sharp focus on every little wrinkle of pink or brown flesh, every hair, even every spot. Most of it did nothing for me, any more than a medical textbook would have done, but one or two worked, where the girls seemed to be coy, or unsure of themselves. The best was one of the younger girls, a natural blonde and really quite fat. She looked shy and, in the shot of her pulling down her ridiculous tarty panties, it actually looked as if she was embarrassed about it, which was really sweet.

Armed with our porn mag and plenty of provisions, we set off south and west, in my car, Monty's being some hideous boxlike thing, which I wasn't going to be seen dead in. The sense of anticipation was wonderful. At the very least I'd end up being made to do something rude to Monty in the woods, and at best I'd have an audience, maybe more, if we took things that far.

He had the map on his knees, giving me instructions as we drove down past Reigate and off the main roads, finally stopping in a pub car park on a country lane. It didn't look very promising, but he explained that it was to make sure the car wasn't noticed and that it was a good way from the wood.

We lunched at the pub, then set off, with the pint of beer he'd insisted I drink making me feel naughtier and more excited than ever, braver too. In the pub we'd been playing a game, looking around at our fellow customers and trying to decide which might be dirty old men and what they'd be into.

The wood was a good half mile away, across fields, and I was glad I hadn't gone for his suggestion of tarty high heels. He still had to pick me up to cross a narrow stream, and my shoes were pretty muddy by the time we got there, but I realised immediately that he'd made the right choice. There was a main road at the far side of the wood, with a lay-by, and it was obvious from the first that people came there for sex.

Monty obviously knew it, because he led me straight to a dip in the ground, which he explained was an old railway cutting. It was overgrown with birch scrub, with a few clear areas, one of which we put the porn mag down in before retreating up the bank to hide. I knew we were likely to be in for a wait, but my heart was hammering in my chest. I wanted to be rude, so I made Monty take his cock out and sat playing with it as we watched.

We could hear the cars on the road, and the change in engine note when one drew into the lay-by. Each time it happened I felt my heart running faster still, but when somebody finally appeared, it was from the other direction. I froze, Monty's erect cock still in my hand, watching as a grey head appeared among the birches. Monty hastily put his cock away.

It was one of the people who'd been in the pub, a very respectable looking man, well dressed and with an air of confidence, even arrogance, about him. I could well imagine him spanking me, bruised bum or not and, as he approached, my excitement rose to the point at which I could barely breathe. He reached the porn mag, glanced at it, and glanced away, his patrician features registering disgust for just an instant.

'No go,' Monty whispered. 'He's a local, I think. I've seen him before.'

I nodded, my heartbeat slowing, with both relief and disappointment welling up inside me. I hadn't realised how strong my emotions would be, and I was wondering if I could go through with it, when we heard the sound of a car stopping in the lay-by once again. Both of us froze, listening.

A door banged, then there was silence, save for another car passing. For a while there was nothing, only for a jay to rise suddenly from the woods, setting my heart pounding. I turned to Monty, but he put a hand out, gesturing me to silence, then to duck down. I obeyed, peeping out from among the leaves. At first I saw nothing, then a movement a long way down the path, where I could still see the first man.

The newcomer stepped out, a businessman, dark suit and red tie, well padded if hardly in Monty's league. I saw him nod to the other man as they passed, and as he came closer I made out his expression, crafty, guilty even, not the look of a man taking an innocent afternoon stroll.

'He's one,' Monty whispered. 'I'm sure he is.'

I nodded, certain he was right. Sure enough, as the man reached the porn mag he stopped, glanced back, forward along the path, then quickly picked it up, folded it and stuffed it into his pocket.

'He's going to pinch it!' I hissed.

'No way,' Monty answered quietly. 'He's probably married. He'll have a quick one, then drop it. That's how it works. Come on.'

The man had moved on, and we followed, staying well down, until he suddenly disappeared into the bushes. Monty stopped me, counted to one hundred, then moved on once more, stealing through the scrub until I caught a flash of red ahead of us and we stopped.

It was the man's tie and, peering closer, I could make him out, seated on a stump, the mag open on his knees, his spare hand squeezing his crotch. A solid lump had risen in my throat, and I exchanged an excited glance with Monty.

'Can you do it?' he asked.

I nodded, unable to speak, and he stood, walking boldly forwards.

The man's reaction was instantaneous, jumping up and stuffing the magazine back into his pocket. I'll say this for Monty, he had guts, because I'd have found the situation impossible to deal with, but it didn't seem to bother him at all.

'Hey,' he called, 'don't go, my girlfriend wants to suck your cock.'

I gave him a prod with my elbow, because I wasn't sure if I wanted it to go as far as that, but the man stopped and turned, hesitant, his face filled with embarrassment and aggression. He was pretty senior, to look at him, probably high up in the management of a sizeable firm, and there was confidence in his bearing despite his guilty look. Timid was not a word I'd have used to describe him. He said nothing, looking at us cautiously, his eyes flicking between Monty and me, or rather Monty's face and my bust.

'We're for real,' Monty assured him. 'I like to watch her with other men.'

The man nodded, slowly, still cautious. He was a pretty big guy, but I could see he was sizing Monty up, wondering if it wasn't some sort of trick. I smiled, trying to encourage him, despite the fact that I hardly felt confident myself.

'So what's the deal?' the man asked.

'Simple,' Monty said. 'She gives you a wank, I watch. If you're lucky she'll suck you.'

'How much?'

'Nothing!' I answered.

'Nothing,' Monty agreed. 'You're getting a freebie.'

'Tits out?'

'Yeah, tits out. Come on, Natasha, show the gentleman what you've got.'

It was happening, and my heart was hammering in my chest as I reached down to take hold of the hem of my dress. I lifted it, exposing my thighs, my panties, my tummy and at last my boobs, which felt very big and very prominent, with him staring at them.

'Nice,' the man drawled, his tongue flicking out to moisten full lips. 'Does she fuck?'

'Only with me,' Monty answered.

'All right, but make her take her knickers off.'

'My knickers stay on,' I answered him, 'but you can have a flash.'

I didn't feel ready to show my pussy, but I turned and popped down the back of my panties, just for a moment, showing him my bare bum. I knew the bruises showed, and I was hoping he'd want to give me a little spanking, which was what I really needed.

'Been at her?' the man demanded of Monty. 'You don't beat her, do you, to make her do this?'

'No,' Monty assured him and I nodded agreement. He didn't seem interested in punishing me, which was a pity, but his hand had gone to his fly.

'All right,' he said, 'I'll do it. Come on, darling, here's what you want.'

He had pulled his fly down as he spoke, and the next moment had flopped his cock and balls out of the opening. I swallowed the lump in my throat, moving forwards as he sat back down on the stump, his thighs wide.

'Rub your tits on it,' he ordered. 'Nice pair, hasn't she?'

'Gorgeous,' Monty agreed. 'Come on, Natasha, do as the gentleman says.'

I was trembling as I kneeled down in the leaf mould, but I did it, cupping my boobs and folding them around the hairy flesh of his genitals. I began to rub, feeling my nipples pop out as they touched his skin.

'Good girl,' Monty said. 'Come on, jiggle them about a bit, give us a show.'

His cock had started to grow, and I obeyed Monty, bouncing my boobs in my hands to show them off. It felt good to be making a display of myself, for my body to be the centre of attention, and I knew I was going to suck him, even as I bent down. I took it in my mouth, a thick, leathery cock, half hard, peeling the foreskin back with my lips. He gave a grunt and pushed it out, filling my mouth.

I was still feeling my boobs, and bobbing my head up and down on his cock. He took it, holding it out for me, then starting to wank into my mouth. I sucked on it, concentrating on the hard feel of his shaft and the cock taste in my mouth, thinking of his fat body and leering face, of Monty watching, fatter still, my boyfriend, my fat boyfriend, watching as I sucked a dirty old man off in the woods.

I needed to masturbate, and I was going to, only to have him whip his cock out of my mouth, give it two last, hard jerks and come, full in my face. I gasped in shock as the spunk splashed in one eye, the second spurt going full into my mouth, with the last of the streamer left to hang from my chin. The third caught me across my nose and in my other eye, blinding me completely before he stuffed his cock back into my mouth, forcing me to suck down the last of his come.

He let his breath out with a long sigh as I swallowed on his cock, then pulled back. I couldn't see, and there was spunk hanging from my lips and my nose, leaving me completely helpless. I heard Monty snigger and I called him a bastard, demanding help.

'Use your knickers!' he laughed. 'He's not going to fuck you now.'

They weren't going to help, so I had to do it, standing to remove my panties and using them to wipe the man's spunk off my face. When I finally got it out of my eyes I found Monty watching me and the businessman standing as he did up his fly. I gave him a dirty look, but he took no notice.

'Good, isn't she?' Monty said.

'Great,' the man agreed. 'See you again, maybe?'

'Maybe,' Monty agreed. 'Could we have our porno mag back?'

'Your mag?'

'Yeah, we put it out so we could find a guy who'd want her.'

'A dirty old man,' I added.

He just nodded, passed Monty the magazine and left, heading back towards the lay-by. I finished cleaning my face, glad we'd decided I should do without make-up, and hung my soiled panties from a twig. Monty grinned.

'Dirty enough for you?' he asked.

'Yes,' I answered him, 'but I wanted to come. I still do. Do you want to fuck me?'

'Not yet, put a fresh pair of panties on, the pale-blue ones.'

'What are we going to do? I don't want to wait for another man, it might take ages!'

'You're going to make an exhibition of yourself.'

'How?'

'Just do as you're told.'

I nodded, eager but a little scared, with my adrenaline running high for what we'd done, what I'd done, and wondering what was coming next. Monty watched as I fished a new pair of panties out of my bag, choosing the pale-blue ones as ordered, and pulling them on under my dress. I felt dirty, excited, and ready for just about anything. He took my hand, leading me back to the path.

'Now what?' I demanded. 'Are you going to make me flash my panties at someone or something?'

'No,' he answered. 'Do you need a pee yet?'

I nodded, understanding immediately.

'Do it, then, in your knickers.'

I was aroused enough, excited enough and, before common sense could get the better of me, I had shut my eyes, letting my bladder relax. I didn't need it all that badly, and it was hard, knowing that it was going to come out into my panties, but I concentrated, struggling to break a lifetime of toilet training, and suddenly it was coming, a dribble, then a gush. I felt it soak into the gusset of my panties, then start to pour from the front, down my thighs, back between my bumcheeks, and spraying out to soak into my dress.

It was that which really brought what I was doing home to me. I could change my panties, I could go pantiless easily enough, but not without my dress, and it was soaking, making it quite obvious that I'd wet myself, exactly the way Monty wanted it. I let it come anyway, all of it, revelling in the dirty, helpless feeling, wetting myself in the full knowledge that people were going to see.

I was sobbing by the time it stopped, and breathing really heavily, so excited, and so humiliated. The whole front of my dress was wet, with a big patch spreading out from below my pussy. The back was wet too, a little, where it had soaked back through my panties, with the wet material clinging to my skin. It was all down my legs as well, and I could smell myself in the air.

Monty was grinning, walking around me as he inspected the mess I'd made of myself. My dress had gone see-through where it was wet, and my panties showed, back and front, the blue material quiet clear through the white. It was obvious what I'd done, so painfully obvious, and he was going to make me show it.

'Dirty bitch!' he said, with immense satisfaction. 'Come on, I want people to see this, lots of them. Try and look sorry for yourself.'

'That won't be hard,' I assured him.

He held out his hand and I took it, letting him lead me along the path. I did feel sorry for myself, very sorry indeed. I was nearly crying with humiliation, and turned on with it, to the point where I wanted him to fuck me with my wet panties pulled aside, right in the middle of the path.

I was going to ask, but at that moment I heard a bird call from behind us. I turned to find the grey-haired man coming towards me. He hadn't seen, but he was going to, and I felt a moment of panic, with a desperate urge to run into the woods and hide myself from his awful, disapproving gaze. Then it was too late. He had seen, smiling in greeting, only for his expression to turn to surprise and disgust as he saw what I'd done.

The shame was agonising, really burning in my head. My tears had started, running freely down my face, and I wanted to fall to my knees and masturbate through the soggy cotton of my gusset, or have Monty fuck me, with my pee-soaked panties squelching against my skin as his fat gut slammed into my bottom. It was too much to bear, and I was pulling his hand, trying to drag him up out of the cutting, in among the trees where he could fuck me at leisure, but he wouldn't come.

'I want it!' I pleaded. 'Now!'

'No,' he answered, 'you're going to be seen by some more people. Come on.'

He had a firm hold on my hand, pulling me along the path, towards the lay-by. I went, thinking of how I must look with my tear-streaked face and my pee-soaked dress, a truly sorry state. I'd done it on purpose too, I knew that, and I wanted to be punished for it, spanked with my soggy panties pulled down, or stuffed in my mouth so that I could taste my own pee while I was beaten.

We reached the lay-by, and a car passed almost immediately, another behind it. I was sure both had seen, but neither slowed. The third one did, an old white Fiat, and I caught the driver's eyes, staring right at me, his mouth slightly open. He'd been old, grey haired and roughly dressed, a retired farm labourer perhaps, or something like that.

'Now bend down,' Monty ordered. 'Show the next one the wet patch on your bum.'

I did it, trembling as I waited for the sound of an engine, then bent, pretending to adjust my shoe, my wet bottom stuck out in full view. The car passed, fast, but slowing fractionally and I knew that one more person had been given an eyeful of my wet seat.

'There's a really good outline.' Monty laughed as he came around behind me. 'Both your bumcheeks show, and it is really obvious what you've done.'

'I know,' I managed, 'but enough showing off. Take me in the woods. Fuck me, from behind, with my wet panties still on.'

'One more,' he said. 'Press your knees together, stick your bum out. Pretend you're doing it. Quickly, there's one coming.'

'I could, a little,' I promised him, getting into the rude pose he'd suggested. 'I'm going to do it! Here goes!'

I felt the pee spurt out as I strained, between my thighs, spattering the back of my dress. The car had passed, and I didn't know if the people in it had seen or not, but it had felt so good, and I was wishing I had more, or worse, to really make a mess of myself.

'Right,' Monty said, 'now for your fucking . . . No, hang on.'

Another car was coming, and as I looked round I saw that it was the old Fiat we'd seen before, only this time he was slowing right down.

'I think we've got one!' Monty said as the car pulled into the lay-by.

'No, Monty, not in this state,' I begged. 'This is for you . . .'

'Shut up and do as you're told,' he answered me. 'He's got to be a dirty old man. Yes he is. I've seen him here before.'

The old man had got out of the car and was trying to be nonchalant, watching me from the side of his eye as he bent, pretending to check the pressure of a tyre. Monty was already walking towards him, and I realised that I had a choice: play along or run back to the pub in my wet clothes. Really it was no choice at all, because I needed Monty to go to the car for my clothes, and into the pub for some water.

He'd reached the man, and was speaking to him, quietly. I'd stayed back, and I watched the man's face, caution turning to interest, and amusement, not the slightest concern. Monty turned, beckoning to me.

'I told him you did it on purpose,' Monty said. 'Take off your panties.'

'Here?'

'Yeah, here. Go on.'

I glanced quickly along the road, then reached up, struggling my panties down under my dress, and off. The man watched, grinning.

'Now take him in the bushes and wank him off, with the panties,' Monty ordered.

I nodded, swallowing once more. The man got up and I took his hand, leading him into the wood, far enough to be sure we weren't seen from the lay-by. I was trembling inside, and he seemed a little nervous, but no more, seating himself on a fallen tree and calmly pulling down his fly. He took his cock out, a stubby, wrinkled thing, very dark-skinned.

'Come on, love,' he said as I hesitated. 'Get wanking.'

'You do it,' I said, still not sure of myself. 'I'll . . . I'll show you my boobs.'

'Make it your bum,' he said. 'I'm a bum man, me.'

I was holding out my wet panties and he took them. He folded them around his cock, really lovingly, and squeezed, making the piddle squirt out from between his fingers. I just watched as he started to wank, pulling at his little cock with my pee running down over his balls. It was mesmerising, so dirty, so open, and I found myself wanting to do what he had demanded. I turned, pushing my bottom out, for all the world like one of the girls in the porn mag, posing myself just so that some dirty old bastard could get his rocks off over the sight of my bare bum.

He leered at me as I looked back, pulling harder at his rapidly stiffening cock. My hands went down, to the hem of my dress and it was coming up, the wet material sticking to my legs as I lifted it, just as I had in front of the businessman, only now I had no panties. The back of my thighs came on show, the tuck of my bottom, everything. I was showing it, my bare bum, stuck out, my cheeks parted to show the rear view of my pussy, wet with piddle, my bumhole too. I could picture myself, so easily, from thinking of the way the girls looked in the magazine, my dress high, my bottom spread, my bare pink pussy lips on show, with the fleshy folds of my inner lips peeping out between them, my bumhole too, with its ring of light-brown flesh around a rose-pink centre. He was staring at me, really intent, while he jerked at his cock, drops of piddle spraying out as he wanked in my little blue panties.

I did it, unable to stop myself, turning and sinking down on the ground, grabbing for his cock and pushing his hand away. I took hold of him, wrapping the panties around his erection, jerking at him, aiming it at my face, with my bare bum stuck out behind so that he could see. He gave a satisfied grunt and reached down, taking my dress and pulling it up, high over my boobs. They came out, but he still pulled, and I had to let go of his cock to let him strip me, peeling it over my head to leave me nude except for my shoes.

Again I folded the wet panties around his erection, tugging at him with one hand as I slid the other back between my thighs. As I found my sex I leaned forwards, taking his cock in my mouth, still wanking, with the wet panty material slapping against my face. I could taste him, the taste of cock, but mixed with that of pee, my own pee, which I had done in my panties, on purpose. He took me by the hair as I sucked, forcing his cock deeper, and I began to rub more firmly, sure he would soon come.

I was going to come myself, at any moment, and then Monty was there, to one side, his cock in his hand, wanking over the sight of me sucking the dirty old man off. He dropped down, behind me, his belly pressing to my bottom, his cock nudging between my cheeks, again, and up my pussy in one smooth motion. He began to fuck me, rhythmically, rocking my body back and forth on the old man's cock, helping me closer and closer towards orgasm, only to slip out and slide up the crease of my bottom, leaving a slimy trail. I slowed my masturbation, waiting for him to put it back inside, only to feel the fat, greasy head push to my bumhole.

The old man had my head down, right on his cock, pressing my face to the sodden panties. Monty was going to bugger me, and I could do nothing to stop him – not that I really wanted to – and was letting my anus go slack even as he pushed. It went in, a little way, my own pussy cream greasing my passage. He pushed again, and for a moment it hurt, with my bumhole straining to accommodate the head of his cock. Then the head was in, and more, forced inch by inch up my bum as I began to gag on the cock that was being forced deep into my mouth.

He got it in, all of it, his fat guts pressing to my naked bottom and lower back, his thighs supporting mine. Again they began to rock me, between them, only now Monty was up my bum, in public, buggering me as I sucked on a dirty old man's cock and masturbated, nude, my body wet with pee, my sodden panties pushed into my face . . .

I came, my bumhole clenching hard on the fat shaft inside it, my pussy closing on empty air, struggling to get as much of the cock in my mouth down my throat as I could. I was shaking my head too, and wiggling my bottom, totally abandoned to them, lewd, wanton, a dirty, eager little slut, being used the way I so badly wanted, the way I needed. It held, wonderfully, with my bumhole locked on Monty's cock and the old man jerking away at my head, fucking it, wrenching at my hair, jerking me up and down and at last grunting in pleasure as he ejaculated down my throat.

The old man held my head while Monty finished off up my bum. He was panting, hard, and jamming it right in, until it had begun to hurt, making me cry out and knocking the breath from my body with each push. His hand came forward, grabbing the soiled panties and shoving them in my face, hard, and with that he came, up my bottom, giving a last deep grunt and holding himself deep inside me until he had drained the full load of his sperm into my back passage.

I just collapsed even as he began to pull out of me, filthy and sore, but really too far gone to care. The bastard cleaned his cock on my panties, in front of my face, so that I could see, then hung them from a tree, as I had with my pink ones.

At last I found the energy to sit up, and it was only then that I realised that there were two other men, watching, well back among the trees, both younger, with guilty, lascivious grins on their faces. They melted away among the foliage when they saw me looking at them, but I knew they'd watched, and that was what mattered.

The old man left, barely saying a word, nodding to Monty as he gave a curt goodbye, and ignoring me completely. I was in a fine mess, but Monty said that there was a stream at the far edge of the wood, and we went there, with me still nude. Nobody saw and, after washing myself and my dress, I sat down on a well-sheltered bit of grass, with Monty keeping watch.

It was only then, with the excitement gone, that I began to wonder about the way the old man had behaved, and other things as well. Monty had said it was a good place, but it all seemed to have gone a bit too smoothly. It was almost as if the men had expected me to perform. Certainly they hadn't showed any great surprise at my behaviour, and that wasn't normal. On the other hand, they had been particularly intrusive, personally, the way dirty old men often are. They'd been more impersonal, in fact, as if I'd been provided for them. In a sense I had, but they couldn't have known that, or shouldn't have, especially the old man.

'You seem to know this place very well,' I remarked to Monty. 'How often do you come here?'

'Now and then,' he admitted.

'You said you'd seen both of them before, didn't you?'

'Yes.'

'More than once?'

'I don't know. I'm not sure.'

'Don't lie to me, Monty. They knew who you were, didn't they?'

'No.'

'You're lying. I can tell.'

'I'm not!'

'Yes you are. That was no accident, two of them so close. And why weren't they more surprised? Come on, out with it. How does it work?'

'I don't know what you're talking about!'

His voice had become really high pitched, and I was sure he was lying.

'Look, Monty,' I went on, 'you know what I'm like. If you tell me the truth I'll probably be all right about it. I enjoyed what we did, OK? Don't tell me, and I'm going back to London.'

'Yeah, all right. I know the old guy.'

'He's a regular here, right, and so are you? I didn't think perverts talked to each other.'

'He a cleaner where I work.'

'He is? Explain, now!'

'Oh, OK. We have this deal, right, at work. I work in Reigate. The guys who're in on it all put a tenner into the pot at the start of the month. We try and bring girls out here for sex, usually in the backs of our cars. The guy who puts on the best show gets the pot.'

His voice had gone low, really sulky, and it was obvious he expected me to be angry. In fact what he was saying was still sinking in as he went on.

'Some of the guys are married, others bring their regular girlfriends. One guy manages to bring a new girl here almost every week. I never have anyone. That was part of the reason I made a move on you in Brighton. We were great though, hey? Two suck-offs, and nobody's ever buggered a girl!'

'That's why you buggered me?'

'Mainly, yeah.'

'Run that past me again, Monty. You're saying that you buggered me to show off to your friends? You buggered me to show off to your friends!?'

Eight

It was a hell of a row, but I knew I was going to lose from the start. It was impossible for me to justify how I felt all right about being made to have sex with complete strangers purely to humiliate me, but not so that he could show his workmates what a big man he was. His argument was that it should be even more humiliating, and it was, so I couldn't really dispute his logic. I still felt used.

In the end my only recourse was to sulk, but even then I was half-hoping he'd put a stop to it with a spanking, the way Percy does. He didn't and, once my dress was dry, we walked back to the car in silence, with me thinking black thoughts and trying to understand my own feelings.

He had no respect for me whatsoever, that much was obvious. To him I was just somebody to use for his fun, a fuck-dolly, to use a particularly crude expression. No, that was wrong, I wasn't somebody to use, but some-*thing*, like the robot he had spoken about. He worshipped my body, yes, but my humanity was not an issue to him.

Unfortunately, it was addictive. He'd made me suck off a guy who made his living sweeping the floor, with my pissy panties in my face, and then buggered me. It was perfect, just the sort of thing I love done to me, utterly filthy and utterly humiliating. Percy might have done the same, but ultimately his loyalty would have been to me, and that was what mattered.

Back at the car I was tempted to tell Monty to piss off and just drive home. I might even have done it, had it not been for the prospect of spending the rest of my weekend dodging Damon and moping in my flat. As it was I drove west, with the radio turned up and no particular destination in mind. Before too long I was feeling better, and telling myself that if Monty was using me, then I could easily be accused of using him. Just because I was the one who got abused didn't change it, after all, that's how I like my sex. In fact it was quite neat, because his behaviour excused mine.

I'd hit the A3 so that I could drive fast, which always soothes my feelings, and it was the look of sheer terror on Monty's face that finally made me forgive him. He was trying to be cool, but his hand was clutching the door handle, and his knuckles were showing white. It just looked so funny, comical really, which restored my image of him as someone safe.

I even began to try and see it from his point of view, and I had to admit that it would have been hard to resist. His workmates undoubtedly took the piss out of him for being so fat, and it would be worse because he was no good with girls. The chance to show me off must have been irresistible, and on the Monday he was going to be cock of the walk, thanks to me. Not only that, but he hadn't forced me to do anything I didn't want to. It was time to make up.

'Don't you know how to deal with a sulky brat?' I asked.

'Eh?' He looked puzzled.

'I said, don't you know how to deal with a sulky brat?'

'What do you mean?'

'What I say. Come on, Monty, show some gumption.'

'You're not cross with me then?'

'No. I'm all right about it, but you should have told me.'

134

'We're not supposed to. Normally the girls don't even know they're being watched.'

'If you want a good relationship you have to have trust. Be honest, that way you get what you want.'

'That doesn't always work.'

'It worked with me, didn't it?'

'It was the first time in years.'

I was about to suggest he'd do better if he lost a bit of weight, about ten stone, but I could see it would make him feel self-conscious. He sounded maudlin enough as it was, so I bit the words back. Anyway, if he hadn't been so fat I wouldn't have gone with him in the first place, which was a fine piece of irony.

'Cheer up,' I told him. 'You're not the one who's supposed to be sulky, I am, and you're supposed to punish me.'

'How? You're doing about a hundred.'

'I'm doing ninety-five, but I'll go faster if you like. Add speeding to my list of offences.'

'OK. I'll spank you this evening, in our hotel room.'

'Good, but you'd have saved a lot of trouble if you'd done it to me earlier, maybe even in the woods.'

'You'd have lost it.'

'Sure, until my bum was all warm and rosy. You've got to take charge sometimes, you know, Monty. Sometimes it's best not to ask. Sometimes it's best to just do it.'

'You get into trouble that way. I do anyway.'

'Yeah, well you have to know when, don't you?'

'How?'

'Body language, little hints in conversation. OK, fair enough, it took me ages to get my first proper spanking, but in future, if you think I need punishment, you don't need to ask. I'll use my stop word if it's not the right time.'

'OK, so how often do you like it?'

'Honestly, Monty! Do I have to tell you everything? What's the matter? You managed all right when I was being your sex slave.'

'Yeah, well, you'd promised to do as you were told.'

'OK then, I'm promising now. As soon as the door closes on our room tonight I'm your sex slave, only no pizza this time.'

'How about knicker-wetting? You liked pissing in your knickers, didn't you?'

'Knicker-wetting's fine, just no pizza.'

We had cleared the air, and built up a fine sense of anticipation as well. I'd wanted him to make me pull off so that he could spank me in the woods, but I was content to wait and let it build up. Until then I'd really had no idea where I was going, but we were nearly at Petersfield, and there was a sort of cross between a hotel and a country pub Percy had once taken me to nearby, the War Down Man, which seemed ideal.

It was very proper for one thing, with the sort of reserved English atmosphere that Percy always says is ideal for spanking girls. I understood what he meant, as it was easy to imagine a bit of discipline being handed out to some wayward barmaid by the landlord, who was a huge, gruff man with an equally surly wife. Not sexual discipline, of course, but that didn't stop me from enjoying the fantasy.

The first thing I did was go up to our room to change, and to wash properly. It was on the second floor, and decorated a rather twee pink, which amused me when I thought of the sort of things we were likely to be getting up to. Discarding the cheap dress and yellow cotton panties, I put on a panty and bra set, with suspenders to match, and black seamed stockings of the sort Percy likes me to wear. I was sure Monty would love them when he got to undress me, or more likely make me strip for him, and I topped it all off with a black Verniece dress. In the mirror I looked both refined and slightly haughty, if not entirely demure, and I knew that the drop to naked, grovelling slut was going to be superb.

The other reason Percy favoured the hotel was for the wine list, which was exceptional, particularly for claret.

Unfortunately Monty thought the prices were outrageous and wanted to drink beer. We would have argued, but he threatened to spank me on the spot if I didn't stop whining, which shut me up. Not that I drank the beer, but I had to content myself with a bottle of some Fronsac I'd never heard of with my pigeon, followed by a half of Rieussec with Stilton.

What that did mean was that I was pretty tipsy by the time we finished. So was Monty, who'd put back several pints of strong beer. We were outside, at a table a fair way apart from the others and sheltered by a couple of straggling bushes, which we'd chosen for the sake of privacy. It was getting rapidly cooler and I was wondering about going in. I'd put my coat on, but he didn't seem to mind, sipping his beer contentedly as he watched the last of the other people go in.

'Right,' he said, rising, 'this'll do.'

'What?' I demanded, an instant before his hand closed in my hair and I realised that he was going to try and put me across his knee. 'No! Not here! Monty! For God's sake, we'll be seen!'

I tried to fight, but he was pulling really hard on my hair. I went down, sprawling across his lap, still squealing and struggling but too shocked to think of saying my stop word until he had twisted my arm hard into the small of my back, rendering me absolutely helpless.

'No, Monty,' I said. 'Not here . . . Amber, Red.'

'You don't get out of it that easily, brat. Nobody's looking, so you get your spanking.'

'No, Monty, come, on, I'm serious!'

I was trying to sound cross, but I could hear the note of pleading in my own voice, then I felt his hand at the hem of my dress and I realised that it was going to be worse than I thought.

'Monty, no!' I squeaked as I felt the cool air on my thighs. 'No, you can't! Not that, not on the bare! We'll be seen! Red! Red!'

He took no notice at all, tugging my dress up, hard, so that I was forced to lift my hips to let it come or risk him tearing it.

'You've got to obey my stop word, Monty,' I babbled as I felt the seat of my panties come on show. 'You have to, Monty! You have to!'

'Stop being such a baby,' he chided. 'I haven't done anything yet. I like your knickers, very swish.'

'Haven't done anything!? You've got my panties on show, in public! You're going to spank me!'

'I know,' he said and his hand came down on my bum.

It wasn't hard, but it was hard enough to make me squeal. He laughed, and laid his hand on my bottom, wobbling my cheeks.

'You're quite chubby, really, here,' he said. 'These knickers make it look fatter. I'm sure you wouldn't want that, so I think they'd better come down.'

'No!' I squeaked, but it was hopeless. He ignored me, taking the waistband of my panties very gently between finger and thumb and peeling them down, slowly, off my bottom, to leave it bare.

'You bastard!' I sobbed as he settled them around my thighs. 'Oh God!'

I was bare bottomed, my panties rolled down, in the garden of a hotel, where anyone might come out, at any moment, and see me getting my bare bottom spanked. My breathing was coming hard, the tears were starting in my eyes and I was cursing Monty, over and over.

'Here goes,' he said cheerfully and brought his hand down across my bum with the full weight of his arm behind it.

I screamed at the blow, really loudly, only for another to land, harder still, and then I was kicking and writhing under a rain of smacks. My free arm was flailing wildly, fist clenched, hitting Monty, the ground, the bench, anything I could find. I was shaking my head too, in pain and humiliation and fear of being seen, my hair flying out to all sides, in utter disarray. My legs were going too, and my hips, bucking up and down, showing off my pussy and bumhole, with my panties stretched taught between my knees. It hurt so much, and I was terrified of being caught, trying to look round at the hotel and stifle my screams as my poor bum was spanked and spanked and spanked.

Monty laughed as he did it, taking great pleasure in my reaction, spanking away with the sound of the slaps ringing out across the quiet of the evening, mixed with my screaming, gasps and tearful sobbing. I thought he'd never stop, that he was determined to get us caught, to make sure that the miserable old couple who ran the place got a good eyeful of my bare red bottom. It didn't happen though, by some miracle, and finally he stopped, letting go of my wrist and letting me roll off his knee on to the ground.

I sat there for a moment, with my bare bottom on the cool, damp grass, just panting and snivelling, until I managed to pull myself together enough to get my skirt down and my panties up underneath it, concealing the evidence of my punishment. That was the moment the landlord chose to come out, doubtless in response to my screams, as he had a pretty peculiar look on his face, but not the fury I'd have expected if he'd really caught us.

He took our plates, asking tersely if everything had been to our satisfaction. It must have been obvious that something was wrong with me, because my face was streaked with tears, my make-up ruined and my dress ruffled, but he said nothing and went back inside.

'You utter bastard!' I spat at Monty. 'Never, ever do that again!'

'It's what you like, isn't it? Sometimes it's best just to do it, like you said.'

'Yes, but not in public!'

'What's public? Nobody saw, not like when you were in your pissy dress, and don't tell me you're not turned on.'

'Of course I'm bloody turned on! Can you even start to imagine how I feel? Spanked in public, on the bare! Jesus, Monty!'

'Well then, you should thank me.'

'No, I should not thank you! It was too risky, and you ignored my stop word! What if he'd come out a moment earlier?'

'He'd have seen a brat getting a well-deserved spanking.'

'Yes, and called the police, or at the very least thrown us out.'

'Well he didn't, so stop whining and say thank you.'

'No, you'll bloody well apologise!'

'No. You will thank me, or I'll do it again. I don't care if we get thrown out.'

'And if he calls the police?'

'I'll take the risk. Now thank me, or you go back over my knee, and this time your dress comes right up, over your knockers.'

'You're not going to do it,' I said, backing away.

'Whatever,' he said. 'I've got the room key, remember.'

He was right. I was stuck. I stood there, glaring at him, until I finally managed to swallow my pride and anger, letting the humiliation of what had to all intents and purposes been a public spanking take over.

'I'm sorry,' I said faintly. 'Thank you.'

'Louder,' he answered, 'and do it properly.'

'Thank you,' I repeated. 'Thank you for punishing me.'

'More.'

'Thank you for spanking me, Monty,' I said. 'And thank you for doing me on the bare. I'd been a brat and I deserved it. Good enough?'

'Once more.'

'Thank you for giving me a bare-bottom spanking, Monty. I was a brat and I deserved it. I'm sorry I made

140

a fuss over it too. You must punish me whenever it's necessary.'

I was really trembling, and biting my lip, with my hands folded in my lap. It was too much for me and, despite my anger, I was genuinely thankful, because I knew I'd be masturbating over the experience for years.

'Good girl,' he said. 'That'll do. Now up to the bedroom and we'll see how sorry you really are.'

'Yes, Monty.'

He took my hand and led me back across the garden, as I wondered what he had in store for me. It was getting rapidly dark, and if he'd wanted to wait a little and then make me go down on him in the garden I'd have done it, maybe even let him fuck me behind the bushes. He seemed to have other ideas, taking me up to the room, only pausing at the bar to order another couple of pints of beer. As soon as we were in he locked the door behind us.

'Strip,' he ordered, 'down to your panties.'

'Yes, Monty.'

He climbed on to the bed, watching me as I undressed. I tried to be shy about it, showing off, but not boldly, shoes, stockings, dress, suspender belt and finally my bra, leaving me in nothing but my black silk panties, standing with my head hung meekly, waiting for instructions. He'd taken his cock and balls out and was stroking them, idly, the way a man does when he knows he's in charge and doesn't need to worry about his performance.

'Right,' he said, 'we're going to play a little game, a game called "It". For you it's a very easy game. Just do everything I say, exactly. Fail and you get a black mark. OK?'

'Yes, Monty. What do the black marks earn me, spanks?'

'Something harder, I don't want you disobeying. You can use your stupid stop word too, but you get a black mark if you do.'

'Cane strokes? Be fair, Monty, you've got to tell me. Remember I'm bruised too.'

'No, but I will. I'm going to whip your tits, tomorrow, outdoors. Now, first, it goes into the bathroom.'

I obeyed. 'It' was obviously me, and added humiliation typical of the mixture of mind games and physical sadism Monty seemed to like. He followed me, stopping at the door with his pint in his hand.

'It climbs into the shower cubicle, and puts the plug in,' he said, and again I obeyed.

'It puts its hands on its head,' he ordered as I stood once more. 'It sticks its tits out.'

I did it, watching him as he stroked his cock.

'Good,' he said. 'Now it pisses in its knickers.'

'Not these, Monty, they're silk!'

'One black mark. It pisses in its knickers.'

'Oh God, all right.'

I shut my eyes, letting my bladder relax, which wasn't hard with a bottle and a half inside me. The piddle started, slowly at first, as I struggled to break my ingrained need not to do it in my knickers, then faster, soaking into my gusset, trickling down my legs, spattering on the porcelain floor of the shower cubicle. I let it all out, the full contents of my bladder, until I was standing in a puddle of warm pee, with my panty crotch soaked, back and front.

'It sits down in its own piss,' Monty ordered, 'and wriggles its arse around.'

I did it, squatting into the puddle so that my bum went right in it, Monty watching as it soaked into my panties. His cock was getting hard, and he was getting to me, badly, and my lower lip was trembling uncontrollably as I wiggled my bottom in the warm puddle. A little more came out, squirting through my panty crotch.

'It takes off its panties,' he said, 'showing its cunt.'

My thumbs went into the waistband of my panties, pushing them down off my hips as I lifted myself, only

142

for my foot to slip in the pee. I sat down squashily in the puddle, my panties half down. Monty laughed. Again I tried, this time kneeling up, with my knees well spread so that he got a good view of my pussy as I took my panties down and pulled them off one ankle, then the other.

'It mops up with its knickers, crawling.'

It was pointless. They were already soaked, but I tried, rubbing them in the piddle with my bum stuck up and turned towards him so that he could see between my spread cheeks.

'It's not doing it properly,' he said. 'Black mark. It sucks its knickers to get rid of the piss.'

I heard my own sob and once more felt my tears start as I picked up the tiny rag of soiled silk. They were dripping pee, and I hesitated a moment, with them held up in front of my face, my mouth open, horrified by what I was about to do. I had to though, and I did it quickly, stuffing them into my mouth, sucking on them and swallowing the piddle.

Monty's cock was rock hard, and his wanking had begun to get urgent. He was still drinking his beer, which made what I was drinking that much ruder – my own pee, sucked out of my panties. I tried to clean up as best I could, but it wasn't easy. My mouth was thick with the taste of pee and my tears were heavy in my eyes as I mopped the filthy floor, repeatedly sucking at the panties and swallowing every drop until at last there was no more than a wet sheen on the porcelain.

'It licks up its piss, all of it,' Monty commanded.

My head went down again, all the way. Poking my tongue out, I began to lap at the floor, sucking up the little pools that had formed where my legs had been. I was making as much saliva as I was swallowing pee, but he didn't seem to care, waiting patiently until I had licked every square inch of the shower floor.

I was breathing heavily, and as I sat up again the first of my tears fell, trickling down my cheek. Monty put down his glass and stepped forwards, reaching down to take me by the hair. I opened my mouth expectantly, but he pulled my face into his crotch, rubbing his cock and balls into it first, and only then stuffing my mouth. For a while he fucked my head, in silence, before pulling out and returning to his pint.

To my surprise he closed his eyes, sipping at his beer. His erection began to go down, slowly, the thick, wet shaft gradually contracting, wrinkling, the head retreating into the foreskin. I waited, pretty sure what he was doing, until at last he had finished his pint. Opening his eyes, he put the empty glass down in the sink. He was grinning at me as he stepped forward, his fat face split into a really evil smirk.

'It lies down,' he said. 'It spreads its cunt.'

I swallowed, hard, rocking back on my heels to spread my thighs to him, with my back to the cubicle wall. My pussy was open, gaping, and very wet, slick with pee and juicy too.

'Black mark,' he said. 'It spreads its cunt, with its fingers.'

My hand went straight to my sex, spreading my lips, wide, to show him the mouth of my vagina. He stepped closer, taking his cock in his hand. Again I swallowed, unable to take my eyes away as he pointed it at my tummy.

'It puts two fingers up its cunt hole,' he said.

I obeyed, sobbing as I slid two fingers up my pussy, holding my hole wide, knowing he could see inside, to the moist, pink tube of my vagina. He pointed his cock towards my sex, leering as he pinched it, holding back then letting go to release a great gush of pee. I cried out as it hit me, hot and wet, full on my tummy, then lower as he adjusted his stream, on to my sex, over my clitty, to the mouth of my vagina, and into it. My hole filled in an instant, urine bubbling out around the stream, splashing my thighs and trickling down between my bumcheeks. I was gasping, overwhelmed by what he was doing, still with my pussy spread wide so that he could piss up me.

My thumb went to my clit, flicking at the little bud as pee gushed out around it. I started to masturbate, urgently, wanting to come while I was still being treated so rudely, so callously, and wanting to be completely soiled, all over.

'In my face,' I begged, 'and do my boobs.'

'Black mark. It shuts up,' he said, but the stream of pee came higher, up my belly again, to my chest, splashing over me as he aimed it at one boob, then the other, leaving them dripping.

My nipples were rock hard, with pee drops hanging from each, the last thing I saw before I shut my eyes tight as he moved higher. His piddle caught my neck and my mouth came open, gaping for it, still masturbating, waiting to come as I was given a mouthful of pee. Then the stream was in my mouth, filling it and running from the sides, splashing from my chin to my breasts, running down over my belly and sides, splashing back over my legs and my arms, my hands as I rubbed frantically at myself, my muscles tensing, coming, in utter, filthy pee-sodden ecstasy . . .

It stopped, just as my orgasm was peaking, breaking it. I opened my eyes in despair, thinking he'd run out, only to find him leaning in close, his cock pinched between finger and thumb. He let go and the full force of his stream burst in my face, exploding over my nose, and up it, in my eyes and my mouth. I tried to swallow, but there was too much and I went into a coughing fit, my eyes stinging crazily, urine spraying out of my nose and bubbling from the sides of my mouth as I struggled to say my stop word, unable to speak or see, choking on his piss.

My head was down, my face out of the stream as I struggled for control. Not that he stopped, but emptied the full six pints' worth of piddle over me, mostly in my hair. By the time I caught my breath it had died to a trickle, but I was soaked, my mouth still full of it, my hair lank and dripping, plastered to my skin. I'd stopped masturbating when he got it in my eyes, but it didn't stop him doing the last of it up my pussy, to leave it trickling out of my open hole as I scrabbled for the shower tap.

I found it, deluging myself with freezing water, which I immediately caught up in my hands, splashing it over my face to wash my eyes out. The stinging died, slowly, to become bearable, then just sore and at last I shook my head and looked up, finding Monty stood back, his cock still in his hand.

'Amber,' I said. 'You got it in my eyes.'

'Black mark,' he said. 'It washes its filthy body, cold water.'

He left the room as I cleaned up, wishing I'd come properly while he was doing it up my pussy or in my mouth. The way he was treating me was freaking me out a bit, but physically I had no complaints – after all, I'd asked him to pee in my face, and it was really my fault that I'd got it in my eyes.

The cold shower left me wet and shivering, submissive, but far from sexy. I dried myself, as Monty hadn't instructed otherwise, and put a towel around my wet hair, returning to the bedroom to find him propped up on the bed. He had his second pint in one hand, his cock in the other, erect again. On the bed was my skin cream. I nodded to him, coming to stand at the end of the bed, my hands folded behind my back, my head hung, ready.

'It takes the lotion,' he ordered. 'It rubs the lotion on its skin. It does it over its tits first.'

I reached down for the cream and unscrewed the cap. My nipples were still hard, and I squeezed out a fat worm of cream on to each, smearing it over my boobs and rubbing it in as he watched.

'It does its tits well,' he said, 'then its stomach and legs, last its cunt bulge.'

I nodded, applying more cream, to my tummy and thighs, my pubic mound, rubbing each bit in until the whole front of my body was glossy with it. It felt good, very sensual, and I wondered why he was being so nice to me. He let me take my time too, creaming myself until I had begun to feel aroused again, enough to want to come. Hoping he'd let me, I began to dab at my pussy, smearing cream between my lips.

'It stops wanking,' he said suddenly. 'It turns round and sticks its arse out.'

I obeyed quickly, equally keen to do it while he wanked over his view of my bum.

'Black mark,' he said. 'Its legs are further apart. Its cunt shows.'

Setting my legs wide, I gave him the view he wanted, the rear of my pussy showing back between my thighs, wide open, with my bumhole on display as well.

'It creams its arse,' he said. 'Round motions, pulling the cheeks apart, then it does its cunt and arsehole.'

I leaned on the wall as I squeezed the tube out over my bum, laying two long worms on my cheeks and a third between them. Reaching back, I began to rub it in, massaging my cheeks and spreading them, letting him see everything, and enjoying both the feel of my bottom and the knowledge of how intimately I was exposed to him. With my cheeks glossy and slick with cream, I poked a finger up my pussy, lubricating the hole, although it certainly didn't need it. I was soaking, my flesh puffy and slimy, very ready for cock.

'Black mark,' he said. 'It stops wanking. It sticks a finger up its arsehole, right up.'

I hadn't been wanking, I'd been showing off for him, but I choked my protest back, instead letting my hand slide up higher into my slimy bum crease, finding my hole and smearing cream around the ring, then up, into the hot, moist cavity of my rectum. He'd said right up so I pushed my finger in, as deep as I could go, until I felt something firm and stopped abruptly.

'Now it wiggles the finger about inside,' Monty ordered.

I obeyed, wiggling the finger about up my bottom and trying to ignore the sudden urge to go to the loo. I really needed an enema, if he was going to bugger me, which seemed very likely.

'It pulls its finger out,' he said, 'and turns around.'

Easing my finger out of my bumhole with a long sigh, I stood and turned. My anus felt open and greasy, while it was all slimy between my bumcheeks and pussy lips. His cock was rock hard, the head shiny with pressure, and I knew it was going to be poked into my body before long, and very likely up my bum. I already felt urgent, and it was going to be really messy. I was going to tell him, but he had seen the state of my finger and was leering at me. I stopped myself.

'It lifts up its hand,' he said. 'Not that one, black mark.'

I knew he was going to make me do something really dirty, something disgusting, and I was trembling hard, praying he wouldn't try and push me beyond where I wanted to go. I knew it would be bad anyway. He was nearly there, his cock-head purple and glossy, his face suffused with blood, leering at me as he wanked over my nude body, over my shame and discomfort. He nodded, then spoke.

'Now it sucks its shit off its finger.'

'No, Monty, not like that . . .'

'It sucks its own shit off its finger. Black mark.'

'No, please . . .'

'It sucks its finger, now! The dirty one, bitch!'

My finger was in my mouth. I was sucking, tasting the thick, fetid tang of my own bumhole even as my other hand went to my pussy, clutching at my lips, spreading

148

them. I found my clit, snatching at it, my knees weak as I sank down, thighs wide, wanking furiously as I sucked and sucked at my dirty finger, coming in utter, exquisite ecstasy.

I was still frigging as Monty pulled himself forwards on the bed. He grabbed me, hard, by the hair, jerking me forwards across the bed, bottom up. He scrabbled round, his hands found my thighs, his cock jamming between my bumcheeks, into my pussy. He gave two quick shoves and pulled it out, and up, to my bumhole, pushing. My anus opened with the rudest, dirtiest squelching sound and he was going up, filling my rectum with penis. I felt my gut bulge and every muscle in my body tightened in a second unbearable climax, and again, screaming and writhing on his cock as he buggered me in my own mess.

He came like that, deep up my bottom while I was still in orgasm. At that instant I'd have gladly sucked his cock clean for him, or anything else he demanded, no matter how filthy. Then I was coming down and his cock was pulling from my bumhole, to pop free, and I was running, staggering on weak knees in a desperate effort to get to the loo.

Nine

I slept soundly, but woke sore and a little guilty, remembering what we'd done the night before. It had been dirty, very dirty indeed, and having done it under orders was no consolation. I'd wanted it like that, there was no use denying it, especially when I could perfectly well have used my stop word.

The fact that I hadn't used my stop word reminded me that I was due for a titty whipping. It was going to hurt, but I didn't mind, as long as Monty left me in peace until I was in the mood. At that moment I wasn't, and he was still asleep, so I washed and dressed, making a thorough job of my oral hygiene, and slipped downstairs, leaving him to lie.

The landlady gave me a pretty frosty reception, and some peculiar looks as she served me. I ignored her, wondering if she had heard me the night before or if she was always like that. Certainly she'd been the same when I'd visited with Percy, but then I'd screamed my head off on that occasion as well.

I was reading a paper in the lounge by the time Monty came down. He ordered a full English breakfast and finished it in no time, waddling out to the lounge to greet me. We paid and left, Monty complimenting them on their bathroom facilities as he waited for his card, which put me into a fit of juvenile giggles as we walked out of the door.

'So where to?' he asked as I started the car.

'There's no point in starting back yet,' I answered. 'Let's go down to the coast.'

'Don't forget you're going to get whipped across your knockers. Nine strokes.'

'Nine!?'

'Nine, I was counting.'

'Ouch! OK, but not too hard. You can make it extra humiliating to make up for it, but I warn you, if you do it in a public place and we get caught, I'm going to say you assaulted me.'

'Still upset over the spanking in the garden, are you?'

'No, but you shouldn't have done it. Still, we got away with it, so I'm not going to make it a big deal. It was nice, thanks.'

'And everything else?'

'No problem. I'm not sure I liked the "It" game, but what you made me do was good, especially in the shower.'

'Great, I always wanted to piss up a girl's cunt.'

'You really are a filthy bastard! You know that, don't you?'

'I like knicker wetting and stuff. I saw a girl piss her shorts once, in the street. She got in such a state over it. I loved it, just watching.'

'You are unspeakable, Monty!'

'And you wouldn't have watched, and enjoyed it?'

'You know I would, but I'd rather it had been me. I tell you what you'd have enjoyed though. A friend of mine wanted to try colonic hydrotherapy . . .'

'What?'

'Colonic hydrotherapy: washing the lower bowel out with water, an enema. It had various benefits, but never mind that . . .'

'I do mind that. What, like sticking a big syringe up your bum?'

'You can do it that way. Using a tube is more usual, with the water running in from a bag. Anyway, my

151

friend, Ami, wanted to try this, but she was a bit shy about it and not really sure what to do. So, I offered to show her. First I did it to myself in front of her, which was wonderful, but not as good as doing it to her. She's really cute, with these big, owlish glasses, and she looked so sweet, with the tube up her bum.'

'And you call me filthy!'

'There's more. She got so turned on by it that we ended up having sex, and she'd never had a girl before! Good, eh?'

'Excellent! So, this colonic whatsit business. Lots of girls do it, do they, and get off on it?'

'Not just women, men too. As for getting off on it, I don't know. Apparently it can become a substitute for sex, like a fetish, but generally it's seen as a health thing, both mental and physical.'

'Sounds like an excuse for being pervy.'

'Not always. For instance, some homeopaths prescribe coffee enemas for liver problems, and red wine enemas for heart disease.'

'You're joking?'

'I'm serious.'

'Fuck me. Weird. I bet some old pervo thought the whole thing up, years ago, just so he could stick tubes up girls' bums.'

'People have been doing it for centuries, millennia. I think the Romans used to do it a lot, or maybe the Greeks.'

'OK, so some Roman or Greek pervo. What's the difference?'

'Not a lot, I suppose. So tell me about the girl in the street?'

'It was ages ago, when I still lived with my parents, in Merton. She'd been running, I think, or doing something sporty. Anyway, she was wearing these tight shorts, stretchy, so they really showed off her bum, which was quite big and really firm, muscley. She was hurrying, running a little, then walking. I was behind her, admiring the view, when she tripped on an uneven paving stone. She went down, right, and as she did some piss must have come out, because I saw the wet patch around her bumcheeks. She hurried on, and I knew she was desperate, so I followed. I'm sure she knew too, because she kept glancing back, giving me these really dirty looks. She was squeezing her thighs together too, in a real state, and when she got to a corner she saw this pub and started to run. She got there, but it had just shut. She was really panicking, hammering on the door and looking at her watch, with her knees really tight together. When I caught up with her I saw the look on her face, totally fed up, like really cross and really uncomfortable, and then she just let it go, in her shorts. I saw everything, right in front of me, with the piss dripping down her legs and making a big wet patch over her fat arse and up her cunt lips.'

'The poor thing! And I'll bet you wanked yourself silly.'

'Sure, and don't tell me you wouldn't have done.'

'I'd have helped her.'

'Yeah, right out of her knickers.'

'No. Well, maybe later.'

He answered with a short, barking laugh. He had spread the map out on his lap, and paused to study it, suggesting I turn left across the face of the downs at the next junction. It seemed as good a choice as any, and I took it, quickly finding myself in winding lanes between chalky banks and through beechwoods. We kept talking, swapping dirty stories as we went, turn and turn about. Monty's were almost all voyeuristic, and some of them were absolutely outrageous.

For the best part of two hours we drove east along the South Downs, until our conversation had done its work and I was wondering if it wasn't time to take my titty whipping. Monty seemed relaxed, aside from the occasional bit of nerves at my driving, but more than once I'd noticed him giving his crotch a sneaky squeeze, and I was sure his trousers were hiding a full erection.

'It could be time for my punishment, if you like,' I suggested.

'Stop somewhere then.'

'Not here, the woods are too open, and you're not doing me on a footpath.'

'I should. I'd love to do it so that some really stuffy people saw, like the couple in the hotel.'

'You nearly did. No, not so risky.'

'You love it.'

'Maybe, but that's not the point.'

'Chicken. After all, I'm the one who'd get into the real trouble.'

'Find somewhere private and you can do it. You can even tie my hands if it turns you on. I think I can trust you enough now.'

He grunted in answer and went back to studying the map, quickly telling me to turn right. When I reached the junction it proved to be no more than a track, leading deeper into the downs.

'Here?' I asked.

'I've got a possible place. It says "Quarry – disused".'

'You think so?'

'It's worth a try. I want those knockers out, now.'

'What, now?'

It seemed safe, within the car, and I did feel like showing off, so I slowed at the corner, quickly pulling up my top, my bra with it, to let my bare breasts loll out. Monty nodded in approval and gave his crotch another squeeze. We drove up to the quarry, my excitement rising simply from being bare breasted, and under his orders.

The quarry was certainly disused, a bowl shape cut into the hillside with ancient rusting gates swinging on their hinges. There were tyre tracks, but no other sign of activity, and I parked, pulling the car into the shade of a tall hedge. It seemed sensible to take a look round, but as I made to pull my top down over my boobs Monty reached out to stop me.

'Uh, uh,' he ordered, 'keep them bare.'

'What if somebody's there?'

'They get to see my bitch's tits. I don't care. Maybe I'll make you suck them off, even let them fuck you.'

'You would too, wouldn't you.'

'You know it. Now, come on, out of the car.'

I opened my door, feeling thrilled but a little unsure of myself. There was no sign of anyone, only birdsong and the buzz of insects. Scrambling quickly from the car, I ran for the quarry gates, clutching my bare boobs in my hands. Monty laughed, following with a last glance back down the track.

It was impossible not to be nervous, even inside the quarry gates. The tyre tracks looked quite recent, suggesting joyriders, as the quarry certainly wasn't in use. If they came back while we were playing I stood a pretty good chance of getting gang-banged, and I could be absolutely certain that Monty wouldn't be able to control the situation.

Inside the quarry it was hot, and very still, with the off-white walls of chalk reflecting back the sunlight and sheltering us from what little breeze there was. At the centre was a shallow pool, the water absolutely still within a ring of cracked white mud. Two cars stood in it, wheelless and sunk to their axles, both burned out. Beyond stood a third, unburned but a wreck, with the windows smashed and the bonnet torn off, with the single word, CUNT sprayed on one side in silver paint. The evidence of the sort of person who'd been there increased my nervousness, but Monty seemed unaffected, with his hands stuck in his pockets as he looked around.

'Perfect,' he declared. 'Right, strip.'

'Strip? What, bare?'

'Yeah, starkers. Why should I let you wear any clothes?'

'In case people come, that's why!'

'I already told you what happens if people come – they get to fuck your posh little cunt. Now strip, bitch.'

I hesitated, not at all sure of myself. Dirty old men are one thing, easy to handle. Lads are another, and the quarry was a lot more open than the woods had been.

'Do you really think it's going to make any difference if I let you keep your clothes on?' Monty said. 'They'll just strip you and fuck you anyway. Come on, Tasha, nobody's going to come, and if they do we'll hear their cars ages before they get here.'

'All right,' I conceded, 'but I want my cheap dress, and you're to tie me lightly. Hang on.'

I ran back to the car, leaving him to amuse himself. I'd put on tight white trousers and an equally tight top, along with a bra that gave plenty of support but was a pig to fasten. The cheap dress was a much more sensible choice – easy to pull off and easy to pull on. I changed in the shelter of the car, hurriedly stripping off my top and pulling the dress over my head before removing my trousers beneath it. I'd chosen the yellow knickers from the three-pack, fairly sure they'd get ruined, and I kept them, running back to find Monty by the unburned car.

'Just what we need,' he said, grinning as he held up something for my inspection.

It was the dipstick from the car, a long rod of flexible metal ending in a smooth ball, still oily. I'd been expecting him to use twigs, but I had to admit it was going to make the perfect titty whip, light but painful, just right to punish a girl across her breasts.

'Right, dress off and up against a tree,' he ordered. 'And we need string, or rope.'

'Use my panties,' I suggested, 'as I suppose I'm going to have to take them off anyway.'

156

'You are,' he said, 'right now. In fact, why aren't you stripped?'

He snapped his fingers, pointing at me. I took the hem of the dress in response, obediently peeling it up and off, to leave myself in panties. Those followed, shrugged down and off, tossed to Monty, who caught them and sniffed the crotch.

'Nothing like the smell of a hot cunt,' he drawled. 'Right, a tree. That one'll do, with the smooth trunk. That way you can slide down to suck on my cock once I've beaten you.'

I went to it meekly, clasping my hands behind the slender trunk. He came behind, to twist the panties around my wrists and tie them off, leaving me bound and vulnerable in the dappled sunlight. My breasts felt huge, and my nipples were sticking up, stiff and sensitive. I was ready, or as ready as a girl ever can be when some bastard is going to whip her across her breasts and then make her suck his penis.

Monty came close to me, trailing the dipstick around the curve of my body to leave a line of old oil running from my hip up to my chest. He stopped with it between my breasts, and pushed, making it flex against my skin.

'Nine,' he said. 'Now don't you wish you'd been a bit more obedient last night and a bit less prissy?'

'I wasn't prissy!' I complained. 'I wet my panties in front of you! I let you bugger me!'

'You were still worried about your precious body,' he answered. 'You should have done exactly as I said.'

With that he lifted the dipsitck, stepping close to press it across my breasts, hard, to make the flesh bulge. I looked down, my lip trembling, as he bent the tip back, leaving another oily line running from boob to boob, just above my nipples. I could see what he was going to do as the rod bent back further and further. At any moment he'd release it, letting the horrid thing snap back across my breasts. The thought of it was making

157

me shiver, my breath coming in ragged pants, tears of panic and frustration welling in my eyes.

He let go. I saw it, a flicker of oily metal and then it had hit me. I felt my flesh jerk and heard my own scream, jumping on my feet, shaking my head in my pain, calling him a bastard. I struggled to recover, only to find him doing it again, the other way around, a touch higher. The agonising process was repeated, the stick drawn back, held, released and again I was squealing and jumping in helpless pain and consternation.

My breasts were already throbbing, and I was breathing really hard. Monty showed no mercy, apparently unaware of my distress. Instead he was just concentrating on my breasts, his piglike eyes fixed on the round globes of flesh with the two oily red lines to show where he had punished me, imposed his perverted will on me.

The third was done low, up under the curve of my boobs, the fourth the same but running the other way. Both cuts set my chest bouncing and jiggling, which really made his eyes pop, and he stopped for a quick grope, stroking them and leaving oily handprints on my skin. Satisfied with his feel, he gave me the fifth and sixth, also under my tits, but harder, which set my tears rolling and had me struggling against the tie of my panties before I regained control of myself.

As he lined up for the seventh I felt a trickle of fluid escape my pussy, running down the warm, dry flesh of my thigh. I hadn't realised I was that turned on, not enough to drip, but there was no denying the reaction of my body. I got the seventh high, right up on the flank of my chest, the eighth criss-crossing it. There was one to go, and as he pressed the awful thing to my boobs I knew it would be the worst, full across my nipples.

He pushed it in really hard, until it hurt, with my breasts bulging out above and below the stick, one nipple popping up over it, the other pressed hard in. The rod came back and I was shaking, mumbling, my breathing deep, wanting to scream and then screaming for real as it cut back, lashing across my nipples. It stung crazily, and I really howled, shaking myself and bawling my eyes out as I sank down against the tree, weak kneed. My boobs were throbbing, sore and welted, the nine long wheals already rising as I slumped down, my head hung low, my knees well spread.

At that point Percy would have paused, to comfort me a little, stroking my cheeks or hair, bringing me to that extraordinary state of gratitude a girl can only feel after punishment. Then he'd have made me suck his cock.

Monty was different. He simply left me sobbing on the ground as he freed his genitals, cock and balls thrust obscenely from his fly. He squatted down, and simply stuffed it all in my face, forcing me to take first his balls into my mouth, then his cock. He was as greasy as ever, and tasted of oil as well as sweat and stale spunk. I sucked it though, not just willingly, but urgently, feeling him grow in my mouth until he was at full erection, which was when he decided to fuck my boobs.

He didn't ask, but just squatted a little lower, cupping my aching breasts in his hands and folding them around his cock. He was touching some of the wheals, his thumbs rubbing my flesh, which stung crazily, making me cry out again. He took no notice, bouncing and jiggling my boobs around his penis, slapping them together and squeezing them hard, rubbing my nipples with his thumbs until I was screaming and writhing my body against the tree. He loved that, grunting as he forced himself against me, crushing me to the tree with his great fat body as he fucked my cleavage, faster and faster, until at last he came, his cock erupting, splashing spunk over my poor, whipped breasts, up my neck and in my face.

As he collapsed back, panting on the ground, I looked down. My boobs were both soiled, their flesh dirty with oil and slick with sweat, each decorated by several thick blobs of come. The welts really showed too, red and angry, displaying exactly what had been done to me. My belly was dirty as well, wet with sweat and oil, while I could feel the come on my neck and one cheek. There was juice under me too, only it wasn't Monty's, but mine, a damp mark beneath my open pussy betraying my excitement.

'Make me come,' I managed.

Monty said nothing, just blowing his cheeks out. His face was red from his exertions, sweaty too, and his breathing really heavy. Obviously he wasn't going to be of any use to me, and even before I realised I was pulling at the panties, jerking one wrist free and putting my hand straight to my pussy. The panties were still on my other wrist, and I caught them up, on to my sex, rubbing at my clitty with the warm, dry cotton. I was close, almost coming, rubbing myself off with my own panties, my other hand on my whipped breasts, feeling them, smearing oil and sperm over the rough ridges where the rod had caught my flesh, soiled and beaten in the hot sun, eyes closed, mouth wide.

Which was when Monty filled my mouth with the full bulk of his oily, sperm-wet genitals, balls and all, forcing it in just as I was coming. My reaction was immediate, and glorious. I'd been right on the edge, thinking of the state I was in, and the man who'd put me in it had stuffed my mouth with his cock and balls. I just came, unable to breathe, gagging on the head of Monty's penis, my hips bucking frantically, my body crushed to the tree by his huge thighs, my face smothered in his fat gut. It was wonderful, going on and on, worth all the pain and risk, a thousand times.

I only stopped, pushing Monty away, because I was in danger of choking. He withdrew, giving me a final degradation by wiping his wet genitals in my face, then stood back, grinning, and staggered a few steps, sitting back heavily against the wrecked car.

'You are hard work,' he puffed.

'Punishing me is hard work? Poor Monty!'

'No need for sarcasm. It was good though, wasn't it? Just a pity your joyriders didn't turn up to watch, eh?'

'Don't joke. I know what it's like to have a load of men take turns with me.'

'You do?'

'Yes, as it happens. It wasn't rape or anything, but they were pretty rough. They stuck candles up my bum and pussy, among other things.'

'That I'd like to have seen.'

'They wouldn't have let you, or at least, they wouldn't have let you join in. In fact, my guess would be, if the joyriders had come, they'd have made you watch while they took turns with me, then made you eat my panties or something cruel like that.'

'Leave them the panties as a trophy then. I wish we could leave a photo.'

I laughed, imagining their faces on finding a photo of me, tied to a tree with my boobs whipped and oil and spunk all over me. Being joyriders, they were probably quite young, teenagers to whom putting a finger up a girl's pussy was a novelty, which made the idea even more amusing. So I used the yellow panties to wipe my pussy and boobs, and hung them on a tree, where they couldn't fail to be seen.

'Neat,' Monty commented.

'Best go then,' I replied, 'before you do end up eating them. No, you need to be careful if you want an audience. Too prim and you might get arrested, too wild and it's likely to get dangerous. Dirty old men are best, and fat boys too.'

I gave him a grin, to which he responded by waggling the dipstick at me. I set about washing in the pool, listening out, but not really worried. After all, we'd been there over half an hour and we hadn't even heard a car engine. On the surface I was glad nobody had come, but underneath there was a trace of disappointment.

In a fantasy, about twenty really horny eighteen- and nineteen-year-olds would have turned up, and just used me, in my mouth, up my pussy, up my bum too, leaving me to bring myself off on the ground with my whole body bruised and sodden with their sperm. They'd have tied Monty up and made him watch too, with my panties in his mouth.

Reality was different, especially when despite my best efforts to wash I was left damp and greasy, with the cheap dress on and no panties. It was getting on for lunchtime, and I needed a clean-up, so I suggested returning to our original plan and driving down to the sea, where I'd be able to find a pub or hotel with some decent facilities.

We ended up in a hotel in Eastbourne, where I managed to sort myself out, even shaving my pussy, which was getting stubbly. Clean and refreshed, I put on my white trousers along with a light top that left my tummy showing, a look which made me feel a lot more confident and a lot less of a slut. Monty had sat in the bar while I changed, and we ate there, looking out across the front.

It was nearly two by the time we finished, and I was already getting a touch of melancholy at the thought of the weekend being over. We had the afternoon, but for me the impetus seemed to have gone out of things. I'd even put on normal panties, heavy white silk, which I knew in the back of my mind meant the end of our fun. After all, I still had a pack of the cheap ones we'd been using as a calling card for our dirty adventures. Monty seemed quiet as well, not saying much until we had returned to the car.

'I bought this,' he said, holding up a small canister, 'while you were in the loo.'

For a moment I thought it was a mini deodorant, only to realise that it was in fact spray cream, the sort used to top cakes. It was obviously not intended for tea, or at least not in the conventional way, and it was impossible not to smile at his sheer enthusiasm.

'I know I've been a bit cruel,' he said, 'so I want to give you a treat, a really nice orgasm.'

'With cream?' I giggled. 'Licked off my pussy, I suppose?'

'Of course,' he said, 'and more. I'll do it among the bushes, up on the Head. Come on, it's a lovely day, and it may be our last chance for outdoor sex.'

'OK,' I agreed, 'but let's walk up. I don't feel ready yet.'

He gave an uncertain glance at the bulk of Beachy Head, but nodded. I gave his fat bottom a slap, which he returned, and we set off, hand in hand, which drew a few peculiar looks, but I found I didn't care. He had used me so well, or at least so thoroughly, that I was beginning to grow fond of him, at least enough to be defensive about people's reaction to me being with him. Anyway, it wasn't as if I was likely to meet anyone I knew.

We talked as we went, once more swapping dirty stories to get me in the mood. Monty's were as dirty as ever, about peering up girls' dresses, spying through windows, even pinching panties from washing lines. He did have morals, of a sort, and drew the line at touching, but I could imagine that he'd left some women pretty upset, which diluted the effect his stories had on me. Much more effective were my own, both from remembering them and from the embarrassing thrill of telling Monty.

By the time we reached the flank of the hill I was feeling more than ready to have my pussy licked in the bushes, while his cock was hard in his trousers, so I knew I was going to get a fucking as well as a lick. It

163

was a good place as well, with lots of thick clumps of vegetation divided by paths. Monty had been peeping there more than once, and knew the layout, taking me high on to the head and well away from the cliff, where there were fewer people.

The place he chose was excellent, a little dip in the chalk, sheltered by a stunted thorn and a ring of bracken and other plants, secure enough for him to fuck me, yet risky enough to give a strong exhibitionist thrill. I wasn't going to strip, not there, and Monty agreed, suggesting I pull down my trousers and panties, rolling my legs up so that he could get to my pussy. It was typical male, and typical Monty – no snogging, no petting, just straight to the pussy. Not that I minded, as I was turned on enough and it was too public for anything leisurely.

So I did as I was told, squeezing down my trousers with my heart hammering in my chest. My panties went too, to my knees, and I rolled my legs up, my bare pussy sticking out, holding myself ready. Monty was kneeling over me, the spray cream in his hand, glancing around one last time before aiming the can between my thighs. The cream spurted out with a rude noise and I felt it on my sex lips, cool and light, a delicious sensation. He didn't just do my crease either, but made a little whorl on my pussy mound, the sort you top a cake off with. Seeing it made me giggle, and he grinned back.

I lay back, relaxing as best I could with that lovely feeling of exposure growing inside me. If anyone caught us they would see me with my pussy bare and creamy, a good rude display. They'd be shocked, or really jealous, with the hugely fat Monty obviously about to fuck me, and it felt good just knowing. My bumhole was showing too, my cheeks well spread, so they'd see my little brown ring, quite nude.

Monty had begun to kiss my thighs, and it was more than I could resist not to pull my boobs out, so up came my top and bra, exposing my breasts, the nipples hard, the whip marks clear on the pale skin. Holding my legs up by clutching my panties, I began to stroke my boobs, thinking how rude I looked.

It was about to get a lot ruder, because he had pushed the nozzle of the can into my pussy. The next moment I heard the hiss of pressure and felt my vagina start to fill, the cream up me but oozing out too, down between my bumcheeks. A bit fell off, right on to my bumhole, and I sighed in pleasure, pulling my legs higher still. Monty's lips found my flesh again, sucking cream from my pussy lips and feeding on me, licking and sucking at my sex, eating up the cream from my body.

His hand had come up, grasping my panties to pin my legs high and free my own hand. I put it to good use, a boob in each hand, stroking the welts he'd made on my tender flesh. He shifted, pulling himself up beside me to feast on my pussy with his fat belly at my shoulder, his crotch near my face. I went for his cock, eager to suck while he fed from my pussy, no longer caring about getting caught.

It took me a moment, and then his erection was out and in my mouth as he swung his legs across to squat obscenely over my head, his big balls dangling over my nose, his massive backside poised above my head. He had me pinned, helpless beneath his weight, my legs flexed wide to accommodate his gut. He was still licking though, and fucking my mouth, driving his cock down between my lips, again and again.

The nozzle was up my pussy once more, jammed well in, the cream squirting out to fill my cavity and burst out before he pulled the can free. It wasn't going to take much more, just a few touches to my clitty. He did it, lapping up the cream, each long slurp of his tongue running full length up my clitty and then I was coming, my mouth agape on his erection, then closed, sucking hard and hoping fervently for a mouthful of hot sperm while I was still in climax.

It didn't happen, and as my muscles went slowly limp he began to fuck my head again, slowly. I let him do it, far from comfortable, but eager to please. Besides which I could barely move at all, never mind get up. He kept licking as I sucked, feeding on my pussy even as I fed on his cock. His licking was getting to me too, and I was wondering if I wasn't going to climax again when he came, full in my mouth, his cock jerking to fill my senses with the taste and texture of his sperm, which I swallowed dutifully.

'Lovely, thank you,' I sighed as he pulled his cock free of my mouth. 'Could you get up, please? You're squashing me.'

'Sure,' he panted, 'just a moment.'

I waited as he got his breath back, busying myself with licking the last few bubbles of sperm and saliva off the tip of his cock where it hung over my face. The cream can was still touching me, cold where it rested between my bumcheeks. I felt him take hold of it, expecting him either to put it aside or give my pussy a last coating, only to have it pressed lower, to my bumhole.

'Monty, no,' I chided, 'don't muck about.'

He answered with a schoolboy giggle and I felt the nozzle tip slide into my already slick bumhole.

'You said you liked enemas,' he said.

'No, Monty, not here,' I said. There was a bubble of panic rising in my throat and no confidence nor command in my voice.

'One day you'll thank me for this,' he said. 'Think of it, Natasha, an enema, in public. What better way to treat you?'

'No! Not that, Monty! It's too rude! I'll mess myself! No, not up my bum, I need to go! Monty!'

'Sorry, up it goes.'

'Bastard! No! Please!' I screamed, but it was too late, he was pressing.

I trailed off with a choking sob as the cream began to squirt up my bottom, an awful, awful sensation, too awful to allow me to speak. My rectum bulged with it as my mouth and eyes went wide with shock and disgust. He'd jammed the can right in, stretching my poor bumhole to bursting point, just to make sure it all went up. It did too, spurting out into my hole until I could already feel the awful heavy sensation in my gut. Monty just kept giggling, even when I found my voice, cursing him and calling him a bastard as my belly began to swell. I was beating on his fat body with my hands too, and trying to kick with my rolled up legs, but I was helpless and he knew it, taking no notice whatsoever as he creamed my rectum.

He stopped in the end, when I bit his cock, not hard, but enough to make him roll off with a squeal not very different from the ones I'd been making. It was too late though: it was up, and as the cream can squeezed out of my bumhole I found myself clenching my cheeks to stop myself having an immediate accident. I had no idea how much cream was up me, maybe the whole lot. It felt like it anyway, heavy and bloated in my gut, filling me with an awful urgency that set the muscles of my bottom twitching, my pussy too. I could hold it, just, with my anus tight and my thighs pressed together, along with a lot of willpower. It wouldn't be long though, and I knew I was going to have to do it in the bushes, with him watching. Fortunately there were plenty of tissues in my bag. I reached for it, only for Monty to snatch it.

'Uh, uh,' he said, wagging his finger. 'Not so easy.'

'What do you mean?' I demanded.

'Pull your knickers and trousers up,' he answered.

'What? No!' I exclaimed. 'Look, Monty, you've done me, OK? You've had your little joke. Now let me clean up. You can watch if you really have to.'

'That's not what I want to see,' he answered me, 'or what you really want to happen, and you know it. Now pull them up.'

'Give me my bag, you utter bastard!' I swore. 'O!
God . . .'

It had nearly happened, and it would have gone right
into my lowered panties and trousers, but I caught
myself in time, panting to regain what was left of my
composure. Carefully, with my cheeks held well apart
so I began to shuffle back, sticking my bottom into th
bracken. Monty lifted my bag.

'Up,' he ordered, 'or I throw your bag over the cliff.'

'Don't be stupid! It's got everything in it. My money
the car keys, everything!'

'Then pull up your trousers. Come on. Who knows
you might make it to a loo.'

He was right. If I walked carefully I might jus
manage to reach the first of the hotels on the seafront
where I could beg the use of a loo. That was better than
doing it in the bracken: more private and less messy
Still I hesitated, with the straining feeling in my rectum
making me just want to let go and get it over with.
would have done it too, only at that moment a dog
appeared among the bracken and I heard a voice calling
for it.

I wrenched my panties up on the spot, my trouser
too, jiggling frantically to make my top fall over my
boobs. I wasn't fast enough though, and I still had one
titty peeping out under my dishevelled bra and my flie
wide open when two heads appeared over the top of the
bracken, both silver haired and female, each giving me
an absolutely filthy glance and turning quickly aside
Monty had got his cock away, and had his back to
them, but he saw my blushes, making his grin broader
still.

I found I'd decided to try to make the hotel, rather
than risk being seen and defying Monty, who was quite
likely to carry out his threat, or something equally
reckless. After all, this was the man who had spanked
my bare bottom in a hotel garden. He had stood up

grinning childishly, beckoning with one finger and taunting me with the bag

'OK, OK,' I said. 'I'll try to make the hotel if it amuses you. Bastard.'

'Good girl,' he answered. 'I knew you'd see sense.'

'You really are unspeakable,' I told him as I stood. 'Ow!'

My bumhole had given a twitch of pain and I doubled up, clutching at myself.

'Just do it,' he advised. 'You like it in public, so you can fill your panties in public.'

'You'd love that, wouldn't you?' I grated.

'Not as much as you would.'

'No,' I answered. 'I didn't mean it, not like this! Ow, my poor bum! Anyway, like I said, I needed to go anyway! Come on, Monty, please, let me go in the bushes and keep an eye out for me. You can watch too! Please!'

I was really begging, but I knew I was only making it worse for myself. He was loving every second of it – my desperation, the pain and panic that showed in my face.

'Uh, uh,' he said. 'I know you. If you really don't want to do it you'll make the hotel. But you do, don't you?'

'No!' I pleaded.

'It should be perfect,' he went on. 'It's safe for one thing. Nobody ever got arrested for having an accident in their knickers, did they? Who would think any girl would get off on such a dirty, disgusting thing, especially a stuck-up piece like you?'

I was shaking my head frantically, but I started to walk, slowly, knock-kneed with the pain, down towards the houses, which suddenly seemed an impossible distance away. I could even see the hotel I needed, but it was too far, I was sure. I was never going to make it. I'd do it in my panties, and everyone would see, and Monty would laugh at me, and when he got me alone he'd watch me masturbate over what I'd done, because I'd do that too, I knew I would.

'Why not just do it?' Monty urged. 'Come on, you dirty little bitch. Do it, shit in your fancy knickers!'

'No!' I grated. 'Never!'

'Come on,' he wheedled. 'Think how nice it would feel, out, filling your lovely clean undies. Silk panties, you said, didn't you? Big, silk panties, full of shit!'

'Shut up!' I yelled.

'Temper, temper!' he taunted. 'People will stare if you shout, and you know what they'll see, don't you?'

He was right, because there were plenty of people in view, and more than one of them was looking at us. They were all going to see, and even if I held it they'd know, sniggering over my discomfort, or feeling sorry for me, which was worse in some ways. That was if I held it.

I walked on, slowly, the tears of consternation welling up in my eyes, the pain in my tummy and around my bumhole growing. It wasn't constant any more either, but was coming in waves, which I knew was a bad sign, fading and rising, fading and rising, each peak worse than the last as I stumbled on over the grass.

Every step was agony, but I reached the main path, struggling to walk properly, ignoring the odd looks from other people. Monty followed, about ten paces behind, no longer taunting me but with his eyes fixed on my bum. It was as if his gaze was burning into me, but I could picture it myself, my cheeks full in the white trousers, which always made them look fatter and rounder, the outline of my panties showing beneath, taut and clean, snug against my bottom.

Another wave of pain came, forcing me to stop, doubled up. My tears came, rolling down my cheeks from closed eyes, the salty taste strong in my mouth as one reached my lips. I really thought it was going to happen, but I held on, the pain fading as I once more stumbled forwards. A man passing the other way glanced at me, his face showing amusement, derision even, then a woman, pointedly looking away.

I managed five steps, counting every one, then ten, before the pain came again. Again I stopped, clutching at my tummy. I couldn't make it, I knew I couldn't, and I sank down to my knees, my bottom stuck out, my head spinning, sobbing aloud, panting. I was going to mess my panties in public, and I couldn't stop myself, my whole being filling with wonderful, blessed relief as I surrendered control, only for the feeling to die with the pain as my shame for what I had been about to do flooded through me.

I got up, forcing myself, telling myself that if I could only hold back five, maybe six times more I would make it. It was silly, though, ridiculous, and I knew it even as I struggled up, walked a pace and sank back to my knees as an agonising pang went through me. It was hopeless. I couldn't do it. I didn't have it in me. With a last broken sob I let my bladder go, my pee exploding into my panty crotch an instant before my anus gave and I expelled the full volume of my enema into the seat of my trousers.

I was sobbing, my face pushed down in the grass as I did it, dizzy with shame and misery as my panties filled and overflowed, the mess trickling out and down my legs, over my pussy too, while pee dripped from my fly on to the grass below. Monty, I knew, was watching, and maybe others, but I couldn't stop it, and it would have been pointless anyway. They'd seen.

Monty had been right, because even as I slowly regained control I found I couldn't get up. I'd soiled myself in public, and it was unbearably humiliating, worse than I'd ever imagined it would be in my dirtiest fantasy. I was crawling, on all fours, the filthy stain spreading out on the seat of my immaculate white trousers, my panties ruined. Yet I wanted more, the culmination of Monty's sadistic act, to finish off, when I could have stopped, abandoning the last, tiny piece of my pride.

What was in my panties and trousers was a mixture of piddle and cream, a disgusting, squashy, oozing mess, but there was worse, and it wanted to come out. I could have held, but I didn't, surrendering instead to the inevitable, bum up, not even bothering to hide it, flaunting it in fact, as I gave in and once more let my bumhole open.

I moaned as I felt it, a great thick piece squashing out against the back of my panties, stretching them, making my trousers bulge out behind. It was going up my crease too, and down over my pussy, but I didn't care. I was pushing now, lost to every vestige of decency as the dung came out, filling my panty seat, the bulge growing behind me in plain view, the moist, squashy mess oozing from the side of my panties, spreading out over my bumcheeks, squeezing up between them and down, into the welcoming hole of my pussy.

That was the strongest, dirtiest bit, feeling my pussy fill, but it wasn't the end. I kept pushing, piece after piece, until I could feel the full, horrid, soggy weight behind me. I knew what it must look like, a great sagging bulge over my bottom, making it absolutely obvious what I had done. They'd seen me poo in my panties, maybe half a dozen people, and all I wanted to do was squat there, showing it off to them. Why I didn't masturbate in it, then and there, I don't know. I wanted to, but some small part of me was still aware of the consequences of showing sexual pleasure. In the end somebody gasped, maybe in shock, maybe disgust, even sympathy. In any case it broke the spell, and the awful situation I was in came flooding back in a great wave of shame.

I just ran, helter-skelter down the hill with my load squashing in my panties as I went. I didn't even know where I was going, just away, away from the people who'd seen me, who knew. It was a blur: grass, then a path, railings and a miniature railway, groynes and pebbles, then water as I plunged into the sea, and under, coming up panting and blowing. The shock of the cold hit me, clearing my head, but I was still in a fine state. People were looking at me, most puzzled, some, who'd guessed or seen, smirking or embarrassed, others sympathetic. Finally someone, a middle-aged matron in a one-piece blue swimsuit, decided to help. She came bustling out, holding a huge pink towel.

She treated me like a messy baby, holding the towel up to shelter me and telling me to get out of my dirty things. I did it, with her watching as if my exposure were totally unimportant as I stripped off. My jeans came down easily enough, my panties with them, peeled down under water with the little waves sloshing up to wet my top. Getting them off was harder, as I had to stand, making a fine show of my dirty bottom, if only to her. She kept watching as I struggled to clean myself and get the worst of the mess out of my clothes, tutting occasionally and casting dirty looks back to the people who were watching on the beach. It wasn't easy, because there was mess in my crease and I had to finger my pussy too, but she waited, very patiently, making sure no one else saw anything at all. I felt pathetically grateful, and more so when she lent me a pair of her daughter's fluorescent beach shorts and a plastic bag.

That was when Monty appeared, with my bag. Everyone was staring by then, and I just had to get away from there. There was the awful process of making Monty buy me new shorts at a stand, changing into them under the towel with everybody in view looking on and whispering, and then I just ran. I was crying again by the time I reached the car, in a real state, yet still fighting down a desperate urge to masturbate.

I would have done it too, a sneaky one in some back street with my hand down my silly yellow shorts, only I was just too angry with Monty to let him see what he'd done to me. Instead I gave him the full treatment: a lecture on respect and understanding and stop words and everything else I could think of. It was pointless though because, although he looked pretty sullen, he knew, and so did I.

Ten

I got back pretty late on the Sunday night, after dropping Monty off at his house. All in all it had been good, but I'd had my fill of him, at least for the time being. My bum was sore, especially the hole, my boobs too. It was nice to have some marks to remind me of what we'd done, but I needed at least a week without being interfered with to get back to normal.

It wasn't just my body either. My head didn't feel straight, what with his 'It' game and doing really heavy things to me in public. It wasn't easy to take and, perhaps more importantly, he never cuddled me afterwards. Percy always does, whatever he does to me and whatever I do to deserve it, and it is very rarely indeed that I'm not back to my usual bubbly self within a matter of minutes.

Both men made a strange contrast to Gabrielle, who was colder still, but so gentle. In fact, if anything, she was too gentle, not really taking charge of me in the way I like, while Monty was too rough, cruel, and not as caring as a good dominant should be. In fact, he wasn't really caring at all, except when he was worried about scaring me off. Percy was the best, without doubt, but just then Percy was the one I couldn't have. Not that I'd had Gabrielle, exactly, but she had given me an orgasm.

Sitting alone in my flat, I actually found I was missing Percy rather badly. I'd understood my need for discipline for a good while, and his ability to fulfil it, but until then I hadn't fully understood how important it was to be comforted afterwards. Monty lacked Percy's confidence, also his skill, and his understanding. In fact, just about everything except the basic desire to punish and humiliate girls.

I was also exhausted, and went to bed with a glass of Armagnac only to wake in the morning with it untouched on my bedside table. I made coffee and poured the Armagnac into it, sipping the hot mixture with a touch of guilty awareness that I was drinking not just first thing in the morning but alone. I felt I needed it though, because in my dreams I'd been back on Beachy Head, running in blind panic with a pound or so of dung swinging in my panties.

The answer was obvious: to come over the experience, which I hadn't yet done. That was always Percy's great thing, to overcome an erotic fear by making it a fantasy. Not that what Monty had made me do hadn't been a fantasy anyway, but I needed that orgasm.

So I closed my eyes and slid further down the bed, letting my mind drift to the feel of hot sun on bare flesh, of hard cocks in my body, or my helpless despair and shame as I was spanked and to the yet stronger emotions of being given an enema in a public place.

I was in one of Percy's big shirts, and that soon came off, then my panties. With my fingers burrowed in between my pussy lips I thought of how it had felt, on the hillside, crushed beneath Monty's blubbery bulk as fake cream was forced up my anal passage. With that thought I rolled over, on to my side, sucking a finger and penetrating my bumhole, wiggling it about inside. I went back to the fantasy, thinking of my pain and angry consternation, struggling to hold myself, dizzy and helpless, then at last unable to hold it any more and expelling my enema into my nice clean white trousers. Worse still, on my knees, deliberately filling my panties

176

with poo in front of half a dozen onlookers, or running in blind panic, as I had been in my dream, with it all sloshing and wobbling in my panty pouch, and even cleaning myself in the sea, filthy from the waist down, near nude, with so many people staring. The huge woman treating me like a baby, watching as I peeled down my soiled panties in front of her.

That was best, only she shouldn't have been so nice. Instead, she should have dragged me out of the water by my ear, telling me I was a filthy little sloven, that I had no self-control. She should have made me change on the beach, no towel, pulling down my trousers to show off my soiled panties, then those too, exposing my filthy bum to the beach. She should have sluiced me down with buckets of sea water, then made me wash my clothes, still bare from the waist down, bent with my bottom and pussy lips showing, my bumhole still dirty. They would have watched, hundreds of people, all delighting in my utter humiliation, and then when I was wet and clean, the big woman would have quite calmly thrown me across her knee and given me the hardest, most painful spanking of my lifetime, in plain view, bare bottom, punished for my filthy behaviour as I kicked and screamed and struggled and blubbered . . .

I came, really screaming it out as the orgasm hit me, so loud that my neighbours were sure to hear. Not that I cared. Masturbation was no sin, neither was having lovers in, not like getting a kick out of filling my own panties with mess. Fortunately they had no way of knowing what I was thinking about, and they were welcome to think it was some slim young man from the city or some respectable, trendy profession.

That brought my mind to Damon, who undoubtedly felt that I had stood him up. With luck it would be a rejection too many, even for him, and he would go his own way. Unfortunately I had a sneaking suspicion that he would do nothing of the kind.

Another person who needed to be considered was Gabrielle. Technically I owed her a body massage and detox, but I was unsure if I wanted to do it. I still felt certain that she had ulterior motives in being so friendly, although it was very hard to accept that she could be so callous as to frig me off if she didn't fancy me, at least a bit.

In the end I decided that it was all too much for that time of the morning. Pouring myself more coffee, I began to get up, only for the doorbell to go before I was dressed. I threw on the first thing to hand, which happened to be the brilliant yellow beach shorts and Percy's shirt, then stuck my head out of the window. It was Damon.

'What are you doing?' I demanded.

'There you are,' he answered. 'Where have you been? You really showed me up at the weekend.'

'How? What are you talking about?'

'The weekend, the Independent Film Forum. You were supposed to come with me, right?'

'No, I didn't say I'd come. I was doing something else.'

'I said I'd pick you up. You must remember. We agreed.'

'No, Damon, you told me. I had other plans.'

'Sure you did! Now will you let me in? We need to talk.'

'No we don't. Just go away. I don't want to see you.'

'You do. You know you do. Look, Natasha, I've had enough of these stupid games. You're behaving like a teenager, with all this hard-to-get business . . .'

He trailed off, his head moving back to look past me. I glanced up, to see my friend Charlotte's head sticking out of the attic-flat window, her hair dishevelled and her face set in a sleepy frown.

'Sorry,' I said automatically.

She gave me a cross look and her head disappeared.

'Look what you've done!' I hissed downwards. 'Jesus, Damon!'

'Let me come up then,' he demanded.

'No!'

'We can do this two ways, Natasha. I can come up, or I can shout at your window. Which is it to be?'

'OK, OK, come up!'

I pulled my head in and marched to the intercom, absolutely boiling inside as I pressed the button. I heard the click of the door opening and a moment later the clatter of Damon's shoes on the stairs. Turning the catch to my own door I stalked back into the living room and threw myself down in a chair, my arms across my middle. Damon appeared a moment later.

'So?' I demanded.

'So we need to sort this out,' he answered. 'Just listen, right? You really embarrassed me at the weekend, deeply, but I'm prepared to overlook that, and all the other girlish crap you've been giving me. You don't need to do that to me, pretending you're not interested and that modesty stuff. I'm a modern guy, I understand female sexuality.'

I tried to glare at him, but it just came out as a sulky look. I wanted to scream at him, to tell him to fuck off, but I just couldn't find it in myself. It was too early, and my head wasn't straight. Instead I just sat there, wondering what I could possibly say to put him off.

'Right,' he went on, 'so from now on, we don't need to get into that any more. I'm coming round tonight, seven o'clock. Put on something from a name, because I'm going to take you somewhere special, really special. It'll amaze you.'

'I don't want to go out.'

'No, Natasha, I'm not going there any more. I'm collecting you at seven, that's it.'

'Look ... look, Damon, I don't want to let you down, please believe me, but the truth is ... the truth is I prefer girls.'

179

'Don't worry, I'll soon have you cured of that.'

'No, really, I'm having an affair . . .'

I stopped myself just in time, remembering that Ami was his PR agent. It wouldn't have been fair.

'. . . Gabrielle Salinger,' I finished.

'Not any more, you're not. You're with me, right? You don't need anybody else. I'll tell her myself if you like.'

'No!'

'Then you must. I've got to run now, you've already made me late. Oh, and I love the Daddy's girl look with the big shirt and the baggy shorts. You're to wear it tonight, for your after-dinner treat. Think about it to get yourself ready. Ciao.'

He went, banging the door behind him to leave me sitting there feeling numb. I'd meant to argue, and normally I would have done. As it was he'd just browbeaten me into accepting the date. I had to go too, because he obviously wasn't going to go away and I didn't want him coming round shouting up at my window again.

My feeble attempt to claim I was a lesbian had fallen flat as well. Worse in fact. I'd really dropped myself in it. He was arrogant enough to tell Gabrielle what I'd said, and I could just see her response, nodding thoughtfully as she wondered if I'd developed an obsession with her because of the detox episode or if I was just mad. There was only one thing for it. I was going to have to call her and explain.

I did, and she must have heard the emotion in my voice, because she suggested coming over to see her immediately. It was an offer I couldn't refuse. I badly needed to talk to somebody, too badly to decline, and under an hour later I was at her clinic in Victoria, sprawled on the black leather sofa she used as a couch. It wasn't technically a professional appointment, but that made it easier still to let go. I told her the whole

Damon saga, from start to finish, and she listened, nodding and making the occasional note.

'It seems,' she said when I had finally finished, 'that he has come to view you as a possession, something which it is his to control.'

'Yes, I realise that,' I told her.

'Therefore, to him, you can no more reject him than a dog can reject its owner. Does he use the word "bitch", perhaps during sex?'

'Yes, always when he's coming. He likes to come down my throat, to make me gag.'

'Again, this is typical. Both are common manifestations of male sexuality, the need to control the female. He wishes to see you as his bitch, implying both doglike loyalty and an inability to restrain your sexual desire for him, although this is unlikely to be entirely at a conscious level. The same is true of the need to make you gag, by which he exerts his control over a crucial life function – your breathing.'

'I'd more or less worked all that out.'

'It is simple, of course. The consequence is that you cannot reject him . . .'

'I can try!'

'No, that is not what I mean. In his own mind you cannot reject him. It is likely that in his mind he sees himself as a hunter, and therefore you as prey. Should you continue to reject him, it is possible that he may become compulsive, calling you at all hours, sending letters, emails, stalking you, making threats . . .'

'I get the picture. So what am I supposed to do?'

'Well, you have the choice of legal action of course . . .'

'No, please. I just don't want to make a big deal out of it all. Anyway, I'd feel he'd won.'

'A common reaction, and in extreme cases legal action may prove counter-productive, increasing his sense of antagonism towards you. You would do better to try to make him reject you.'

'I'd already thought of that one. That's why I told him I was a lesbian. He said he'd cure me!'

'No, this was the wrong choice. By claiming to be a lesbian you merely provide him with a reason to accept your rejection of him, on your terms. You provide only an added challenge. He needs to make the rejection himself, on his own terms.'

'I see, but what can I do?'

'Initially, you must discover what he finds unacceptable in women. For instance, many men have a strong need to feel that a woman is theirs alone, that she has been 'pure', 'inviolate' before. In their minds they are conquering a woman by taking her virginity, after which it is easier to view her as their possession.'

'Not Damon, he gets off on me being a slut. Anyway, that's another thing he used to call me when he was coming.'

'It is a common alternative, taking pride in the possession of a highly sought-after woman. To further the analogy of hunter and prey, he sees you as a trophy.'

'Definitely.'

'Should you prove socially unacceptable you would cease to be a trophy. Yet you are slim, beautiful, educated, rich . . .'

'Thanks, Gabrielle, you know how to cheer a girl up. Not rich though.'

'No? You own a flat in Primrose Hill, a sports car. You have, I suspect, private means?'

'Well, Daddy pays for a few things – the flat, the car.'

'Wealth is relative. To Damon Maurschen you appear rich.'

'Whatever. So what, I've got to put on ten stone to get rid of him, or give everything to charity? No way!'

'No, this would only be seen as an attempt to evade him, to prevent your capture. In any case, it would be wrong to pay so high a cost.'

'Dead right.'

'No, it is essential that he does not realise you seek to escape . . .'

She went on, but I wasn't really listening. An idea had occurred to me.

Damon picked me up at seven, by which time I was nearly ready. He had asked for designer clothes and I'd gone to town for him – shoes, stockings, suspenders, bra and panties all handmade by the best names, and topped off by a crimson Gaultier gown I'd bought in Paris, beautifully cut to show off my back and tummy, but high enough to cover the mess Monty had made of my boobs. The colour worked with my hair, which I'd put up in a gold fillet, Athenian style, along with jewellery set with rubies, including one for my tummy piercing. The moment I stepped from the front door Damon's expression changed to smug satisfaction. He'd caught me.

'Hi,' I greeted him. 'Do you like it?'

'You look beautiful,' he answered. 'As a woman should for her man.'

I smiled, simpered really, and slid myself into his car, which was some Japanese four-wheel drive thing. He started off, turning south, then west on the Euston Road and out on to the flyover. I'd expected somewhere in central London, and was wondering what he was doing, until we passed the M25. It seemed certain that he'd decided to take me to *Le Beaunois,* which was even better than I'd expected. Perfect in fact, because Percy had known the owner since before I was born.

Not that I said anything, allowing Damon to have his moment of glory as he finally turned off an Oxfordshire lane and parked in front of the long Cotswold stone building with its great gnarled vine twisting up around the windows. I oohed and aahed a bit to show how grateful I was, and allowed him to take my arm.

'The vine is supposed to be nearly a hundred years old,' he said, as we approached the door.

'Eighty-three,' I answered. 'It's a Pinot-Noir, supposedly grown from a cutting stolen from *la Romanée-Conti* itself at the end of the First World War.'

'Your subject, of course,' he said. 'Natasha!'

The grapes were showing full colour, and I'd picked one, popping it into my mouth in full view of the man coming to meet us at the door. He was tall, grey haired, with an air of absolute propriety, sending Damon into immediate stumbling apologies for my behaviour, which were ignored.

'Nearly ripe,' I pronounced. 'Not bad for an English summer. Good evening, Louis.'

'Miss Linnet, good evening,' Louis answered. 'A pleasure to see you again. Sir.'

He finished with a polite but minimal bow to Damon, then ushered us inside, still talking.

'Your usual table is taken I fear. Had I known, of course . . . yet there is another within the conservatory, if you care to take it?'

I nodded, following him past the main dining room to the glass and iron space of the conservatory, where he showed us to a table that looked out over the countryside, with the lights of Oxford in the distance.

'An aperitif, perhaps?' Louis suggested, sliding my chair in beneath me. '*Cristal*, perhaps?'

'Mineral water, please,' Damon put in.

'Poor Damon's driving,' I said. 'I will though, a half of that *Vaudésir* ninety-nine if you have it?'

'Certainly, Miss Linnet.'

Louis left, beaming and I picked up the menu to hide my smile.

'You've been here before?' Damon asked.

'Once or twice,' I admitted. 'My uncle likes to bring me here. I'm sorry you can't drink, the wine list is spectacular. The house used to belong to a Major Allens, the man who pinched the vine cutting. When he died and Charles bought the place they took over the cellar. There are things you wouldn't see outside an Oxford college.'

'I thought you said that man was called Louis?'

'Louis is the cellerman, the manager too. Charles is the owner. Now, what shall we have? Foie gras of course. They have the La Seigneurie.'

'I don't see that.'

'Oh don't worry, they've always got some. Louis will dig it out for me. We'll have it pan fried, with an *Yquem*. I do hope they've got some of the 'sixty-seven left. First though, oysters, which will go nicely with the Chablis. Oh, and there's grouse, we can't miss that, and they have the most wonderful chocolate dessert, which means we'll have to have Banyuls. I will anyway. I'm really sorry you can't too. Couldn't we get a cab back or something?'

'To London?'

'I don't see why not.'

'No, don't worry. I'm happy with mineral water.'

'Suit yourself.'

Damon was going to say something, but went quiet as Charles himself appeared with my half bottle of Chablis. He was his normal unctuous self, full of flattery for me and ignoring Damon almost completely. I was sure the only reason he'd never made a pass at me was out of respect for Percy, and I could tell from his questions that he was trying to find out if we were still together. It was rather fun, but I answered evasively, not wanting to make Damon jealous.

When Louis returned along with a waiter I gave our order, everything I had planned, including the 'sixty-seven *Yquem*, of which Damon obviously had no idea of the price. Damon added his, going for much lighter choices and declining the foie gras. Louis waited, the ancient notebook that contained the Major's original stock list in his hand.

'Would you care to?' he queried, holding it up to me with a smile as the waiter left.

'Naturally,' I answered, and turned to Damon. 'You don't mind, do you, darling?'

'You go ahead,' he assured me, smiling back.

'With grouse then,' Louis said, 'perhaps the *Clos Vougeot* 'sixty-four from Jean Gros? Or Louis Remy's *Chambertin* 'fifty-nine, which is truly superb.'

'Thanks but no,' I answered. 'I almost never get the whole bottle to myself, and Damon's spoiling me. I'll have *Chambertin*, but the Leroy 'forty-nine.'

'Magnificent, of course,' he answered, casting a quick glance towards Damon.

Damon gave no outward sign of having understood, which made it pretty certain that he hadn't. Soon afterwards the oysters arrived, and I tucked in, enjoying myself immensely, filling the shells with Chablis and pouring the contents into my mouth, which drew an indulgent look from Charles and one of disapproval from Damon.

I began to flirt with him after that, as the alcohol slowly warmed me up. With two and a half bottles to drink I was going to be almost under the table by the end, but that was fine, and I soon had my shoe off so that I could stroke Damon's leg under the table, and even press my toes to his crotch so that I could feel the soft mass of his cock and balls beneath.

That left him smiling, and half erect by the time I took my foot away, pretty agitated too. I could just imagine what he was thinking, of stopping in a lane on the way back, making me suck him until I gagged on his cock, maybe fucking me over the back seat. I didn't want to hurry though, and lingered over the meal.

The combination of foie gras and 'sixty-seven *Yquem* was exquisite, the grouse and *Chambertin* 'forty-nine better still, with the wine everything it was supposed to be and maybe even the finest I had ever tasted. Naturally I had to let Charles and Louis have a glass each, but the rest went down me. By the end of the bottle I was feeling mellow to say the least, even a bit mean. The ice that followed to break the meal cleared my head a little, but only until the arrival of the chocolate pudding and a 'seventy-eight Banyuls Grand Cru, which left my head spinning and my pussy so wet I was wondering if I'd leave a damp patch on the chair, a thought which just made me giggle. I still managed a glass of Armagnac, after which I was wondering how I was going to manage to stand up.

Damon was stone cold sober, but seriously randy. He could see how drunk I was, and he knew I'd be grateful, and up for anything. I was too, even though I was wishing my companion had been Percy, or Monty, so that they could give me a bloody good spanking for my behaviour. It was what I needed, and it was at that point, completely drunk, that I realised why I hadn't been able to get my head around what Monty had done to me. He should have punished me for it, or somebody should have done anyway.

The appearance of the waiter with the bill drove the thought from my head and I sat back, watching Damon's face and sipping my Armagnac. He took the folder, opened it, scanned down the list of items with a little mean frown, then stopped, his mouth coming slowly open.

'I think there's some mistake,' he said.

'Sir?' the waiter enquired.

'Here,' he answered, pointing to the bill.

'No, sir,' the waiter responded. 'I believe that to be correct.'

'Eight thousand, five hundred pounds? For a bottle of wine?'

'The *Chambertin* 'forty-nine, sir, yes.'

'Is that all right?' I asked sweetly. 'I'm sorry, Damon, darling. You did say it was OK. It was really special.'

He didn't answer, just staring at the bill. I bit my lip, trying to look concerned and not to giggle as with

187

leaden motions Damon drew a credit card from his wallet. He was white in the face, and his hand was trembling as he tucked it into the folder. It was time to play my ace.

'Sorry, darling,' I whispered as the waiter withdrew. 'I didn't realise it was a problem.'

'Didn't realise?' he said weakly.

'Oh, I'm sorry,' I said. 'I really am. That was so thoughtless of me. Would you like me to get it? I don't mind. You can treat me another time, to the *Borscht* maybe, that was nice.'

He shook his head, staring after the waiter like a man watching the bailiffs drive his car away. At that point I actually felt sorry for him, he looked so grief-stricken, and I told myself it would only be fair to give him his blow job, or whatever he wanted.

'Never mind then,' I said, reaching out to take his hand and dropping my voice to a whisper. 'I'll make up for it in the car, properly.'

'For nearly ten thousand pounds?' he said.

'Aren't I worth it?' I asked.

I never discovered if he thought I was, or rather if he was prepared to lie, because at that moment the waiter came back to say that Damon's card had been rejected. Damon went red, stammering apologies as he leafed frantically through his wallet, taking out a second card, and a third.

'This might cover it, just about,' he said. 'Look, Natasha, you might have to lend me some.'

'Don't be silly,' I chided. 'I don't expect you to pay if you can't. Here, take it off my card, and ten per cent, of course. Make it a round eleven thousand.'

'Thank you, Miss Linnet,' the waiter answered, taking my card.

He went back to the reception area, where I saw him speak briefly to Charles, whose eyebrows rose a fraction. Louis appeared and took my card, passing from sight as I turned back to Damon, who looked as if he was about to be sick.

'I'm really sorry,' I assured him. 'That was so thoughtless. I've had my eye on that *Chambertin* for ages, and they've only got two bottles left from the original case. I had to have it, or some overpaid footballer would have drunk it and not appreciated it at all. I'm sorry, Damon.'

Louis returned my card in person, with Charles too, helping me with my coat and fussing round me as we left. I was fairly sure they wouldn't have taken the full amount for the wine, and even if they had I knew my card would stand it, even if it was going to mean some serious grovelling to Daddy. Not that it would be the first time, and he always forgave me. Damon never said a word, climbing into the car and starting it as I waved a giggly goodbye.

'That was glorious,' I said, stretching to push out my boobs. 'Now you can drive somewhere quiet and I'm going to give you the longest, nicest suck you've ever had, to say sorry. You can do it right down my throat too, so I choke on your lovely big cock. You like that, don't you?'

He didn't answer, his face set as the lights from the restaurant swung across it, then in darkness as we moved out into the lane. I reached out to squeeze his cock, nuzzling his arm with my face at the same time.

'Careful!' he snapped.

'Don't be sulky,' I wheedled, pulling at his fly. 'Come on, pull him out. I want to suck him and swallow your spunk.'

'Look, stop it, you'll cause an accident!' he said urgently. 'Look, I'm not sure I feel like sex. Let's just drive back.'

'Oh come on!' I pleaded. 'I won't touch, I promise, not until you can pull over. The old A40's the place. Hardly anyone uses it, and there are lay-bys where you can get right off the road.'

'You know a lot about it.'

'Well, yeah. You're not the first, you know.'

'I thought you said your uncle took you there?'

'Oh no, not uncle James! I don't go down on him! What a thought! That is so funny! I bet he'd let me if I offered though, eh, Damon? No, not uncle James, silly, but I did do his son, not Anthony, the younger one, Richard. Wasn't that naughty of me, sucking my own cousin's cock? Or was it, I can't remember if you're supposed to or not. Then there was Eustace what's-his-name, you know, his father's an Earl or something, and that black guy, the rapper, you know, with the funny hats. Actually, that was a bit of a let-down, because his cock wasn't all that big, not as big as I expected anyway, from what he said. He was good though, he really knew how to handle me. He made me suck him for just ages, and when he came he did it all over my face and made me lick it up off his fingers. Would you like to do that, Damon, darling? Would you like to spunk in my face and watch me lick up your lovely thick come?'

'Right!' he shouted and jammed on the brakes.

I jerked forwards against my safety belt, crying out in shock, even as his hand locked in my hair. My head was wrenched down, into his crotch, as he struggled to get his fly down. It came, and my mouth was filled with soft, salty flesh, his cock and balls jammed in, hard. He was cursing, calling me a slut and a bitch as I mouthed at his cock, trying to suck properly. His hand was twisted hard in my hair, really rough, which was just what I needed – to be forced to suck cock until he spunked in my mouth, then made to swallow.

Only I didn't get it, because for all his urgency and all my efforts I couldn't get him hard. I tried, nibbling on him, licking the underside, rolling his foreskin back to suckle on the head. Nothing worked, while he was getting more and more angry, until the grip in my hair had become more painful than sexy. He turned the interior light on so that he could watch me suck, and popped my boobs out of my dress, groping them really hard, but it made no difference.

Finally he pulled me off, and that was when he saw my whipped breasts. The expression on his face immediately set hard, scaring me into babbling a string of apologies and accusations. He put his cock away, his jaw set and his eyes tight. I really thought he was going to hit me, and put my hands up to protect my face, but his hand went to my safety belt catch.

'Out,' he said.

'Out? Here?' I demanded.

'Out,' he repeated, 'before I really lose my temper with you, and believe me, you wouldn't like that.'

'But . . .'

'Just . . . just get out!' he yelled, jerking at my door handle. 'Fuck off out of my life you drunken slut!'

'Jesus, Damon!' I managed, but the door was opening and he was shoving at my shoulder, really hard.

I went, tumbling out of the door, just managing to get one foot on the ground, only to stumble and sit down hard. Something hit my legs, the door slammed and I was left sprawled on the ground, staring after the departing tail lights of his car. I hadn't expected him to react so badly, and for a moment I was too shocked to do anything but lie there with the stars spinning slowly around my head, and then I started to laugh.

It had worked beautifully – the one thing that I had been certain his ego would be unable to tolerate. I'd made him feel inferior, in a way that no amount of tantrums and long letters of rejection could ever have done. He knew he was good looking, and clever, and more together than any silly little girl. Nothing I did would ever disabuse him of his arrogant self-confidence. He also knew he couldn't afford ten thousand pounds for dinner, and he hadn't imagined I could either. Then I'd paid, casually, easily, with a thousand-pound tip for good measure. It wouldn't have worked with Monty. He'd have probably spanked me in front of everybody and made me pay the bill as well. Percy would never even have let me. With Damon it had worked, perfectly. In fact it had worked too well. I'd expected him to have his fun with me, even spank me, or at least fuck me really hard. After all, I deserved a spanking, surely?

It was just so funny. It was pitch black and my head was reeling with drink, but I didn't care. I was in the best possible mood, drunk, horny and seriously pleased with myself. I could not stop smiling, or giggling, and it wasn't until a car passed that I realised my boobs were still out of my dress. The car stopped, not surprisingly, and a head appeared at a window, looking back at me.

'Are you all right?' a male voice asked.

'No,' I admitted. 'I'm not. Help.'

After that it was a blur. Eager hands helped me into the back of the car as I babbled thanks, and I think I offered to suck all their cocks for them. I certainly asked for a spanking, because I remember their delighted laughter at the idea and pats on my bottom. They were well-off students, some dining society, who'd been at the restaurant, and seen what had happened, which they thought really funny. They were drunk too, except the driver, who I only had a vague impression of, and who may even have been a cabbie.

They were pretty sneaky about it at first, but the two in the back with me had a good feel of my boobs in the darkness. They were shy too, or at least reluctant, but I wasn't going to let them get away with it, and I soon had their cocks out, one in each hand, wanking them. I remember the guy in the front looking back, his bow-tie undone and his mouth open, demanding his turn. I remember the driver grumbling about them taking advantage of me and me telling him not to be a prat. I remember my boobs being pulled out again, and the flash of a camera. I remember the first one coming, and

I think I sucked his spunk up as he told me I was a good girl. If the other man came, I don't remember.

Suddenly we were among houses, then stopping, and I was vaguely aware of stumbling from the car, being helped through a wicket gate, up a stone staircase, into a big room panelled in oak, pulling off my clothes, sitting giggling on the floor. There was a man in a dinner jacket and shirt-tails, no trousers, watching me and tugging at his cock. It was the guy who'd been in the front, I think. Whoever he was, he thoroughly took advantage of me: malt whisky and sex, for hours.

I got spanked across his knee, in just my suspenders and stockings, kicking a bit but giggling like anything. I vaguely think that went on for ages, but then it was cock-sucking, and having my cleavage fucked, before it went up my pussy, and finally my bumhole, at my own request, I think. I know I got made to suck it afterwards, because I came like that, frigging off with his dirty cock in my mouth, which was just the perfect end to the evening. After that came oblivion.

Eleven

When I woke up I didn't even know where I was. It was doubly weird, because in my dreams I'd been back on Beachy Head again, so that one moment I seemed to be on grass with the sky over my head, and the next in a bed with an ornate plaster ceiling above me.

It turned out to be Oxford, a room in one of the old colleges, and my companion was an eighteen-year-old. He was in a fine state, desperately eager to please, almost worshipful, which was odd considering he had enjoyed me so comprehensively the night before. Not that I cared, letting him make coffee and fetch hot croissants from the town while I nursed my head and a sick feeling in my stomach.

Fortunately they'd had the sense to rescue my bag, which was what Damon had thrown out of the car after me. So when my knight errant finally said he had to go to lectures I was able to take a fast bus back to London, falling asleep again before reaching the edge of the city.

I awoke in Victoria Coach Station, feeling worse than I had the first time. The place was crowded, with lights and bustle and noise, bus brakes and the hum of traffic, all of which seemed to go straight through my head. I'd cleaned up well enough, but I was still in an expensive evening gown, which was now drawing some amused looks from people, even though in Oxford nobody had seemed to notice.

What I wanted was a bath, clean fresh sheets and sleep, preferably for about a week. What I got was Gabrielle Salinger, emerging from a newsagent with a copy of the New Scientist in her hand and an infuriating air of brisk efficiency about her.

'Natasha? You look dreadful!' were her opening words.

'I know,' I answered. 'I . . .'

'Come up to my flat,' she continued. 'Lie down for a while. Sleep if you like.'

Once again she was making me an offer too good to refuse. The prospect of a cab journey back to Primrose Hill, undoubtedly with some greasy cabbie drivelling at me, was suddenly unbearable. I accepted her offer, returning to her flat, where she helped me undress, made me drink a pint of water and put me to bed.

My third awakening that day was the least painful, but by far the strangest. The first thing I focused on was a huge pink rabbit, as big as me, with long fluffy ears and an expression of sentimental stupidity on its face. I lay staring at it, probably looking just as vacant, wondering where I was and how it fitted in with being made to drink water, in the nude, by Gabrielle Salinger, which was my last memory.

When she'd put me to bed it had been dim and I'd been too sleepy really to take in my surroundings. Gabrielle's clinic was all black leather and chrome, with white walls, and so was her flat, along with stark black-and-white art photographs in plain frames. The giant pink rabbit couldn't have been more out of place, but in what I assumed to be her bedroom it fitted perfectly. Except for the odd touch of white or lemon yellow, everything was pink – the walls, the carpet, the furniture, the curtains, the bedclothes, everything. There were mirrors too, large ones on three of the walls and several smaller ones, all framed in pink.

My first thought was that Gabrielle had a daughter, but she had never mentioned one, and the room was far too neat to be a child's room, too perfect. Everything was just so, set exactly in its place, from the family-sized container of baby powder on the shelf to the huge collection of cuddly toys. They were particularly disturbing, because all of them were staring at the bed, hundreds of coloured glass eyes, fixed on me where I lay. There was a phone too, in pink, and a clock radio, also pink.

I still hadn't managed to get my head around it when I heard the click of a door catch. A moment later Gabrielle came in, in a grey wool two piece and a silk blouse as smart and severe as ever, except for the expression on her face. She looked shy, timid, biting her lip as she pulled at a finger.

'Hi,' she said, sitting down on the side of the bed with an embarrassed smile, then spreading her hands. 'So now you know.'

'I do?' I asked.

'About me,' she said. 'You will play, will you not? Please. Maybe not now, but soon, please?'

There was real entreaty in her voice, almost desperation, and as it began to sink in I found myself gaping at her. She gave me her embarrassed smile again, her big pale eyes wide and hopeful behind her glasses, uncertain too.

'You want me to be a baby for you?' I asked. 'A grown-up baby?'

She shook her head, shyer than ever, as if she was about to burst into tears.

'You want to be a grown-up baby, for me?'

She nodded, twisting her fingers together in nervous embarrassment.

I could have been nasty, I could have laughed, but I knew how it felt to want something really badly when it's just not acceptable to society. It had been so hard to find someone to give me the discipline I needed, and I could guess that if Gabrielle was into infantilism it would be harder still. I smiled and took her hand, squeezing it as her uncertain expression faded to the most beautiful smile.

'I will make coffee then,' she said, bouncing up from the bed, 'and we will talk. Black isn't it?'

'With honey,' I answered, and was left to contemplate the sea of pink around me.

The contrast could not have been more absolute, and I was still struggling to take it in. Her true personality was the exact opposite of the impression I'd formed of her, yet with hindsight I felt I could understand. For all her severity she had always been gentle, very caring, prepared to go to enormous lengths to help. It was a good disguise as well, which she used in the same way I feign distaste for older men when in fact I find them best suited to my sexuality.

It wasn't that far away from my own fantasies either. Certainly not too far to understand. Helplessness appeals, and being cared for, and I could well see the appeal of old-fashioned nursery discipline. It was a good fantasy, and one I'd happily have indulged in, although preferably as the grown-up baby myself. What I wouldn't have done was go to the obsessive lengths Gabrielle's taste in decoration suggested.

I also understood why she'd been so determined to get in with me. She knew I was into spanking, and enemas. I'd thought her curiosity was professional. Obviously I'd been wrong. It didn't take a genius to work out that I'd at the very least be understanding about playing at grown-up babies. She'd been right.

Somehow it didn't seem right to drink coffee in her playroom, so I got out of bed, still naked, and walked into the main body of the flat, seeking the bathroom. The first door I opened led into another bedroom, and a very different one: neat, feminine yet cold, the sort of room one of Monty's fantasy girl robots might have lived in. Evidently it was the official bedroom. The remaining door had to be the bathroom, as neat and cold as the rest of the flat, bar that one special room.

I peed, washed my hands and splashed water into my face before taking a grey silk robe from behind the door. By then Gabrielle was in the living room, on the sofa with her shoes kicked off, pouring coffee into little chrome-plated cups. I sat opposite her, waiting until she chose to speak.

'I had hoped you would understand,' she said, completely direct. 'You do, yes?'

'Sure,' I answered. 'It's cute.'

'And you would play with me?'

'Yes. OK, so I'd rather be baby, but I don't mind being nurse. We can take turns, maybe?'

'Maybe, yes. I had hoped you would want to take charge, solely, as you did with Ami Bell?'

'I prefer to be on the receiving end. With Ami I had to take control, or nothing would have happened.'

'I understand. Often this is the way.'

'I thought you'd have known, after Jo. Jo Warren?'

'I should not really say this, but Jo was not altogether clear in her explanations. Her sexuality is very repressed, more so than Ami's.'

'But she told you I wanted her to spank me?'

'She said you equated pain with pleasure, in the form of corporal punishment. You will understand if I do not explain the details of her case?'

'Of course. So you thought I wanted to spank her? That I'd scared her?'

'Essentially, yes.'

'That's actually quite funny. I mean, there's no way I would do it to her unless she wanted it. There's no way I *could* do it to her unless she wanted it!'

'Physically no. That is not important.'

'Yes it is. It's just not the same for me if I don't feel that the person punishing me is genuinely in control.

Like you. I thought maybe you wanted to dominate me, to control me, when you wrapped me in the cling film for my enema. After all, you saw my spoon bruises.'

'That was a legitimate therapy.'

'Including frigging me off?'

'Yes.'

'Do you do that to other clients? Masturbate them?'

'You know I cannot possibly tell you that. But yes, orgasm can be highly therapeutic, in many ways. You were aroused, also.'

'Well, what do you expect? You put me in tight restraint. You gave me an enema, you made me pee myself. You must have known it would get to me.'

'You see the cling film as restraint?'

'Well yes, don't you?'

'Not necessarily.'

'Oh. Fair enough, I suppose. So tell me, your masturbation therapy or whatever you call it. Jo Warren?'

'That would be to betray her confidence. It is an important technique for release of tension.'

'And Jo's as tense as they come. Fine. That screws my head up. I mean, how can she get in such a state over an offer of lesbian sex then casually let you frig her pussy once a month!'

'As I say. It is a therapeutic technique.'

'Sex, Gabrielle. One girl masturbating another, sex, S-E-X.'

'Not at all . . .'

'Well it is to me.'

'This is an old-fashioned idea, related to the repression of female sexuality, male too, perhaps more so.'

'It's still sex.'

'Not necessarily. You are very focused on the sexual responses of your body, Natasha, much more so than most.'

'Perhaps. So why did you take me so far at Haven?'

'To become closer to you. In the hope that we might talk, that I might find in you an expression of my needs, and your own.'

'Well you have, sort of.'

'Thank you, Natasha. You maybe understand how important that is to me.'

'Yes, I think I do. You'll need to explain the details though, with the whole baby thing. Do you want me to humiliate you, sexually?'

'No, humiliation plays no part in it.'

'It does for me.'

'That is not uncommon, especially in very confident women. When I first saw you I thought you were repressed, and unable to open yourself due to low self-esteem. Had you told me everything, I would have understood.'

'I know that now. Look, I'm going to tell you something very intimate, and you can tell me if it fits in with your fantasy.'

'Very well.'

'This man I've been seeing . . .'

'Damon Maurschen?'

'No, and incidentally, I think I'm rid of him, thanks to your advice. This is another one. It doesn't matter who he is. What does matter is that he's into female humiliation.'

She nodded, folding her hands in her lap and leaning forwards, listening intently.

'He um . . . he did something really cruel to me. He made me poo my panties, in public.'

Again she nodded. I'd expected a bit more reaction.

'It was my fault,' I went on. 'I'd egged him on, sort of, or at least he thought I had. The humiliation was dreadful, mind-numbing, as I'm sure you can imagine, but it turned me on, so much, although it made me angry too. The thing is, that I didn't manage to come, although I wanted to. I was just too cross to let him do it. I dreamed about it that night, and masturbated in the morning, only it wasn't him I came over, or what he made me do, but this big woman who rescued me. She just took over completely, helping me clean up, making sure I was decent. In my fantasy she punished me too, but that's not the point. I think maybe that feeling, of just being taken charge of, is what you want to get, yes?'

'Yes, exactly. If you would behave to me as that woman did to you, it would, I think, be perfect.'

'Then wet yourself.'

For one instant her eyes showed surprise, no more. Then she took her glasses off and closed her eyes. Her mouth went loose as she relaxed down into the sofa. Her legs began to part, the neat grey skirt riding up her thighs, to expose first stocking tops, then the taut white crotch of her panties, stretched over the gentle bulge of her pussy. I realised immediately that she was shaved, because I could see every detail of her sex lips. Suddenly those details were a great deal clearer as a tiny wet patch appeared at the centre of her pussy, growing, spreading, the cotton pulling tight to her sex as a little fountain of pee sprang from the middle to run down over the clean white cotton and on to the leather beneath.

She was wetting herself, right in front of me, Miss Perfect herself, Gabrielle Salinger, with pee spurting out through her little cotton panties, all over her sofa. I watched, absolutely delighted, until she had finished, by which time she was sitting in a big puddle of pee. Her panties were sodden, her skirt and stockings too, soaking it slowly up. She still had her eyes closed, with her face set in an expression of abandoned bliss, and her thighs were wide open, showing me everything. She'd gone straight into role, without a moment's hesitation, peeing somewhere just so totally inappropriate. It was only fair that I returned the favour.

'Honestly, Gabrielle!' I exclaimed. 'You know you should go on the potty when you haven't got a nappy on.'

'Sorry, *Bobonne*,' she answered, and stuck her thumb in her mouth, throwing me a really sulky look. 'Which means a nursemaid in French, and call me Gabby.'

'Got it,' I answered quickly, then went stern. 'In the bath, Miss Gabby! Now!' I ordered.

I had grabbed her by the wrist before she could answer, pulling her to her feet. She took her thumb out of her mouth, but her sulky look intensified as I dragged her towards the bathroom. She came, trailing after me with reluctant steps as the pee dribbled down her legs, leaving a line of little puddles and wet footprints behind her.

We came to a stop in the bathroom, and she once more put her thumb in her mouth. I twisted the taps to full and turned on her, folding my arms across my front. Her skirt was soaked, and she looked pathetic, standing in her own slowly growing puddle with her thumb in her mouth and her big eyes wide.

'Off with your clothes, young lady,' I snapped. 'All of them!'

'Yes, *Bobonne*,' she answered, her hands going tentatively to her skirt.

I watched her strip, first peeling off her pee-soaked skirt and stockings, then her panties. I ignored the temptation to stuff them in her mouth, as it wouldn't have been in role, but it was more than I could resist to plant a firm smack on one wet buttock.

'I've a mind to make you clear it up,' I snapped. 'Certainly you shall be spanked, don't think you won't.'

'No, *Bobonne*, please, no.'

'Yes, and firmly, on your bare bottom. How will that feel?'

She didn't answer, just looking more sulky than ever and sucking on her thumb. I considered putting her straight across my knee, or the edge of the bath, but thought better of it, reserving the pleasure of spanking her until later in the game. Instead I waited as the bath filled, making sure it was as hot as she could possibly tolerate. That made her squeal when she got in, and the look on her face when she stuck her bottom in the water was something else.

I pretended to ignore it, taking a long-handled bath brush she had and smearing soap on it. She waited, just looking at me with her lovely pale eyes, her skin going gradually pink. Her nipples had come up, firm and proud on top of her tiny tits, really sweet, and just ripe for tweaking. I did it, pinching each between thumb and forefinger to make her squeak again and fold her arms protectively across her chest.

'As if it could possibly matter who sees those,' I chided. 'Now, scrub time, so you can put your hands on your head, right now.'

She obeyed, and I began to scrub, her arms first, then her chest, making her screw her eyes up in pain as the stiff bristles caught her nipples. Her tummy came next, and her legs, before I made her turn over and stick her bum out of the water, with her pussy showing, wet and shiny between her thighs.

I did her whole body, twice, scrubbing vigorously to get the soap up into a thick lather, then again, until her skin was bright pink all over and really glowing. Once scrubbed, I made her stand to be inspected, stark naked and soaking wet in front of me. Her body was lovely, firm and slim and smooth, maybe not really meaty enough, but just right for the role. Her bum looked particularly sweet – small and firm, with the little round cheeks flushed cherry colour, just as if she'd already been spanked. I wanted to beat her, and it was tempting to use the bath brush, but I was sure she'd howl and held back, again delaying my pleasure.

With her clean, I ordered her out of the bath. She scrambled quickly out, and ran, her wet bottom jiggling behind her, into her special bedroom. I followed, towel in hand, to find her sat splay-legged on the floor, pussy on show, totally indifferent to her nudity, with a big pink dummy in her mouth. I wrapped the towel around her back, and spread a plastic sheet I'd noticed in one corner on to the floor. She crawled on immediately, rolling over on to her back.

She was breathing quite heavily, and it was obviously getting to her, but I knew better than to rush it. So I set about drying her, rubbing her all over with the towel and trying not to pay too much attention to her little boobs and the soft contours of her bottom and hips. She did as she was told throughout, never complaining and allowing me to move her body as I pleased, regardless of how blatant a show it made of her pussy or bottom.

Once she was dry I put the towel away and took down the big container of baby powder I'd noticed on the shelf. She was on her back by then, legs spread wide, pussy open, a very tempting position. Too tempting in fact, but I forced myself to do her neck, tummy and legs before moving to her boobs. I did both at the same time, shaking powder on to them and smoothing it in with my hands. Her nipples were rock hard, and as they moved under my fingers she gave the softest of sighs, hardly audible, but enough to tell me that she was getting seriously aroused.

It was pussy time, so I shook out more powder, on to the bare swell of her mound, then between her legs, over her sex. Instead of rubbing, I patted it in, very gently, smacking her pussy to send up little puffs of powder. That drew another sigh from her, as she set her legs as wide as they would go, offering herself to me in complete abandonment.

It wasn't what I wanted. Smacking her gently on each thigh to make her put her legs down, I had her roll over, bum up. That was what I wanted, her gorgeous little bottom, bare and pink. I did her back first though, and her neck, then a few little bits I'd missed, like behind her knees, saving the real treat until last. Finally my target was the only bit unpowdered, pink and smooth, her cheeks open just enough to let me see her bumhole and the crease of her pussy.

I put the powder on, giving the container a good shake over each cheek to leave them crowned with little piles of white powder. She was quite still, waiting, but trembling ever so slightly, so that her cheeks quivered as I slowly began to rub the powder in, stroking and smacking gently, distributing it evenly, until just her crease was left. I used more powder for that, plenty of it, down between them until her flesh was white and it had begun to make little drifts in the crevices of her bumhole and between her pussy lips.

She looked so sweet, with her little powdery bottom and shaved pussy. I couldn't hold the role of stern, detached nurse any more. I needed to touch, sexually, and she was simply too good to resist. Besides, I knew ultimately that I was supposed to bring her off. So I had a good feel of her freshly powdered bottomhole, holding her cheeks apart to get at it. She gave no resistance at all, simply sighing quietly as I tickled the little hole, which twitched in response, tightening, then going loose to show a wet, pink centre.

I eased her thighs gently open, displaying the rear of her sweet little pussy, with the neat folds of her inner lips peeping out from between the outer. She was wet, her flesh puffy, with a little white fluid escaping from the mouth of her vagina. I touched it, easing my finger into the opening and bringing it out wet and glistening. She sighed again, lifting her bottom ever so slightly. I gave her a little more powder, on her pussy lips and into the tiny wet hole at the centre of her anus, rubbing it in with my fingers to make her sigh again.

She was ready to come, I was sure of it, so I began to stroke her bottom, smoothing my hand over the powdery cheeks, grazing the wrinkled pink bumhole with my thumb each time, while my other hand cupped her sex, my thumb on her vagina, then up it as my fingers found her pussy lips, tickling, the nail of my longest finger on her clitoris. She reacted all right to that, sticking up her bottom and sighing aloud. I went on stroking and tickling, watching her react as her muscles started to twitch, her bottomhole tightening, her pussy too, starting to pulse as she moaned, deeply, her bottom coming up, her buttocks squeezing, her thighs going tense and her pussy clamping hard on my thumb as she came, once, then again, with the sweetest little cry of passion as it hit her.

I was pretty turned on myself, and wondering if I should make her lick me. The fantasy wasn't complete though, and nor were her bedtime preparations. She needed to be in a nappy, which was something she was bound to have. Sure enough, there was a big packet of them, tucked neatly away, grown-up size, but girly pink. I pulled one out, opening it and trying to work out how it fastened. She stayed still, watching me and sucking her dummy, her feet kicked right up to her powdery bottom.

Finally I managed to figure out the nappy and went back to her, rolling her over by her legs. She went, and I took her by the ankles, lifting her legs so that I could slide the nappy under her bottom, parting them to pull it up between, and lying her down once more to fasten it. We'd been playing since she'd wet her panties, but the nappy really made the difference. Before the game had been mainly in my head, now it was much more real, and she did look ever so sweet, with her little titties bare and the soft bulge of the puffy white material around her hips and bottom.

In her place I would have felt utterly humiliated, bathed and powdered and put in a nappy by a stern nurse, humiliated but also protected, the same feelings the woman at Eastbourne had given me. I'd have looked just as cute too, and it would have been great to be masturbated the way I'd done it to her. As I put the changing things away I was wishing it had been me, most of all for what was coming next: her punishment.

She must have known she wasn't going to get away without a smacked bottom, but I wanted to torment her. So instead of dealing with her then and there and having tears before bedtime, I simply finished dressing her, in a frilly pink nightie with matching panties I found in the wardrobe, and put her to bed with a kiss.

It was obviously my duty to clean up, so I went back into her living room and did the best I could for the leather sofa. The surface was treated, so her pee hadn't soaked it, but it had run down the back, which made it really hard to get at. I persevered though, because I knew I could choose my own reward, and by the time I'd finished I knew that if a girl had ever earned herself a spanked bottom it was Gabrielle.

She was going to get it too, over my knee, bare bottom, which was the best way to spank a girl in a nappy. There hadn't been a squeak out of her since I'd put her to bed, and I was actually wondering if she'd fallen asleep. I gave her the full treatment anyway, walking in without turning the light on, so that my silhouette was backlit from the living room. It took a moment for my eyes to adjust to the nightlight, but when they did I found her looking at me, her big pale eyes wide and trusting, the dummy moving in her mouth as she sucked.

'Right,' I announced, 'spankies time for you little Gabby, bare bottom.'

Her eyes went wider still, and the dummy dropped from her mouth as she scrabbled back against the wall, pulling the covers up over her head.

'No nonsense,' I chided. 'Come on out, and if you're good about it maybe I'll let you keep your nightie on.'

She stayed firmly under the covers, with just her feet showing at the bottom.

'Gabby,' I warned. 'No nonsense, I said. You know you deserve this. You've been naughty and you must take the consequences, so out you come, and we'll pop those little frillies down and it'll all be over in a trice.'

Still there was no reaction, then her head appeared briefly, only to vanish again beneath the covers.

'OK, Gabby,' I said, 'if that's the way you want it. Right, come here you little brat!'

I grabbed her ankle, and pulled hard. She squealed, clutching at the covers and her pillow as I dragged her down the bed, really frantic, trying to keep herself bum downwards. I took hold of her foot and twisted, forcing her over, on to her face, while she squealed and pleaded and beat her fists on the bed. She went though, all the way, and I planted a firm smack on the back of her thigh, making her squeal louder still.

Her bum was up, and I could have had her, seated on her legs or back. I wanted her across my knee though, always the best way to spank a girl. So I sat down, lifting her legs and swinging them around, before taking her by the middle and dragging her back across my lap. She fought, but ineffectually, clutching the pillow with one arm and beating on the mattress with the other, and I soon had her in correct spanking position, bottom up over my legs.

I was really enjoying myself, full of sadistic glee as I admired her rear view, with her nappy bulging out the rear of her frillies and plenty of pert pink bumcheek at either side. So I took her firmly around her waist for a feel, stroking her thighs and bum, then patting the seat of her nappy, only to realise that it felt suspiciously heavy.

'Have you wet, Gabby?' I demanded.

'*Oui, Bobonne,*' she said, ever so softly.

'Well you needn't think that's going to stop you getting your spanking,' I told her, 'or having your panties pulled down. Nappy too.'

'*Non.*'

It was the most pathetic little squeak, but it only made my grin wider as I took hold of the back of her frillies and peeled them slowly down. The waistband was elastic, and snapped against her thighs when I let go, making her squeak again. She was shivering, and making little mewling noises, but she had stopped fighting. I let go of her waist to unfasten her nappy, tearing the tabs loose and lifting it to expose the soggy interior and her little pink bum, with a wet patch under her cheeks. She gave a little sob as it was exposed and I took her around the waist again, hard, lifting my knee too, to bring her bum up higher.

She was a fine sight, with her frilly nightie ridden up over her tiny little boobs and the nappy turned down with the panties, in a tangle of pink frills and squishy white stuff. Better still, I could see our reflection in the mirrors, a grown-up baby about to get a spanking from nursie, from three different angles. It was an immensely satisfying sight, and after a moment admiring the view I decided that she was ready. I put my palm to her bum, flat, wobbling the little cheeks, pausing to tickle her bumhole, lifting my hand, and bringing it down across her seat with all my force.

I'm a cry-baby about spankings, but she was worse. She really howled, bawling her eyes out and kicking like anything, throwing her body from side to side and thumping the bed. I loved it, and it just made me worse, spanking away merrily, as hard as I could, with her lovely little bum bouncing and wobbling under the smacks. In the end I had to stop because my hand was stinging. Not that I was going to let her off. I was enjoying myself too much. Holding her firmly in place, I leaned across to get at the chest of drawers. I was hoping for a hairbrush, but I found something better – her baby bottle, full of milk, and a big tub of cream.

What to do came to me immediately. I tightened my grip on her, determined not to let her get up. She was still crying, and she must have realised she was in for something worse because she started to fight again, weakly, but enough to force me to cock a knee up between her thighs and curl my leg around hers, locking her in place. It also spread her legs, really wide, showing off her bumhole, just the way I wanted it.

She was going nowhere, so I showed her the bottle, shaking it. Her mouth came open, hopefully, but I shook my head and showed her the cream, at which a look of horror slowly came across her face.

'What a clever girl Gabby is!' I said. 'She know's where this is going, doesn't she? Up her little botty, to leave her nice and clean for the night.'

'*Non!*' she squealed immediately. '*Non, Bobonne, non!*'

She started fighting again, for real, but I held on tight, sure that if she actually didn't want it she wouldn't still be talking in nursery French. It was a hell of a struggle though, but I held on, clutching her to me as I twisted the lid off the cream. I stuck a finger in, dropped the pot and snatched opened her bumcheeks, forcing them wide despite her best efforts to clench. She couldn't do it, her thighs were too wide around my knee, and I got my creamy finger to her bumhole, and up, deep into the hot, slimy cavity of her rectum. I buggered her with my finger for a bit, just to torture her, then made a grab for the bottle, stuffing it between her open cheeks. I actually saw the teat go in, sliding up her creamy little bumhole despite her frantic efforts to keep it tight. She'd been squealing all the time, but the noise she made when her bumhole popped was like a steam whistle, and ever so full of consternation and despair, just the way I like it.

'*Non, Bobonne, non, pas le clyso!*' she pleaded.

I squeezed the bottle, and up it went, the thick, creamy baby milk squirting up her bumhole to the sound of her long wail of utter frustration. I was laughing, I couldn't stop myself. It was just so good, to see her long legs kicking and her little tight bottom clenching and unclenching as she struggled to stop me giving her the enema. She was pleading too, and well in tears, but I took no notice, feeding the entire contents of the bottle up her bum, before pulling the teat free to leave her anus to shut tight, with just a little white fluid trickling from the hole.

'Spankies time again, Gabby!' I crowed, dropping the bottle.

She gave a little wail of protest, but she was too busy keeping her bumhole shut to really make a fuss. The new position had left her pussy spread over my thigh, so I pulled off her wet nappy and took her panties right down, leaving them around one ankle. Her flesh was now against mine, pussy to thigh, so that as I set to work again each slap pressed her bare sex on to my leg, rubbing it. I come that way during spankings, and I could see no reason why she shouldn't be the same. She tried to hold back, she really did, but she was getting there, whether she liked it or not, and losing control of her sphincter too, because soon little spurts of milk were jetting from her bumhole with each smack.

It really was a pathetic sight, watching her try so hard to control herself. I knew it was going to fail too, and sure enough, her reaction soon started to get wanton, rubbing herself on my leg, sneakily at first, then blatantly, her little bum going up and down, her cheeks clenching and unclenching, all the while bouncing to the spanks. Her clit was right on my thigh, deliberately, her muscles were tightening, her cries changing tone, and she was coming.

I knew what was going to happen, and sure enough, her bumhole opened as she lost control of her muscles. Out came the milk, all of it, spurting over the bed and my thigh and the floor in one big gush. She really screamed at that, calling out my play name and suddenly kicking her legs wide, just as a second spurt erupted from her bumhole, up into the air, falling back to splash over her bottom even as my hand came down for the last time, spattering droplets of dirty milk in every direction.

She was done, thoroughly, and she lay limp, utterly submissive, snivelling faintly, her pink bottom stuck high, the milk trickling down her skin, making no effort at all to get up or to cover herself. On the other hand, I wasn't, and my pussy was tingling. There was a patch of my own wet under my bottom and my nipples were rock hard. I needed to come, and being nurse wasn't going to stop me making her help.

'Right, Gabby,' I snapped, 'I think you know what nurse needs now. On your knees.'

I let go of her waist, rolling her on to the floor. She sat down with a bump, looking up in surprise, then shock as I caught her by the back of her neck. Sliding forwards on the bed, I spread my thighs, pulling her into me, her face to my pussy. She gave a last squeak of protest, and then I had her nose against my clit, using it to masturbate on as I twitched her head from side to side. Her feet were kicking, and she was beating her clenched fists on my legs, but I didn't care. Her bottom was stuck out too, the cheeks wide, with a little puddle of milk on the carpet behind her, flaunting herself, ever so rudely.

'Stop fighting!' I spat. 'Lick, you little brat, on my bump.'

She obeyed, lifting her head as I relaxed my grip, her tongue lapping out to send me straight into ecstasy. I shut my eyes, picturing what I'd done: bathing her, powdering her, putting her into her nappy, spanking her. I would have come, but she transferred her attention to my pussy hole, probing with her tongue, then lower, cleaning up my bumhole with her tongue tip, ever so gently. It felt glorious, and my head was swimming with pleasure as her arms came up, around me, taking my bottom in her hands and pulling herself into me.

There was no fight left in her, she was licking not just willingly, but wantonly, with her tongue lapping on my sex, one moment up my pussy, then on my clit, on my bumhole again, up it, and at last back to my clit as I took my boobs in my hands and lay back on the bed. My eyes were closed, my head full of images of spanked, powdery female bottoms, panty crotches tight over shaved pussies, running with pee, little neat bumholes, a girl nude except for a bulging pink and white nappy, only it wasn't Gabrielle, but me, as I came in an absolutely blinding, perfect orgasm that lasted and lasted.

Twelve

I'd been gone from my flat for two nights, but it felt like a week. In the meantime I'd got rid of the awful Damon Maurschen and had a really extraordinary sexual experience with Gabrielle Salinger. That meant two of the biggest problems in my life sorted out, and in a very satisfactory way. Not surprisingly I was in a good mood, better still after I'd played back my answering machine messages and discovered nothing from Damon.

Most were work, but Ami had rung, to say that she and some others were getting together that evening to watch old films and generally have a girl's night in. She obviously wanted to restore our friendship to its previous footing, and it was just the sort of relaxing evening I needed, so I decided to accept.

The last message was one from Percy, typically inefficient, with a long spiel about the quality of the vintage in Bordeaux that ended in a click as the memory ran out. He hadn't said when he was coming back, or even if he was going to stay on and watch the sweet wine grapes come in. If so it was going to be a pain, because I was missing him, and my bottom had almost recovered from the spooning enough for one of his well-judged sessions with a school cane.

I fantasised over that in the bath, masturbating lazily as I wondered how I should dress to greet him, and how it would feel pulling down my panties for him again, to take six across my bare bottom before a leisurely suck of his little cock, or riding on it, sat astride his lap with my bottomhole full.

Afterwards I managed some work, if not much, spending most of the day surfing the net until it was time to go to Ami Bell's. Chris had gone over to Europe for some football match or other, which was why she was alone, with the flat to herself. I was a bit concerned about how we'd get on, so I waited until I was sure some of the others would be there, but Gabrielle had done her job well. Ami was completely relaxed with me, not distant at all, and if anything more friendly than before I'd seduced her. She even cuddled up to me on the sofa while we watched *Silence of the Lambs*. It was really cosy, and I was even wondering if the two of us might not end up in bed together again when I got the most horrible shock.

I'm not really into horror films, and I'd never seen it before, but I was well into the plot, with the victim at the bottom of a pit and the psycho, Gumb, looking down on her with the poodle in his arms. Then Gumb began to speak – '*It rubs the lotion on its skin. It does this whenever it is told.*'

It took a moment to sink in, as the girl answered, and again Gumb spoke – '*It rubs the lotion on its skin or else it gets the hose again.*' It was the 'It' game, or rather it was obviously where Monty had got the 'It' game from. He'd used it on me for sex, which was just horrible.

I just couldn't handle it, at all. I didn't even understand why it was so upsetting, except that sex ought to be intimate, trusting, however dirty it got. In fact, the dirtier it was the more intimate it became. Monty had betrayed that intimacy, twice, in the garden and on the cliff top, and I'd forgiven him, because it had been so good, for me. This was different. He'd used our intimacy, my trust for him, putting something in my

215

head which hadn't been there before, something that came from a really, really nasty motif.

Not that I imagined Monty was actually a psycho for a minute. After all, I'd given him plenty of opportunity to show his true colours if he had been. What mattered was that he had used the motif, on me, but even that I might have handled, if he'd only told me first. He hadn't, and finding out came as a real shock. It made me feel sick, and I had to leave the room.

As I stood, trembling, by Ami's sink, with a big glass of water in my hand, I tried to rationalise it away. I was telling myself that Monty might have thought up the idea on his own, that he hadn't meant it to freak me out so badly, that I was being silly and it was just a game, all sorts of things, but none of it made me feel any better. He had made a link between my sex play and a particularly nasty horror film, and even if he hadn't meant to, it was an awful thing to do. I'd thought he was being nice when he made me rub cream into my skin. I'd been wrong. It was the worst thing he'd done to me, by far. Worse than fucking me while I was being sick, worse then making me suck dirty old men's cocks, worse than pissing up my pussy, worse even than the public enema.

The next morning I was feeling a bit better about it. At least I was able to sit down and look at the thing objectively, instead of purely in terms of my emotional reaction. From Monty's behaviour, especially the 'It' game, it seemed clear that he actually did want to see me as a thing, to be used. OK for sex, but still. That just was not me, and I knew that I was going to have to get rid of him.

Unfortunately, there was the uncomfortable knowledge that I was being a hypocrite. After all, most of the pleasure I'd taken in him had come from the humiliation I felt at having sex with him, and if he'd known that he would have been really hurt.

So it wasn't like Damon, who should have known when to take no for an answer. Monty was too much for my head, but I didn't feel right about just cutting him off. To add to that, I was going to have to do something anyway, once Percy got back, because I just wouldn't have the time for both relationships, and there is only so much abuse my poor bottom can stand. Monty was going to have to go, but gently.

By the time I'd reached that conclusion I was sitting at my computer, in my big shirt and beach shorts, idly checking through an article and sipping coffee. When my intercom went it was quite a shock, and for one awful moment I thought it was going to be Damon, until I heard the door open. Only one person announces himself that way, and sure enough, as I opened my flat door I found Percy, puffing his way up the stairs with a huge bunch of flowers and a magnum of *Crémant*. Immediately I was happy, hugging him and taking the flowers, then ushering him quickly into my flat.

'You're supposed to be in Bordeaux,' I said as I closed the door.

'Not at all,' he answered. 'Didn't you get my message?'

'I had a message about vintage conditions, but the memory on my answering machine ran out halfway through.'

'Damn fool contraptions. I crossed on Monday night, by the St Malo ferry.'

'Oh right, well nice to see you anyway. I'll get some fresh coffee going.'

I kissed him and gave his crotch a gentle squeeze, which he returned with a pat on my bottom. Walking into the kitchen, I bent to get milk, displaying my bright yellow beach shorts, which I'd been using as nightwear.

'What in heaven's name are you wearing?' he demanded.

'Beach shorts,' I answered. 'It's a long story, and a very dirty one. I'll tell you when I'm in the right mood.'

'I look forward to it,' he said, 'but for now, there is the small matter of a bottle of *Chambertin* nineteen forty-nine.'

'Yes?'

'Yes. I'd promised Louis I'd ring through my vintage report, and he tells me you were at *Le Beaunois* the other night, with a young gentleman.'

'No gentleman. Damon Maurschen, an admirer, now ex.'

'Never mind him. You drank the last bottle of that *Chambertin*.'

'The second last.'

'No, a group of businessmen drank that a few weeks ago. Now, you know you can misbehave all you like, but I really think you might have waited until you were with me to drink that bottle.'

'Sorry, Percy.'

'Well?'

'Oh, all right.'

I knew what he wanted, and it was fair. With what I hoped was a look of meek resignation on my face I leaned across the kitchen table, lifting my bottom.

'Good girl,' he said calmly. 'Now down with those silly shorts.'

Reaching back, I turned up my shirt-tail and pushed my shorts down over my bum, feeling that little jump of humiliation which always comes with exposing myself to him, however often I do it. I know how he likes me too, and set my feet apart without having to be told, stretching the shorts taut between my thighs and giving him a prime view of my pussy and bumhole. I knew that wasn't all he could see.

'Been smacked?' he enquired, taking a casual squeeze of one cheek.

I nodded.

'What with?'

'A big spoon, and by hand. I think the marks are all left over from the spoon.'

'This Maurschen fellow?'

'No. He wouldn't know what to do with a girl's bum. Another man.'

'You have been busy. Still, you look like you're ripe for a few more, which is just as well. Right, back in, bottom up, let's have that little hole pointing at the ceiling.'

I obeyed, making the display just one little bit ruder. He loved my bumhole showing, and it was more than likely that was where his cock would be going once he'd beaten me. I looked back at his red face, his balding head, the bulge of his gut: the perfect image for my discipline, to bring my humiliation to a glorious peak as he buggered me, then to cuddle me.

He took a while to inspect my bottom, gave it a couple of gentle pats, and left the room. I knew he'd gone to fetch the cane he always keeps at my flat for just such an occasion, leaving me with my bare bottom sticking out, wriggling my toes in anticipation of what was to come. Not that it was unexpected, but normally he'd have waited until the evening, once I'd got a few glasses of wine inside me and was in the mood. This was a punishment.

The cane was an evil looking thing, long and thin with knobbles and a crook handle at the end, a rattan, which he'd bought specifically for my discipline when we'd first started to play together. It stung like anything and, when he returned, flexing it in his hand, I felt the familiar weak feeling in my stomach and a lump rising in my throat.

'Six,' he announced, 'although it can hardly be said to fit the crime.'

I braced myself as he lifted the cane, still looking back, and trying to fight down the rising panic at the thought of the pain he was about to inflict on me. I do like it, I adore it, but caning hurts.

I screamed at the first cut, and kicked my legs so that my shorts fell down. Percy paused to pick them up, holding them up to my face. I opened my mouth obediently, letting him stuff them in, crotch first, so that I could taste my own sex. It was to stifle my screams, but it was humiliating too, with the rag of yellow cloth hanging from my mouth as I once more pushed my bum up and out.

The second was delivered low, right across the fat of my cheeks, again making me jump and kick, the shorts falling from my mouth. Patiently, Percy paused again, rolling them into a tight ball and forcing them into my mouth, to leave me gaping wide with just a little yellow cloth showing in the opening. That left me breathing through my nose, bringing my sense of panic to a fresh peak as he drew back the cane for the third cut.

It was harder, and lower still, just above the groove where my bumcheeks join my thighs, a really sensitive spot, right over my pussy, and agonisingly painful. My eyes went wide and I blew my breath out through my nose, kicking wildly, then jumping up and down on my toes until the unbearable stinging began to dull. I was really panting as I got back into position, and my skin had started to flush on my boobs and tummy, as well as around my sex.

Seeing me come on heat so fast, Percy gave a dirty little chuckle, and squeezed his crotch as he lined up the fourth stroke. I could see he was getting hard as I braced myself, thinking of his cock inside me, and then once more it was all pain and the uncontrolled jerking of my body as the cut came down, higher, but harder still, to leave me gasping and trembling.

I could feel my pussy growing warm and urgent, and the pain had become more hot than sharp, a state it normally took longer to get to. I was sticking my bum up higher too, only half consciously, and as much in an instinctive need to flaunt myself for entry as for the cane. Percy knew full well what was happening and chuckled again, before bringing down the fifth stroke.

Once more I bucked, but with less violence, and I was sticking my bum up again even before my breathing had come back under control. He brought the sixth stroke down, another one across the meat of my buttocks, and as I slumped across the table I was feeling both relief and disappointment that the punishment was over.

Well, not over, because no man worth his salt canes a girl and doesn't come over it, even if it's only to put his spunk across her beaten bottom. Knowing Percy, it was unlikely to be anything so perfunctory. Sure enough, he had hung the cane over the back of a chair and was bending to look in the fridge.

'Lard? Butter?' he demanded. Sure enough, I was going to be buggered.

I pulled the shorts out of my mouth, finding them wet with saliva.

'Neither. There's some olive oil in the cupboard, extra virgin.'

He grunted, rising to open the cupboard and pull out the bottle of oil, glancing at the label as he turned to me. It was going up my bum, and he was reading the label, which made me giggle, only for the sound to turn to a squeak of pain and alarm as he took me by the ear, hard between finger and thumb, pulling me up. I went, squeaking with the pain, as he dragged me out of the kitchen and into the bedroom, throwing me down across my bed.

I scrambled into a crawling position, bum up, knees well apart, showing him everything. As he groped for his trouser buttons I lifted my shirt high, tucking it up under my neck to leave my boobs swinging bare beneath my chest. He kneeled on the bed, watching my bum all the time, and popping his buttons, one by one, the olive oil bottle clutched in his other hand. I gave him a wiggle and stuck my tongue out.

His cock, already half hard, came free of his fly, sticking out above his disproportionately large balls. I opened my mouth, hopeful for a suck, and he waddled forwards, on his knees, letting me take it in my mouth as his hand went to my bum. He fondled me as I sucked, stroking the cane wheals, then my cleft, my pussy, slipping a finger up my hole, then to my anus, tickling me as I sucked him to erection. It felt lovely, and my eyes were shut in bliss, revelling in the taste and feel of the cock I'd missed so much. He was smaller than Monty, or Damon, with a thin shaft, not that impressive maybe, but perfect for girls' bumholes.

Which was where it was going: up mine. He had stopped fondling me, and was pouring the olive oil out into his hand, his face set in a frown of concentration. A little spilt over, the thick, yellow-green fluid running down over his hand to splash on my back. Then he had slapped it on to my bottom, full between my cheeks, and I felt the cool, oily sensation on the skin around my anus. He rubbed it well in, bumhole and pussy too, frigging me a little before a single fat finger found my bumhole and pushed inside. I stuck my bottom out, sucking harder as he invaded my rectum, lubricating me for the lovely slim cock in my mouth.

He let me suck for a moment more as he put the bottle down, then pulled free. I sank lower, pulling a pillow down the bed so I could cuddle it as I was buggered. My bum was right up, high, with olive oil pooled in my open anus, ready for buggery. Percy took me by the hips, pushing down to get me at the right height for entry, his cock slipping up into the crease of my bottom. I sighed, burying my face in the pillow, waiting to have my anus popped, only for him to slip it up my pussy, very easily, and start to fuck me.

I'd thought he would bugger me straight away, to make it more of a punishment, but I wasn't complaining. It was nice, and he was well up me, with the firm, fat swell of his stomach pressing to my beaten bottom, fucking me with little, short pushes of his cock. It didn't last long though, and as he pulled himself out of my pussy I once more braced myself for anal entry.

This time I got it, the head of his cock pressing to my juicy bumhole as I relaxed, letting my anus open with that awful, helpless feeling of being about to poo myself rising up, until he was in me and I was firmly plugged. Once in, he put it up slowly, push by push, pulling my ring in and out as I gasped and panted into the pillow. My whole body seemed to be filling with cock, right up to my head, with each push until he was right in, his balls squashed to my empty pussy, his shaft stretching my ring wide, with me breathless and abandoned.

His cock was up my bottom, a dirty old man of over sixty, buggering me as I kneeled on my bed, everything showing, my boobs quivering to his pushes, my smacked buttocks bouncing to his thrusts, stripped, caned and now buggered. It was ecstasy, nothing less, and as I slid my hand back to find my pussy I also knew that I could count on him to keep his cock wedged firmly up my bum until I reached orgasm.

It was going to happen too, very quickly, almost more quickly than I wanted it to. I couldn't stop though, rubbing at my clitty, slipping a finger up my empty vagina, touching the junction between cock and bumhole, then back, to my clitty. He was getting faster, and harder, his balls squashing on my hand with each push, hurting me a little, just enough to be perfect as I concentrated on the utter, delicious humiliation of allowing a dirty old man to cane me, bare, and bugger me. And what was I doing? Crying? Trying to fight? No, I was frigging my pussy, masturbating my rude, wet little cunt . . .

I came, screaming out in pure, perfect ecstasy as my bumhole squeezed hard on Percy's erection. It was more than he could stand and he immediately jammed it in, right up me, making me scream again, to a second peak, then a third, at the wonderful, utterly dirty thought that he had just spunked up my bottom.

He drained it into me, puffing and panting, with his hands locked in the soft flesh of my hips. I kept frigging, stretching out my orgasm as long as I could, until at last he had finished and we slumped together on the bed, exhausted but happy, kissing, lightly, then open mouthed as he took me in his arms to comfort me. Eventually he got up and I rolled on to my front, reaching back to stroke my sore bottom.

'Ow!' I said. 'Satisfied, I hope?'

'Absolutely,' he assured me. 'Especially as I have nearly a whole case of the stuff put down. In fact I've promised Charles a bottle to replace the one you drank, so you needn't worry about the bill.'

'That's worth six of the best, just about,' I joked.

'We can easily make it a stroke a pound,' he suggested.

'Eight thousand five hundred cane strokes! Double ow! Not even from you.'

'Well I dare say we'll get there eventually anyway.'

'Promises, promises. How does my bum look?'

'As a girl's should: well caned. Damn fine piece of work actually, if I say so myself. Go and look in the mirror.'

I did, and he was right. My bottom was well marked, and all six wheals were flat, parallel and evenly spaced. Each stroke had fallen just so, across both buttocks, with the teardrop marks where the end had caught me still on my cheeks. It was perfect, and with my bum stuck out it was better still, with my bumhole wet and juicy, the skin around it shiny with oil, a little sperm running out of the hole. A really lovely image of a punished girl: caned and buggered.

That was what was so good about Percy, one of the things anyway. He had caned me to perfection. In fact, if there was such a thing as a manual of technique for caning, the way teenage girls' magazines have them for make-up, my bottom would have made the perfect illustration for the 'finished' picture.

Not that any such thing had occurred to me during my caning, when it was all pain and humiliation and the anticipation of sex. Yet I'd soon have been complaining if he'd caught my thighs, let alone the base of my spine. Of course he hadn't. The victim shouldn't have to worry about her tormentor's skill. With Percy I never did, which is one of the things that makes him a master of the art.

So I was thoroughly pleased with myself afterwards, well and truly punished, and well and truly fulfilled. Well and truly buggered as well, but if my bottom was bruised and my anus throbbing and sore, it was in the nicest possible way, and I knew it would keep me horny all day, and probably longer.

It also put Monty's abilities into very clear perspective, especially in terms of my reaction. He was going.

I'm certainly a brat, and I can be a bitch, I suppose, but only when people make me behave that way. Monty deserved better, and he was going to get it. It would have been so easy to tell him to get lost, and all he had was my mobile number, nothing else. It would have left me feeling bad though, which I hate. I'd still have done it, in different circumstances, but as it was, I had a solution.

I'd enjoyed the grown-up baby game with Gabrielle, but it hadn't been perfect, and I knew it hadn't been perfect for her either. Afterwards she had told me I'd been a little rough with her. Her ideal was strict but fair, spankings when she needed them, but only then. Unfortunately, having control over her, but only within the boundaries of her fantasy, wasn't really enough for me. Head trips are all very well – crucial, in fact – if sex play is going to rise above mere animal response. They're not everything though, and for her game to be any fun for me I'd had to have the physical contact, plenty of it, and rough. I do like being in charge, sometimes, and I like to punish.

225

Besides, I wasn't really sure how a dominant was supposed to get her kicks in a game of grown-up babies. It's easy with corporal punishment, because you can always make the victim lick pussy to say sorry, or to thank you for punishing her, or sit on her face as part of the punishment, with her tongue up your bumhole, whatever. Pee games are easier still, because she can lick while you do it in her mouth. After the scene I'd played out with Gabrielle it was different, and hard to see how I could have done it without breaking role. After all, what should a nurse do after bedtime? Go and drink gin in front of the TV?

What she needed was somebody who was more dominant and less sadistic, who liked the control for its own sake. Fortunately I knew just the man, her perfect partner. Well, not perfect – far from it in fact – but with enough common ground between them for each to get a lot of fun out of it. Just the thought of Monty and Gabrielle together was enough to put a huge smile on my face, while it would also salve my conscience. So it was perfect, for me anyway, which was what mattered.

It took me the rest of the week and three long phone calls to persuade Gabrielle that she ought to meet a complete stranger, and a man at that, with a view to him being her nurse. In the end I succeeded, but only on the proviso that I'd be there too and that we would all meet on neutral ground.

Monty was a lot easier. When I suggested that he might like to dominate another woman, and me at the same time, I thought he was going to come on the other end of the phone. He wanted to know everything, at once, but I told him to calm down and wait for me to call back with the arrangements.

All that was fine, except for one thing. Neutral ground was all very well, but we could hardly play grown-up babies in a pub or restaurant. A hotel was better, but we needed complete privacy, and a fair bit of equipment. It also had to be far enough away from any form of public transport to give me the time I needed if it looked as though Gabrielle was going to freak completely when she found out what Monty actually looked like.

So it had to be somewhere well out of town, where I and, if necessary, Gabrielle could maintain our anonymity. It also had to be safe, comfortable, with en suite bathrooms and preferably decorated in pink. It was the pink that set me thinking of the War Down Man. The room Monty had tormented me in had been pink, very pink. It was also miles from anywhere, and they didn't even know my name as I'd never actually paid a bill there. The couple who ran it might be surly, but both Percy and Monty had had me screaming and they hadn't interfered, so obviously they believed in leaving guests to their own devices. That or they were both stone deaf. Monty knew it too, which made it easier to arrange the meeting. In fact it was perfect, except that it was where he'd played the 'It' game on me, but I felt I could put up with that as long as he didn't expect to repeat it.

I called both of them again, on the Friday night, and arranged everything, then rang the War Down Man from a call box to book the rooms, insisting on a double in pink. It was all set, and as I walked back to the flat I was feeling both the thrill of sexual anticipation and of the game I was playing. It even seemed a pity to be getting rid of Monty, but then I didn't have to, because if he and Gabrielle worked together there was every likelihood they'd let me join in again, so I'd have the best of all worlds.

In the morning I collected Gabrielle from her flat. She was nervous, not surprisingly, but less so than I would have been. What I didn't want to do was spring Monty on her as a complete surprise, so once we were out on the A3 I told her that Monty was pretty fat, and very much a pervert. To my surprise she simply shrugged and gave me a five-minute lecture on not allowing myself to be influenced by society's concepts of the ideal. I wasn't going to argue with that, so I gave her the whole story, or most of it anyway, certainly enough to give her a clear idea of what he was like. She listened without a word, just steepling her fingers, as if I was on her couch. Only when I had finished did she nod thoughtfully and speak.

'His need to objectify women comes from his fear of rejection by real women, probably built up across a series of experiences, each of which will have fortified his attitude. The solution is simply to be open and trusting, demanding the same in return.'

I was going to say I'd tried that, only to realise I'd done nothing of the sort. In many ways Monty had been right not to trust me. Yet if I had told him the truth, he probably would have hated me for it. Certainly he'd have refused to play. He had pride, after all, of a sort.

'As a fetishist yourself your must understand the frustration of being unable to easily express your sexuality,' Gabrielle went on. 'For you this applies only to your desire for those sexual preferences not broadly acceptable to society, as is also true for myself. For your Monty this is likely to apply to the full range of sexual experience. Was he overweight as an adolescent?'

'Search me, I always avoided the topic. I got off on him being fat because it was so unacceptable, to humiliate myself.'

'I see. Regardless, what we must do is build trust and hope it is returned.'

I didn't answer, smiling to myself and remembering how it had felt to be sat on by him while whipped cream was squirted up my bumhole. She might be right, or not, but she seemed to be up for it, which was what mattered.

She went on talking, explaining her ideas of sex and society, which centred on the need for greater openness and understanding. I agreed, by and large, although I had to point out that if everybody was completely open and understanding nothing would seem naughty any more, which would take half the fun out of it. I had to explain, and ended up telling her some of my deepest secrets, even one or two things Percy didn't know. Now it didn't matter any more, because when you've changed a grown woman's nappy for her, you can be sure your own secrets are safe.

What did annoy me a little was how coolly she took it. I told her how I'd sucked off a tramp to prove my own willpower to myself, how I'd let Percy stuff my anus and vagina with food and how we'd shared it, even how I'd first masturbated while filling my panties on a toilet in a French hotel. All of it she took quite calmly, as if I was talking about the weather.

I was determined to get some sort of reaction out of her, so as we came out on to the section of good road beyond Hindhead I put my foot down. It had terrified Monty, but not Gabrielle. My car is supposed to be able to do one hundred and sixty, and I got to just over one hundred and thirty before I lost my own nerve and slowed down. If Gabrielle noticed she didn't show it. A robot would have shown more emotion, and it occurred to me that perhaps she really was perfect for Monty.

We got to the War Down Man in easy time for lunch, and shared a bottle of Chablis with our salad. The landlord was as miserable as ever, showing us up to the double room we'd booked, then the single. The single was good, but the double was perfect, a long attic room looking out across the downs in one direction and on to a leaded roof in the other. There was a large bathroom, with both bath and shower, twin four-foot-six beds, and as much pink upholstery as we could possibly have wanted.

We talked for ages, very intimately, discussing everything from the geology of Alsace to why men are so often obsessed with buggering girls. Nothing happened, but slowly the atmosphere between us became warmer and more sexual. By five I felt ready to start, Monty or no Monty, but it was Gabrielle who made the first move. She had sat down on one of the beds, and was bouncing gently, with a distinctly mischievous look on her face. I was immediately wondering what she was up to, and it was impossible not to smile.

'Shall we put our nappies on?' she suggested suddenly.

'Shouldn't we wait for Monty?' I queried. 'After all, he's sure to want to put us in them. Or do you want to play together first, with me?'

'In a way. I have been thinking, of what you said about the pleasure of being naughty. You enjoy it so much, and I am not sure that I understand, but I do not want to be dismissive. I would like to try.'

'Great. What would make you feel naughty then?'

'I do not know. This is what you must show me.'

'OK ... first rule then, naughty is when you know you can handle the consequences. If you can't it's just plain dangerous. Going with no panties under your dress is naughty, so is streaking if you don't mind being arrested. Peeing over each other is naughty. Wearing a nappy aged twenty-seven is naughty.'

'Going with no underwear I would find free. Streaking has little appeal for me. Peeing over each other is an intimate sharing of bodily fluids. Being in a nappy represents security.'

'If you say so. So what were you thinking of, in nappies?'

'Perhaps going outside.'

'Outside!'

'Yes. In skirts perhaps, so that we know, and people may guess, but they cannot be sure. With strangers to see, there would be no security. It would feel naughty, I think.'

'Naughty! It would be terrifying!'

'It would? With Monty you have had sex with strangers, which is greatly more dangerous.'

'Yes, but they wanted it. We were on equal terms. To others I was just another person out for a walk. I was scared stiff when he gave me my titty whipping in the quarry.'

'On Beachy Head, people realised that you had soiled yourself.'

'Yes, but it was an accident. It looked like one anyway. That's the good thing about panty-wetting and stuff. Nobody knows you've done it on purpose. Any girl might mess her panties if she was embarrassed enough about pulling them down where she might be seen. Anyway, Monty forced me, remember. I'd never have had the guts to just do it! Wearing a nappy is different. Everyone will know, and they'll guess we're kinky!'

'Why?'

'Well obviously! I mean, why else would we do it? Rubber incontinence pants are far less obtrusive.'

'It is in your mind, and mine also, that it is sexual. Others will not know.'

'I just wouldn't dare!'

'I would.'

'Jesus, Gabrielle, it's not that you don't understand, it's that you're too liberal, and a sight too cool! In public, in a nappy!?'

'On a country lane, a footpath even, on a September afternoon.'

'There'll be people about, believe me. And what about the miserable old git at reception?'

She merely shrugged, and began to undress, pushing her jeans and panties down over her hips with one smooth motion. Her shoes went with them, her top and

231

bra followed and she was nude, rolling back on the bed and catching her legs up to make a fine display of her shaved pussy. I pulled a nappy from the bag in her luggage, unfolded it and put it on her, a lot more easily than I had the first time. Again there was that sweet shock of transition from naked girl to grown-up baby, something everyday to something exquisitely naughty.

'Thank you,' she said. 'It always feels better to be put in them. Now, a summer dress maybe. It is warm enough, I think.'

I sat down to watch, feeling more and more impressed by her, jealous too. It was so daring, and she was being really cool about it. There was no question about whether people were going to guess either. The dress she had chosen was loose, very floaty, in lightweight cotton, and pink. She had no bra underneath it, showing off her perky little tits in a way that would have been quite daring enough for most girls. The nappy was something else. It showed in outline as she moved, quite clearly when the light caught her dress in the right way. It amazed me, especially considering how private she was about her fetish, but she seemed to be determined, giving me a twirl to show off before slipping on a pair of sandals and declaring herself ready.

'I know it's not likely,' I said, 'but what if someone you know sees you, a client maybe?'

'That is easy,' she answered me. 'I will explain that it is a new therapy, called practical regression, designed to reduce the stress inherent in adult life by making a symbolic reversion to an infantile condition. Believe me, I will convince them.'

She was right. She would. In fact, if she'd told me before I knew she was into being a grown-up baby, I wouldn't have batted an eyelid. I'd have had to suppress a giggle perhaps, but I'd never have guessed the truth. She was too cool, too detached, to be into anything so perverse, and she was too clever to get caught out.

'I want to do it too,' I said suddenly. 'Wait for me, Gabby.'

She smiled and bounced down on one of the beds, lying back to watch as I stripped. I knew my nerve would fail me if I didn't hurry, so I pulled my clothes off as fast as I could. Nude, I rolled back on the bed, holding my legs up as she had done. She stood up, taking a nappy, and caught me by the ankles.

I relaxed, letting her take over, with the most beautiful sense of erotic humiliation washing over me as she tucked it under my bum. She was quick, obviously practised, opening my legs, curling the nappy up between them and fastening it off with quick, precise motions. I stood, to look at myself in the mirror, nude, save for the puffy pink and white nappy around my hips. It looked cheeky, and rude, and improper, all the things I like, especially from the rear, with my bum stuck out towards the mirror. How Gabrielle could not see it as naughty was beyond me.

'You enjoy flirting with yourself, I think,' Gabrielle remarked.

'I never really thought of it that way,' I said, 'but yes, I get off on the sight of my own body. Don't you?'

'It is what I have been doing for years. Why do you think I have so many mirrors in my bedroom?'

'Well you can show off for me now, too, and Monty. Shall I wear the white dress, or a skirt and top?'

'The white dress.'

'It's very light, the pink of the nappy might show through.'

'Good, and no bra. You must show your breasts.'

'Mine are a lot bigger than yours, Gabby. They'll really show.'

'All the better.'

I put the dress on, quickly, before I could change my mind. The nappy did show underneath, my boobs too, both really prominent, yet the white dress gave such an innocent image that it didn't seem tarty at all. I could feel my embarrassment though, really strong, so strong I wasn't sure I could do it.'

'We go,' Gabrielle announced, opening the door.

I hesitated, but she took my hand and I stumbled out on to the landing, with my stomach knotting inside me. There was nobody about, but I could hear voices in the lobby below. Gabrielle shot me a glance, smiling, and set off down the stairs, quickly, with her dress bouncing behind her to hint at what she was wearing underneath with every step. I followed, trying to keep close to her, down one flight, the next, the last and we were in the lobby, where the landlord was booking in a group of four American tourists.

'Good evening,' Gabrielle said sweetly, smiling at a fat man in a gaudy shirt who was looking our way.

'And a very good evening to you too, Miss,' he replied, including me with a nod and a grin.

I responded in kind, trying to play it cool, but as I walked past, I caught a change in his expression, just for a moment. I nearly tripped over their luggage, catching myself just in time by skipping sideways and clutching at Gabrielle's shoulder.

'Beg pardon, Miss,' the man said, and pulled his bag to the side. In doing so he gave himself a prime look at our rear views.

He had to have noticed. I felt the blood rushing to my face, and I scampered quickly to the door and out. Gabrielle followed, at a leisurely pace, until we were out of sight, when she burst into giggles.

'Wonderful!' she exclaimed. 'Just wonderful! Did you see the look on his face?'

'Yes!' I answered. 'He must have seen. I'm sure he did!'

'He may have guessed,' she answered. 'He may not. That was exciting, and yes, I think, naughty.'

'Very naughty! You're going to get us thrown out!'

'I do not think so. It is good to have a partner, Natasha . . .'

'Playmate.'

'Playmate, as you say. It is very good. Thank you.'

She kissed me, which gave me a lovely warm glow of contentment. I was still filled with embarrassment, but I was buzzing too, with all the feelings of daring and naughtiness I enjoy, really strong. Gabrielle seemed much the same, and there was a glint of mischief in her eye as she took my hand, leading me quickly across the road to where a footpath sign pointed along the edge of a wood.

'Where are we going?' I demanded.

'I don't know,' she said. 'Maybe just to walk, maybe to show off a little. It feels good, like this. I have never been outside in my nappy, never.'

'Nor have I!'

'Come then, let us enjoy it, and decide what to do with your Monty.'

'You choose, it's your thing.'

'Very well. There are many games I play with myself, and yet more fantasies.'

'Tell me.'

'My favourite, I think, is to be fed at the breast. I take my bottle of course, in reality, although not usually in my bottom.'

I laughed and slapped her bum, on the soft padding of her nappy.

'I'm not being nurse,' I reminded her. 'You can suckle me, but another time.'

'I look forward to it. You have beautiful breasts, and large enough to play as nursemaid.'

'Thank you, Gabrielle. I suppose I should take that as a compliment. What then?'

'Just to play is good, but needs no help. I would like my nappy changed, and perhaps to have my bottom spanked. We could perhaps have Monty teach us to use the loo?'

'Potty training? Perfect, and so dirty. That's naughty, surely?'

'Maybe, but not perhaps so naughty as this. We are out of sight of the hotel, so kiss me.'

She held her arms out and I came into them, letting our mouths meet in a gentle kiss that quickly became passionate. I knew we could be seen from the road, but I didn't care. Snogging other girls is not something I'm prepared to keep private. Nor was she, obviously, because she was getting rude, one hand on my bum, the other around my back, holding me tightly, very tightly in fact, and then I realised that her fingers were inching up my dress, showing my legs.

'Hey!' I protested, pulling my head back as my nappy came on show. 'No! Gabrielle!'

'Be a good girl, no tantrums,' she chided. 'There is a car coming. Do you want them to see you making such a fuss?'

'No, I . . .' I squealed, but it was too late.

It was showing, the big pink bulge over my bum, unmistakably a nappy, and she had my arms, tight. I wriggled, struggling, but only succeeded in making more of a show of myself, wiggling my bottom as she hoisted the dress right up high, showing it all, waist to feet, my lower body bare but for a big pink nappy, wriggling in a silly little dance as I fought to escape.

I heard the car, and turned to look, catching a glimpse of the driver, a big, ginger-haired man, staring right at me, no more than fifty yards away. Then it was past, hidden by a hedge and she had let me go, and was skipping back, laughing.

'Now that is naughty!' she crowed. 'Yes!'

'Naughty!? I could kill you, Gabrielle!'

'*Du calm.* Do it to me if you are cross. Come on, show the next car that I am wearing a nappy.'

'You'll cause an accident!'

'Yes, maybe we should not. Spank my bottom instead, in the wood.'

'No, you'd like that too much, and being shown off. You're going to say sorry though, my way. In the wood.'

She ducked through the fence, giggling, and I followed. I took her hand, leading her a little way in, just far enough to be sure we weren't seen from the road. It still wasn't safe.

'Kneel,' I ordered.

She obeyed quickly, pulling her dress up so as not to soil it as she went down in the leaf mould.

'Good,' I said. 'Now show you're sorry. Kiss this.'

I turned, glancing quickly around as I hiked up my skirt, and quickly tore the tabs on my nappy loose and let it fall, showing her my bare bum. She responded immediately, kissing one cheek, then the other.

'Uh, uh, not like that, Gabby,' I said, pulling open my cheeks. 'On my bumhole, that's how a girl should say sorry.'

She hesitated for only a second, and then I felt her face press to my bottom, her puckered lips touching me, to plant a firm kiss full on my bumhole.

'Much better,' I said. 'That's the way. Now once more.'

Again she did it, right on my ring, this time flicking her tongue out to lap at the tight little hole. I wanted more, but a sudden birdcall from the direction of the path brought our dirty little game to an end. She helped me fasten the nappy, both of us in fits of giggles, before we scampered quickly back to the path.

I was absolutely flying, high on pure, wanton pleasure, and so was she, laughing and stopping occasionally to kiss as we walked back towards the hotel. We would have ended up in bed, and never mind Monty, only as we came out on to the road I saw his awful car, just parking.

'Monty's here,' I said, pulling her along by the hand. 'Come on.'

She ran after me, reaching Monty just as he was heaving his bulk out of the driver's seat. I kissed him as soon as he was upright, and stood aside to give him a clear view of Gabrielle.

'This is Gabrielle,' I said. 'Gabrielle, meet Monty, my pet pervert.'

He grinned, showing a trace of uncertainty as his eyes flicked over her body, then mine.

'We have nice breasts, you think?' Gabrielle asked.

He coloured slightly, but managed to nod.

'And you like our dresses?' she went on.

'Sure,' he said, his eyes going lower.

A puzzled expression suddenly came over his face. I giggled, pulling my dress tighter to my front to show the outline of my nappy. Gabrielle did the same, cocking one hip out to make the bulge of the material unmistakable. His frown stayed, for a moment, then changed to a look of astonishment.

'You're wearing nappies!' he said. 'Both of you!'

'We like nappies,' I answered. 'Don't you like us in nappies?'

'Yeah, kinky. But outdoors? Haven't other people realised?'

'Maybe, but they don't know what we're going to do in them, do they?'

'Fucking hell. What do you want me to do?'

'Play with us, of course.'

'Both of you? At the same time?'

'I think that's what I said before.'

'And you'll do it to each other, in front of me?'

'Yes, of course.'

He blew his cheeks out, his whole face beaming.

'Not yet,' Gabrielle said. 'First we talk, and we eat, a good meal. I will order.'

'Now? It's only just gone six.'

'We eat now, and no salad. Jacket potatoes, two each, filled with cheese, and chocolate cake for dessert.'

'Sounds good,' Monty put in. 'Who's for a beer?'

'Not beer for us, cider,' Gabrielle said firmly. 'It is a better diuretic.'

'Don't muck about, do you?' Monty said. 'Let's go in then. I'll get the first round.'

We turned for the pub, Monty putting his arm around first me, then Gabrielle. When neither of us tried to pull away he let his hands wander lower, squeezing my bottom through the seat of my nappy, hers too. I let him have his feel, only gently taking his hand away when we reached the door.

'Later,' I said. 'We don't want to give people ideas.'

'Yeah, right,' he said, 'and women go around in nappies all the time, I suppose.'

'It's a therapy,' Gabrielle said, and gave him the full explanation.

It made him laugh, and that broke the last of the ice. We ordered our dinner, as Gabrielle had suggested, and in no time the two of them were chatting away as if they had known each other for years, and intimately. Because it was so early we had the dining room to ourselves, and Gabrielle began to explain her grown-up baby fantasy to him, only for the group of Americans to appear and choose the table right next to ours.

That stopped us talking openly, but Monty seemed to have caught on to the basic idea, and when the food arrived he fed her most of her potato with a spoon. From then on I was absolutely sure it was going to work. Just being in our nappies was enough to keep a permanent sexual tension, and having him know. I relaxed, drinking the two pints of cider Gabrielle had made me order, followed by a half of their Rieussec with my cake.

By the time we finished it was quite obvious that it was going to happen, and we went straight upstairs, catching a last curious look from the Americans as we went. In the room we locked the door behind us and drew the curtains on the windows looking out to the front, throwing everything into a pale pink-orange light.

'So what's the deal?' Monty asked, sitting down heavily on a bed.

'We'd like you to play a game with us,' I told him, 'like your role-playing games, only very naughty. You're going to potty train us.'

'Potty train you?'

'It's simple,' I explained. 'You're supposed to teach us to use a pot instead of going in our nappies.'

'We don't have a pot.'

'Use the loo,' I went on. 'You can make us pose on it and all sorts of rude things. If we do pee our nappies you're to change us, and spank us too. Don't forget to spank us.'

'I won't. Count on it,' he answered. 'Do I get to fuck you?'

'Sure.'

'Up your arseholes?'

I glanced at Gabrielle.

'If it amuses you,' she told him. 'We are yours, to look after, to chastise as you think necessary, to treat as you please. Please do not be too rough, but if I should cry while my bottom is being spanked, you are not to stop.'

'Me too,' I added.

'So none of these stop words?'

'Well, yes,' I said, 'but we'll try very hard not to use them.'

'I do not need such a thing,' Gabrielle said.

'Are you sure?' I asked her. 'He can be pretty filthy.' She shrugged.

'You'd better get your dresses off then,' he said. 'Shoes too.'

Gabrielle responded immediately, reaching down and peeling her dress up and off. Monty licked his lips as her titties came on show, nodding to himself in satisfaction.

240

I followed Gabrielle's example, stripping quickly, kicking off my shoes. Shaking my hair out, I stood bare in front of Monty, Gabrielle beside me, both nude but for our nappies, with his piggy eyes feasting on our bodies.

'You both need fucking,' he said, 'but playtime first, as that's what you want. So, what to do while we wait for all that cider to work through? You'll tell me when you're going to wet, won't you?'

'A little more in role, please,' I suggested. 'You're supposed to be our nurse.'

'Nurse?'

'Well no, I suppose not. What then?'

'Actually, I don't really feel comfortable about you playing babies. Couldn't I be a wicked uncle who's forced his sixteen- and eighteen-year-old nieces to go around everywhere in nappies?'

'Yes please, perfect,' I answered eagerly, then glanced at Gabrielle, who shrugged and nodded. 'This will be naughty, believe me,' I told her.

'I will try,' she said, 'but I would still like to be trained, or something, so I am punished when I wet myself.'

'Leave it to me,' he smirked. 'This is the deal. I've told you I'll fuck you if you take your nappies off, so you've got no choice but to go to the toilet in them. When it happens, I'll use it as an excuse to punish you.'

'Yes please!' I repeated. 'Say yes, Gabby darling, please?'

'Yes,' she said firmly. 'It is different, but maybe I should try harder to learn.'

'Right, outside, you two.'

'Outside?'

'On the roof, I said. I want you to feel exposed.'

'We will be!'

'It's quite hidden. Now out there, do as you're told, or does my cock go up those little virgin cunts?'

'No, please, but couldn't we put tops on, at least, just in case?'

241

'No, it's a warm day. I think you can go in just your nappies.'

I went to look out of the window, and sure enough, there was an expanse of flat lead roof with red tiles sloping up beyond it. Either end looked out over fields but, if anyone did see, they would be too far away to realise we were in nappies. They would see that we were topless though, and that's the sort of showing off I've never had a problem with.

So I climbed out, Gabrielle following me. The lead was still warm from the sun, the air too, and I stretched, just luxuriating in my nakedness. It felt so daring, so rude, standing on a rooftop, nude except for my nappy, especially with so little chance of really being caught. It wasn't going to be long before I wet myself either, because the cider was already getting to me, making my bladder tense if not yet painful. Monty looked totally happy, just watching from the window with a big grin on his face and his hand on his crotch. I could tell he was erect, but he didn't seem in any hurry to get it out. I put my arm around Gabrielle, on the slim curve of her hip, and she returned the gesture.

'I'm sure the pig wants us to wee in these horrid things, just to make us feel even more awful,' I said.

'I do not mind, actually,' she answered. 'It feels nice, comforting, but I don't want that horrid cock of his anywhere near me.'

'Nor do I!' I assured her. 'You are a pig, uncle Monty, to make us go like this.'

'I'll take you into town like that if you don't mind your language,' he said. 'Titties bare and all.'

'Pig! Oh, Gabby, I need to pee. I'm not sure I can hold on much longer. Hold me.'

She took me in her arms, folding me in until our bodies were pressed together, chest to chest. I could feel the pressure in my bladder, but I held back, letting the moment build. It was my first wet nappy, in well over twenty years anyway, and I wanted to enjoy it. Gabrielle was holding me really tight, and stroking my neck and hair, my back too. I kissed her, on the mouth, again, and we were snogging, holding on really close, really lovingly as I felt my pee start to come. I pulled back, letting her watch my face as the pressure grew and at last I let go.

'Oh God, I'm doing it, Gabby. In my nappy. Cuddle me.'

I stood still, the warm pee flowing out of my body, down between my pussy lips and around the tuck of my bum, soaking into the nappy. Gabrielle held on tight, kissing and stroking me, and whispering into my ear, murmuring soothing words in French, calling me her pet and her sister and telling me not to be scared. I let it all come, flowing out into my nappy, until the material felt warm and soggy around my pussy and bum, with the same heavy feeling I'd had when I messed in my panties.

'I'm full,' I said as it finished. 'Feel it. Then you.'

Her hands went down immediately, cupping the sagging bulge of my wet nappy in her hands. She began to go down, kissing my neck, my breasts, my tummy, then the front of my nappy, nuzzling her face against it. I held her head against myself, letting her nuzzle and feel my bum and the pee-soaked pink material encasing it, until at length she sat back on her heels, looking up me, ever so sweet, with her big grey eyes behind the glasses.

'My turn,' she said. 'I can't hold it any more. Watch me.'

She tumbled over, turning her back to me with her bottom stuck out and her knees apart, looking back over her shoulder. I sank down to get a better view, slipping a hand between my legs to feel the weight in my own nappy. Gabrielle's eyes met mine, then closed.

'I can feel it coming,' she said. 'This is lovely. It is coming out, now. Watch me, watch me do it, Tasha.'

Her mouth came open in a low sigh and I heard the hiss of her pee as she let it out. The back of her nappy quickly began to bulge, growing heavy with piddle, and as a familiar scent caught my nose I realised that wasn't all.

'Oh you're not!' I said. 'Gabby!'

She just nodded, and sighed again, clenching her bottom, then relaxing once more. In the window Monty was watching, his eyes round, his hand on his crotch, rubbing at a very obvious erection. Again Gabrielle squeezed, and I saw the bulge in her nappy grow bigger, and once more, so that the load began to pull the nappy down her hips, exposing the very top of her bottom cleft.

I just had to touch, so I cupped my hands beneath her bottom, feeling the weight of the load in her nappy, lifting it, and squashing it against her bum and up over her pussy. She moaned in pleasure, sticking it out, and I felt it start to swell once more as another piece came out.

'That's all,' she said. 'Now you've got to do it, Tasha, the same, for me.'

'Cuddle me, then,' I demanded. 'I'll try.'

She turned immediately and came into my arms, our breasts squashed together, our mouths meeting, opening, to kiss, hard, our tongues twining together. I was stroking her neck and back, and her hands went lower, touching my nappy, one hand slightly down it, to caress the little V at the top of my bottom crease. I came in closer and her hand slid down further, between my cheeks, to tickle my anus. I let it relax, wondering if she wanted me to do it in her hand, but she pulled back, kissing me on the nose.

'Just do it, now,' she whispered.

It was more than I could resist, and I knew I could manage. I leaned into her, my head to her chest, my arms tight around her. She put a hand to my neck, stroking my skin and my hair, the other going down

244

again, along the curve of my spine, on to my nappy, cupping my bottom. I shut my eyes, sighing, and as my mouth came open so did my bumhole, slowly, pushing out, spreading around the head of a fat, hard piece of dirt. I nearly came as I did it, just from that feeling of utter, glorious wantonness, the dirty, irresponsible delight of doing my business in my nappy instead of a toilet. There was more too, and all the time Gabrielle held me tight, cuddling me and whispering to me, until I'd done it all, and my nappy was as heavy and soggy and filthy as hers.

We went on cuddling, stroking each other and kissing, again and again letting our hands stray to the obscene bulges in each other's nappies. I was revelling in it, and I could tell she was too, in no hurry, just enjoying the sensation of having each other to hold with dirty nappies on, full nappies, heavy with pee and dung, squashy and wet around our pussies and up our bottoms. Not just that, but we were on a rooftop, bare to the sky, breasts showing, so open, so exposed.

Only when a light aeroplane went overhead did we stop. Not that they could have seen anything, except maybe two topless girls snogging, which was enough to send me into a fit of mischievous giggles as we broke apart. We stood up, grinning at each other, her eyes full of mischievous delight, mine too. We'd really done it, together, and now we were going to get punished for it, spanked and fucked by dirty old uncle Monty, which was just what we deserved. He was still at the window, only now he had his cock out, erect, his balls too, bulging from beneath his shaft.

'Sluts,' he said. 'Little dirty sluts. Inside, both of you. You need changing, then spanking, after that it's time to pop your cunt cherries.'

'Pig!' I spat, but I climbed in at the window willingly enough, with only a little discomfort as I sat on the ledge and squashed the mess up into my crease.

'Bathroom floor,' Monty ordered. 'Gabby first.'

She went, very meekly, her head hung as she walked to the bathroom. Lying down on the shiny pink floor tiles, she put her hands behind her head and her knees up, waiting. Monty took a fresh nappy, and the packet of baby wipes we'd brought, and followed her in. I watched from the door as he changed her, my own load hanging heavy in my nappy, feeling utterly humiliated and aroused to the point where I could hardly hold myself back from frigging.

First he pulled the tabs free at either side of her nappy, then pulled her legs up, holding her by both ankles, then one so that he could peel the nappy away from her pussy. It fell away, landing on the floor with a squashy sound, and I could see everything, a real mess, all over her pussy. I pinched my nose, making a face at her, and she stuck out her tongue in reply.

Monty made fast work of her, wiping her pussy clean before lifting her by the ankles to get at her bumcheeks. He left her hole until last, polishing the little ring until it was pink and glossy, then poking a finger up for good measure. She took it all without flinching, even while he was feeling around up her bum.

Personally, I couldn't stop giggling, despite the smell, until he turned round to remind me that I was next, which shut me up. He was going to do to me what he'd just done to Gabby, to see my dirty bum, and clean it too. The humiliation was unbearable, just thinking about it, and then she was up, sent into the corner with a smack on her bottom, and he was nodding to the floor.

I got down as he put her dirty nappy into a plastic bag, and adopted the same vulnerable position she had. My breathing was low and heavy, my stomach fluttering as he turned to me. He pulled the tabs open, one by one, peeling them loose. He took my legs, lifting them, which squashed my load up my pussy, making me cry out in surprise and disgust.

'Big baby!' Gabrielle chided, obviously familiar with what had just happened to me.

I barely heard her, because he'd dropped one leg and was pulling at my nappy, lifting it, letting it drop, and it was all showing, the whole revolting mess, all over my pussy and bum, and pretty smelly too, with Gabrielle holding her nose and giggling. Monty had the wipes, and was pulling my legs apart, spreading my dirty pussy. He touched me, dabbing at me, on my pubic mound, on my sex lips, and into the groove between them, right on my clit, once, twice, three times, and I just came.

It hit me so suddenly, and so hard, a really intense orgasm, built on my exposure, my humiliation, the whole dirty game, everything coming together in one glorious climax. Fortunately he had the sense to keep dabbing at me, rubbing my clit until I'd had enough and moved my hand down to push his away, after which I just lay still, letting him manhandle me as he pleased, cleaning my pussy, my bum, and fingering me in both my holes as well. He saw my cane marks too, and commented on them, but I told him Gabrielle had done it and she had the sense to keep quiet.

We went into the shower after that, together, soaping ach other as he watched, tugging at his cock, which had gone limp while he was changing our nappies. It had been good, wonderfully good, but it wasn't over, as neither of them had come. That was how I'd wanted it, although it had been accidental, but in any case I was sure still to be expected to play. He was hard again by the time we finished our shower, and gloating over our naked bodies. We held on to each other, pretending to be afraid.

'Now a spanking for both of you,' he declared. 'Side by side, over the bath, both of you, now!'

We scampered across, quickly positioning ourselves over the bath, bums lifted high, and legs together, our pussies showing in the mirror behind us. He came around, brandishing his cock.

'Get your backs in, I want to see those arseholes,' he ordered. 'That's better. Boy I am going to enjoy fucking you two. Right.'

He closed in, his podgy hands going to our bums, fondling us, his fingers everywhere, including up our pussies. Both of us were soaking, and I could hear the little wet noises as he poked and probed.

'Bitches on heat,' he said. 'Taste yourselves.'

His hands came forward, sticking two fingers, wet with slimy white pussy juice, right under my nose, another two under hers. I sucked automatically, tasting my juice, and watched Gabrielle from the corner of my eye as she did the same. He stepped back, pulling his fingers free, and again I felt his hand on my bum, this time with the palm flat against my cheeks.

An instant later he hit me with a swat that sent me sprawling across the edge of the bath. I squealed in pain and surprise, but it didn't stop him, his hand twisting hard in my wet hair as he forced me down, smacking me again and again. My control went instantly. Screaming, kicking and thrashing, I was beaten firmly, my bum turned to a burning ball of tender flesh, until at last I burst into tears and he stopped, as suddenly as he had begun.

I staggered upright, my mouth wide, rubbing at my poor bottom, just in time to see him take Gabrielle firmly around the waist. I knew she had a low pain threshold, and sure enough, from the first smack she was howling, and in tears almost immediately. He didn't care, he beat her well, his big, heavy arm going up and down like a piston, spanking and spanking as she howled and kicked and struggled, tears streaming from her eyes, begging and pleading for him to stop, of which he took not the slightest piece of notice. In the end he stopped when his own hand started to get sore, leaving her to slump down, sobbing, with her bottom a rich, deep pink all over, just like mine.

I gave her a cuddle as he recovered his breath, and helped her up. She was still crying, but she didn't complain, just turning her back to the mirror to inspect her bottom. He grinned at her expression as she saw what had been done to her, and held out his cock.

'Cunt time,' he announced gleefully. 'Which one wants her cherry popped first?'

'Do me first, you beast,' Gabrielle answered. 'Leave her alone.'

'You're both going to get it,' he said, 'right up, or else I'll use your arseholes. Tell you what, you can choose. You first, Gabby. What's more precious, your cherry or the old chocolate starfish?'

'I can't take that,' she said. 'Not in my bottom.'

'Cunt then,' he said. 'Over the bog, backwards, I want to watch you piss, and I'm going to fuck you while you do it. Can you do it?'

Gabrielle nodded, and I watched as she mounted the loo, clutching the cistern, with her red bum stuck out, her back curved in to make a real show of herself, pussy and bumhole both flaunted. Monty was stroking his cock, which was nearly back to erection. I took it, pulling at the thick shaft as we watched Gabrielle. She was looking at us too, back over her shoulder, her mouth slightly open, her pale eyes half-lidded.

Her pee started to come, drips, a little gush, a stream, splashing into the water beneath her. Monty moved forwards, my hand slipping from his cock, taking her firmly by the hips. His gut squashed out against her trim buttocks, the expression on her face changed and I knew he was in her, his big, ugly cock moving in her neat little pussy, in and out, jamming her against the cistern with each push. Her pee was still coming too, running off his balls as he fucked her, splashing on to the toilet seat and floor.

She was moaning, and giving out little sharp cries as her body jerked to his thrusts. He did her hard, really pumping into her, with his whole body wobbling as he moved. I'd always been the one he was up, so I'd never realised just how obscene it looked when he was with a girl, especially Gabrielle, like something out of a kitsch sci-fi movie.

I'd have masturbated, but she didn't, taking the pounding until at last he withdrew, standing back, panting, his cock slimy with her juice. I swallowed, knowing it was my turn, and wondering if I could manage it up my bum.

'Well, Tasha?' he puffed. 'Your sister's been popped, so what's it to be, cunt or arsehole?'

'Not my pussy, you pig,' I answered. 'You can't!'

'Then it's your arsehole,' he smirked, 'and I'm going to grease the ring with your sister's cunt juice. Get over the bog, stick it out.'

I got into the same lewd position Gabrielle had been made to adopt. He positioned himself behind me, and I shut my eyes, my whole body trembling as I let my bumhole push out, opening, wet and mushy, an easy target for his penis. His hands took my hips, and he pressed up to me, jamming me against the cistern, his belly squashing out against my bottom, his cock pushing between my cheeks. He nudged it lower and for a moment it went up my pussy, then out, smearing slimy juice up between my cheeks and on to my bumhole.

'Got you,' he said, and pushed.

My anus spread around the head of his cock, stretching, with a twinge of pain, despite my being so sloppy. He grunted and pushed again, making me gasp as the head went in, my sphincter closing on the neck. Again he pushed, forcing in a little more, and yet more, stuffing my poor aching bumhole with penis, until at last the full, fat length was jammed up.

'Fucking great feeling,' he grunted. 'Nothing like one up the dirt box, eh Tasha?'

I managed a weak moan in response and he began to move inside me, slowly at first, then faster, quickly leaving me breathless, then panting as he began to pump into me the same way he had treated Gabrielle, harder and harder, crushing me against the cistern, my breasts slapping on the cold porcelain. I was screaming and thrashing my head from side to side, in pain but ecstasy too, with my bottom hot and wet under his belly, wanting to masturbate but unable to get my hand to my pussy for fear of having my face pushed into the wall. It slowed, leaving me gasping in relief, only to see Monty reach out beside me and pull off a long piece of toilet paper.

'Get this in your mouth, you noisy bitch!' he spat.

I made to protest, only to have it jammed in between my teeth and wadded firmly into my mouth, leaving the last piece hanging out. Again he began to bugger me and, as I glanced sideways, I found that I could see him in the mirror, on top of me, his toadlike body pumping into my little bottom, my boobs swinging and, worst of all, a piece of bright pink loo paper hanging from my mouth.

He was getting hard again too, pushing me back against the cistern, hurting as he shoved himself over and over into my bowels. I knew he was coming towards orgasm, but I didn't know if I could take it, or if my ring would tear. It felt like it, absolutely on fire, but I couldn't speak, couldn't stop him, about to get the full load of his sperm in my gut . . .

He stopped again, suddenly, really panting. His thumbs went to my bottom, spreading my cheeks as he pulled slowly out. I was sure he hadn't come, and I looked back, finding him red faced and gasping, his cock sticking out from his trousers like a pole, slimy, but with no trace of sperm.

'Are you all right, Monty?' I asked.

He sat back, on the edge of the bath, panting hard, his fat face crimson, shaking his head.

'I can't,' he puffed. 'I can't make it. Ow, my legs! Shit! I'm sorry, Tasha.'

'Do not worry,' Gabrielle said, and as she sank down to her knees I realised that she was going to suck him.

I had to watch, her pretty face, so delicate, so genteel, as she opened her mouth to take in that huge, dirty cock, a fat man's cock, a cock that had just been used to bugger me, stuffed up my bumhole in my own mess. She was going to do it though, her long, elegant fingers closing gently around the base, pulling it forwards, towards her mouth, kissing the obscene, bulbous head, and then it was in and she was sucking.

Monty leaned back, bracing himself against the bath, still struggling to get his breath. It came, and then he was grinning with absolute glee as he watched her. She moved a little, fully between his open legs, setting her knees apart and sticking out her bottom to show off her sex. Her head came up, off his cock, leaving it glistening with her saliva. She'd sucked most of it, but not the base, and as she poked out her tongue to finish the job I knew I had to have my share.

I got down, crawling quickly over, doglike, on my hands and knees with my tongue lolling out. Gabrielle saw, and moved to let me in, holding Monty's cock out for me. I took it in deep, sucking down the thick, salty flavour, feeling the fat head push into the back of my throat. Gabrielle's arm came around my back and I pulled off, offering his cock to her. She took the head, and I began to lick the base, finishing the job of cleaning his cock up until my mouth was full of my own earthy taste.

He was breathing hard again, but with pleasure, as we shared his cock, licking, sucking and wanking, at his feet, both nude, both wet and juicy, holding each other and feasting on his dirty cock, until at last it jerked, he grunted, and came, full in Gabrielle's face, all over her glasses and her nose, in her mouth too. She gave a little shocked cry, dropping his cock and I caught it, pulling it towards me even as the second spurt erupted, over my nose and into my open mouth as I took him in, sucking and swallowing, over and over, draining him down my throat, until at last he could stand it no more and pulled me off by the hair.

Gabrielle and I turned immediately to each other, our mouths opening, licking at each other's faces. She cleaned my nose and I hers, then her glasses, licking up the spunk and smearing it across the lenses. I giggled at the sight, sure she couldn't see a thing, then our mouths came open and we were kissing, sharing the taste of his sperm and the rich, dirty tang of my bottom. Her hands were on my boobs, then lower, under my belly as we rolled the sperm together in our mouths. She found my clitty, dabbing at me, even as I slid a finger into her pussy. We closed, tight, cuddling and frigging, my thumb on her clitty, her body wet with sweat against mine, the spunk on her face smearing over my cheek, and once more I was coming, and so was Gabrielle.

It all came together in my head as my orgasm rose, the whole glorious filthy game, wearing the nappy, playing with Gabrielle, cuddling her on the roof. Peeing in my nappy and watching her fill hers with dirt, doing the same myself, and the feel of the squashy, soggy mess against my skin. The utter humiliation of being changed, of coming as Monty wiped me clean, the shower, the cock up my bottom, and at last my lovely Gabrielle to share a mouthful of fat Monty Hartle's spunk as we came together in beautiful, blinding ecstasy. It was such a good orgasm, together, kissing and frigging, with the mixture of sperm and saliva running down our chins, on to our breasts and the floor. Being in front of Monty was good too, our fat uncle Monty, watching his two dirty little nieces, ravished and spoiled, getting carried away with each other on the bathroom floor.

We took a break, to rest and clean up, including such essentials as mouthwash and brandy, all of which we had packed. We had beer too, which Monty and I guzzled and Gabrielle sipped. I was getting tired, although Gabrielle seemed full of energy, and Monty was obviously determined to make the best of his luck. He had stripped off, and was lying on one bed, idly playing with himself and watching us. We were on the other, me nude, Gabrielle in frilly pink panties and a short nightie, gently petting each other, which was doing wonders for his cock. It was time for me to go, almost.

'You know your "It" game, Monty?' I said casually. 'Where did you get the idea?'

'From this scene in *Silence of the Lambs,*' he answered. 'This guy . . .'

'I know,' I interrupted, 'and it wasn't very nice. Horror and sex don't mix. Now come into the bathroom.'

'Why? What are you going to do?'

'Don't be awkward, or I won't let you play with me any more. Come on.'

I got up and took his hand, trying to pull him up. He came, fortunately, because he could just as well have dragged me down over his knee. I led him into the bathroom, Gabrielle watching from the bed.

'On the floor. Kneel,' I said.

'What are you going to do?'

'Kneel down, Monty.'

He kneeled, reluctantly, his expression full of uncertainty as I straddled his legs, my pussy just inches from his face. I took him by the hair, pulling his head back and moving closer still. His tongue appeared, lapping at my pussy.

'Uh, uh, none of that,' I chided. 'Just open wide, like a good boy, otherwise no more games, and I mean that.'

His mouth came open.

'Now this,' I said, 'is for the "It" game. Drink up.'

I let him have it, right in the face, the full contents of my bladder, which had been building up since I'd first wet my nappy. Just watching was great, with the pee bubbling out of his mouth despite his best efforts to swallow, splashing over his face and body too, until he was absolutely running with it, and sitting in a big puddle. Best of all was his expression when I'd finished, his face screwed up in absolute disgust, his eyes shut tight, his throat working as he swallowed his last mouthful.

'That's one,' I said, still with my hand locked firmly in his hair.

'And two?' he asked.

I turned, presenting him with my bare bottom, my crease open over his mouth.

'Kiss my bumhole,' I demanded.

'Hey, come on, that's your kick.'

'Kiss my bumhole, Monty.'

He kissed, his thick lips pressing to my anus.

'Good boy,' I said. 'That was for spanking me in public. Now three, for making me mess in my panties. Open wide.'

'No!' he squeaked.

'Open wide, Monty. Just think, no willing little playmates any more.'

'Please no. Not this, I . . .'

I skipped back, laughing, and bent to kiss him. He looked absolutely horror-struck, but his mouth had been open. He would have let me do it, in his mouth, or at least try to. However he had treated me, however little respect he gave to me, that showed just how much I was worth to him.

'He has my seal of approval, Gabby,' I said, patting him on the head. 'What are you up to?'

She was standing in the doorway, looking sheepish. It was quite obvious that she'd had an accident, with the crotch of her frillies wet and taut across her pussy.

255

'I've been naughty,' she said, 'I've wet my bed, and, and, oh dear . . .'

She just did it, standing there as we watched, completely filling her panties, far more than before, the rear pouch bulging until the weight was simply too much and they fell down, around her ankles, landing squashily on the floor.

'Here we are, Monty. She's all yours,' I said, and threw him the baby wipes.

NEXUS NEW BOOKS

To be published in April

WHIP HAND
G. C. Scott

Richard and his German girlfriend Helena continue to live out their private fantasies of submission and domination, with all the elaborate touches that their England rural idyll can afford. Even Helena's imperious aunt Margaret no longer wants to spoil the party – or does she? As Richard's tame dominatrix she seems to want nothing more than to join in their fantasies. But can Richard be sure that she doesn't want to keep him all to herself? The latest in G. C. Scott's powerful series of novels about the reality of male submission.

ISBN 0 352 33694 3

SLAVE-MINES OF TORMUNIL
Aran Ashe

Leah, the pretty young slave from the Citadel, has been claimed as body-slave by Josef, the handsome outlander who must now assume the responsibility of training her in the Tormunite ways of lust. Together they embark upon a quest for the lovely milk-slave Sianon, reportedly abducted by soldiers as a vessel for their pleasure and cruelty. Josef's worst fears are confirmed when he discovers that Sianon is being held in the notorious fleshpots of the mines of Menirg. The third novel in Aran Ashe's classic *Chronicles of Tormunil*, some of the finest erotic fantasy fiction ever produced.

ISBN 0 352 33695 1

THE INDIGNITIES OF ISABELLE
Penny Birch writing as Cruella

Nineteen-year old Isabelle is a refined young woman of cultish tastes and a deep sexual yearning which she's yet to reveal. The pleasures of domination and the female form are obvious to her, but now, in her first year at university, she's set to discover that there are many more excitements of the flesh. As she traverses the pathways of willing sexual degradation, Isabelle's sensual education is about to begin. A Nexus Classic.

ISBN 0 352 33696 X

To be published in May

INNOCENT
Aishling Morgan

Innocent tells the story of the young and faithful lady's maid Cianna and her haughty mistress Sulitea. Shipwrecked in the kingdom of Alteron, Cianna must wrestle other women for the entertainment of the masses. But as the fur flies in her world of gladiatorial combat, the distinction between her bizarre sport and her life is confusingly and thrillingly blurred. A filthy gothic fantasy tale from the author of *Pleasure Toy*.

ISBN 0 352 33699 4

UNIFORM DOLL
Penny Birch

Jade is usually a confident young lesbian, very aware of what she wants, and what she doesn't. Unfortunately her taste for being bullied can very easily get out of hand, and when she decides to compete with her filthy uncle Rupert in collecting the uniforms of sex partners, they quickly do. What starts out as a playful if provocative hobby leads to her finding herself obliged to accommodate men as well as women, and ending up in a seriously sticky mess – literally.

ISBN 0 352 33698 6

ONE WEEK IN THE PRIVATE HOUSE
Esme Ombreux

Jem is a petite, flame-haired, blue-eyed businesswoman. Lucy, tall, blonde and athletic, is a detective inspector. Julia is the slim, dark, bored wife of a financial speculator. Each arrives separately in the strange, ritualistic, disciplined domain known as the Private House. Once they meet, nothing in the House will be the same again – nothing, that is, except the strict regime of obedience and sexuality. A Nexus Classic.

ISBN 0 352 33706 0

If you would like more information about Nexus titles, please visit our website at www.nexus-books.co.uk, or send a stamped addressed envelope to:
  Nexus, Thames Wharf Studios,
  Rainville Road, London W6 9HA

Nexus

NEXUS BACKLIST

This information is correct at time of printing. For up-to-date information, please visit our website at www.nexus-books.co.uk

All books are priced at £5.99 unless another price is given.

TIE AND TEASE	Penny Birch	☐
	ISBN 0 352 33591 2	
TIGHT WHITE COTTON	Penny Birch	☐
	ISBN 0 352 33537 8	
THE TORTURE CHAMBER	Lisette Ashton	☐
	ISBN 0 352 33530 0	
THE TRAINING OF FALLEN ANGELS	Kendal Grahame	☐
	ISBN 0 352 33224 7	
THE YOUNG WIFE	Stephanie Calvin	☐
	ISBN 0 352 33502 5	
WHIPPING BOY	G. C. Scott	☐
	ISBN 0 352 33595 5	

Nexus books with Ancient and Fantasy settings

CAPTIVE	Aishling Morgan	☐
	ISBN 0 352 33585 8	
THE CASTLE OF MALDONA	Yolanda Celbridge	☐
	ISBN 0 352 33149 6	
DEEP BLUE	Aishling Morgan	☐
	ISBN 0 352 33600 5	
THE FOREST OF BONDAGE	Aran Ashe	☐
	ISBN 0 352 32803 7	
MAIDEN	Aishling Morgan	☐
	ISBN 0 352 33466 5	
NYMPHS OF DIONYSUS £4.99	Susan Tinoff	☐
	ISBN 0 352 33150 X	
PLEASURE TOY	Aishling Morgan	☐
	ISBN 0 352 33634 X	
THE SLAVE OF LIDIR	Aran Ashe	☐
	ISBN 0 352 33504 1	
TIGER, TIGER	Aishling Morgan	☐
	ISBN 0 352 33455 X	
THE WARRIOR QUEEN	Kendal Grahame	☐
	ISBN 0 352 33294 8	

Period

BEATRICE	Anonymous	☐
	ISBN 0 352 31326 9	
CONFESSION OF AN ENGLISH SLAVE	Yolanda Celbridge	☐
	ISBN 0 352 33433 9	

Samplers and collections

Nexus Classics

A new imprint dedicated to putting the finest works of erotic fiction back in print.

- - - - - - ✂ -

Please send me the books I have ticked above.

Name   ....

Address   ....

                ....

                ....

                .... Post code....................

Send to: **Cash Sales, Nexus Books, Thames Wharf Studios, Rainville Road, London W6 9HA**

US customers: for prices and details of how to order books for delivery by mail, call 1-800-805-1083.

Please enclose a cheque or postal order, made payable to **Nexus Books Ltd**, to the value of the books you have ordered plus postage and packing costs as follows:

UK and BFPO – £1.00 for the first book, 50p for each subsequent book.

Overseas (including Republic of Ireland) – £2.00 for the first book, £1.00 for each subsequent book.

If you would prefer to pay by VISA, ACCESS/MASTERCARD, AMEX, DINERS CLUB or SWITCH, please write your card number and expiry date here:

....

Please allow up to 28 days for delivery.

Signature ....

Our privacy policy.

We will not disclose information you supply us to any other parties. We will not disclose any information which identifies you personally to any person without your express consent.

From time to time we may send out information about Nexus books and special offers. Please tick here if you do *not* wish to receive Nexus information.   ☐

- - - - - - ✂ -